FEAR

A CURVY GIRL ROMANTIC SUSPENSE

F-BOMB: CURVY VIGILANTES
BOOK 6

MARY E THOMPSON

BluEyed Press

FEAR

F-BOMB: Curvy Vigilantes, book six

Copyright © 2023 Mary E Thompson

Cover Copyright © 2023 Mary E Thompson

Cover Photo from depositphotos, Copyright © envivo

Break (Mask) from depositphotos, Copyright © K3star

Published by BluEyed Press, All Rights Reserved

Ebook ISBN: 978-1-953879-41-7

Print ISBN: 978-1-953879-42-4

Audiobook ISBN: 978-1-953879-43-1

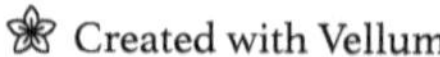 Created with Vellum

F-BOMB: CURVY VIGILANTES

Say hello to the Curvy Vigilantes, a group of plus-size women who protect their city. They have no training, but they don't need it. All they need is the desire to right wrongs and to protect the ones they love... and maybe some help from the men strong (and smart) enough to fall for these kick-ass curvy women.

F-BOMB: CURVY VIGILANTES

Forsaken (subscriber exclusive)

Fury

Framed

Feign

Fierce

Fatal

Fear

Flee

Fracture

Faith

SUBSCRIBE NOW AT MARYETHOMPSON.COM

To every woman who has ever doubted her own strength... you can do anything and you are powerful beyond your imagination. Never give up.

1

EDIE WARREN WAS DONE LETTING FEAR RUN HER LIFE. SHE was done being afraid of every damn thing. She'd stared the devil in the face, then snuck out the back window when he wasn't paying attention.

Damon Street wasn't the only devil, though. Not by a long shot. And Edie was going to take down the other ones. The little devils who helped those evil bastards get their hooks into innocent victims. And the devil who held her captive far longer than a few days. The one who held her for months.

That was the one who cost Edie's cousin her life. If Edie had never gone missing, Tonya wouldn't have dug into her disappearance and been in the wrong place at the wrong time and gotten killed for it.

Edie was done hiding and being afraid and letting others fight her battles for her. She was going to fight her own.

She slid the black mask from her pocket and onto her face. She closed her eyes and inhaled deep, ignoring the scents of urine and vomit in the alleyway where she hid.

The mask made Edie strong. It connected her to the other women she knew. Her friends. The Curvy Vigilantes.

Edie was just one of them. They were fighting to make their city a better, safer, brighter place. Niagara Falls, New York, was one of the most beautiful places on earth, but the seedy, nasty evil that had taken control of parts of it was ruining the beauty of one of the Wonders of the World.

Edie was ready for it to stop.

A door opened down the alley, twenty feet or so from Edie. She waited until the man leaned against the brick wall and took a drag from his cigarette. He blew out a long breath, the smoke dancing in the air above his face for a second before it dissipated and disappeared into the mild evening air.

Edie moved closer to him, her sneakers silent even in the trash filled space. She wore dark clothes and was all but invisible.

The man froze, cigarette perched between his lips, breath stalled in his lungs. "Who's there?"

Edie was close enough to see the fear in his eyes. "Did you sell drugs to a teenager last week?" she growled.

He laughed. Actually laughed. "What if I did?"

"Then you're going to pay for your crimes," Edie whispered.

He snorted. "And you think you're going to make me?"

"Yes, I am," Edie said, not wasting any time before she rushed the man. Her quick move from the dark caught him off-guard, and the knee she slammed into his nuts had him on the ground in seconds.

Edie pulled a zip-tie from her boot and grabbed the man's wrist before he had a chance to regain his footing. She held his arm against the pipe running down the building and secured him to it.

"You bitch," he spat, half-heartedly tugging on the zip-tie.

Edie got in the man's face. "The kid you sold those drugs to died because they were laced with garbage. You made an extra buck and a fifteen-year-old never woke up again. So use whatever language you want, but trust me when I tell you I'm not the worst piece of trash in this alleyway right now."

Edie walked away, the bastard shouting after her the entire time.

"Nine-one-one. What is your emergency?" Mackenzie Chambers asked. Mackenzie was Edie's friend and confidant, but she was also a professional and had a job to do.

"Alleyway behind Jester's Bar. There's a present waiting if the police can get there quickly enough. He might know a thing or two about that overdose last week."

Mackenzie sucked in a breath. "Can you tell me who you are and how you know this?"

Mackenzie hated when Edie called in her prizes, but Edie wasn't going to go through all the work of finding out who was involved in the drug trafficking in the city without handing the scumbags over to the police. "Just a concerned citizen. Trying to do my part to clean up our beautiful city."

"Be careful, please," Mackenzie said. She couldn't say Edie's name or hell would rain down on Edie. Probably on Mackenzie, too. But Mackenzie knew Edie's voice and always told her to be careful.

Technically, what Edie was doing wasn't legal. But she was willing to work outside the law if it meant delivering justice for the silent ones. The ones whose voices were stolen from them. The ones who'd never speak for themselves, or anyone else, ever again.

Edie hid across the street and waited for the police car

to come screeching up the street. The red lights flashed bright and drew the attention of everyone awake that time of night. When the cop walked the man out of the alley in handcuffs, the criminal insisting he was innocent, Edie smiled to herself and knew she did her part for the night.

Tomorrow was another day.

PRYCE MURPHY KNEW EXACTLY what he'd find when he got the call that another gift was left for the police. He broke every traffic law in the book to get there before the *present* found a way to get free and get away.

But he was still there when Pryce arrived, the zip-tie holding him to the pipe nearly split in half from the guy's work. His wrist was raw from the effort, but he insisted he was innocent. That he had done nothing wrong. That "the bitch in all black had the wrong guy."

"We're going to take a ride anyway," Pryce told him. "Have a chat."

The guy grumbled, but he was smart enough not to resist arrest. He wasn't quiet about it, though, shouting the whole time Pryce walked him out of the alley and into the backseat that he didn't do a thing.

Pryce guided the guy into the car and scanned the crowd. Whenever the cops showed up, the residents came out in force. A few were faces Pryce knew, people he'd be able to speak to another time. He nodded at Mr. Pickens, who owned the corner store. No doubt the sirens woke him up. Then there was Ms. Moore, who was definitely not sleeping and absolutely still working. Pryce didn't bother her, even though prostitution wasn't legal. As long as that was the worst she did and she answered any questions he asked, she was an ally.

Pryce walked around his cruiser and looked at the rest of the crowd. He was good with faces, but there were definitely new ones. And there were plenty of people in the shadows, hiding from his curiosity as they fueled their own.

Without a reason to ask any of them questions, Pryce got behind the wheel and waited. Another car was on the way to process the scene, and Pryce had to make sure they knew what he knew.

"I didn't do anything," the guy in the back insisted again. "That lady has no idea what she's talking about."

"What does she think you did?"

"Sold drugs to that kid who died. But I don't do that shit. She's got it all wrong."

Pryce nodded, playing along like he agreed with the guy. "Mistaken identity."

"Yeah, man. Exactly. She don't know me. Never seen her before."

"And you were never around that kid, either. No reason to suspect you."

"Right. I don't know her."

"Sara hung out with a rough crowd. She probably got something from a friend."

"Tara," the guy in the back said.

Pryce met his gaze in the rearview mirror and nodded. "Right. My bad. I didn't know her either."

The guy sputtered his excuses as the other car pulled up. Pryce ignored him and got out.

"What do we got?" Officer Maxwell asked as he met Pryce on the sidewalk.

"Another gift. Guy insists he's innocent."

"Don't they all?" Maxwell chuckled. He was a decent

cop, but a bit of a jackass, in Pryce's opinion. Not that he disagreed with what Maxwell said.

Pryce nodded. "Yep. Even knew her name was Tara and not Sara."

Maxwell snorted. "Dumbass. What's the scene look like?"

"Couldn't see much. Dark alley, zip-tied to a pole. Can smell the cigarette on his breath, so likely a stub down there somewhere, but could be thousands of them."

"Did you get the zip-tie?" Maxwell's partner, Dempsey, was quiet until then, but he looked over Pryce like he could see the zip-tie.

Pryce nodded. "In a bag. I was ready for it."

"Gotta love our friendly neighborhood vigilante. Tying up the bad guys and letting us know where to pick them up." Dempsey rolled his eyes. None of them were fans of the vigilante.

"Yep. Gave this one a shot to the nuts, though, so assault isn't out of the question," Pryce told them.

Maxwell winced. "Damn. I'm rooting for her."

"Not me," Pryce growled. "She's outside the lines. She's going to be the one we have to rescue one of these days."

"Nah, she's good. I'm starting to have fun on nights again. After all that shit with Damon Street, things were tense. It's time to put the bad guys away and know we're making the city better. She's doing the same."

"Yeah, well, I'm not so sure about that."

Maxwell rolled his eyes and backhanded Dempsey's chest. "Well, we'll go check out the alley. Enjoy your night, Murphy."

"You, too." Pryce shook his head. He wasn't popular. That was what happened when you were a suspect as a rookie cop. It didn't matter that he'd been exonerated. He still had a stain and had to stick far from the line. One toe out of place and he'd be on the other side of the line for good.

And Pryce did not want that to happen.

The guy in the back grumbled the entire way to the station. When Pryce booked him and put him in a cell, he asked when he'd get his phone call. Pryce assured him someone would be in soon.

"Your partner strikes again, Murphy?" Foster called out.

Detective Drake Foster was a thorn in Pryce's side. He'd gone from beat cop like Pryce to detective in record time and had never forgotten bringing in Pryce for questioning. Or let him forget it.

"She's not my partner," Pryce growled.

Foster chuckled. He looked around the station, ensuring he had the attention of everyone there.

He did.

"Well, it's funny how you're always first on the scene. You're always the one to collar the guys she picks up. And you never seem to know anything about what's going on."

"Aren't you the detective? Shouldn't you be the one figuring it all out? Or did I forget that was part of my job now?"

Foster scowled at Pryce, the blow landing exactly as planned. Foster pushed off the edge of the desk and leaned back. He crossed his arms and glared at Pryce. "It's hard to do my job when one of my own is hiding things. You know how the system works and you're keeping her just outside it."

"Bullshit," Pryce snapped. "I'm not doing a thing to help her. I don't know anymore about her than you do."

"Bullshit," Foster parroted, a smirk lifting the edge of his lips.

Pryce shook his head and turned toward the hallway leading back outside. "I'm on duty. And some of us have to actually work for a living."

Foster called out, "I hope your partner doesn't get picked up before you can warn her we're onto her."

Pryce ignored the dig and kept going. He deserved that one, maybe, but it didn't make it easier to swallow.

Pryce got back into his car and returned to where he picked up the guy. The other cop car was gone and nothing was out to prevent someone from going down the alley. Pryce parked at the front of it, mostly blocking the entrance, and got out of his car.

He shined his flashlight around the small space as he walked. He wasn't sure if he'd find anything else, but he wanted to get a look at the scene before too much time had passed.

The pipe was rubbed clean where the zip-tie had been wrapped around it. The heels of the guy's boots dug up the gravel, leaving grooves behind. Nothing else seemed to have been touched. But the woman had to have been back there, waiting for the guy.

Pryce moved deeper into the alley, looking for places to hide. A dumpster was the perfect cover if you knew the person you were looking for wouldn't come down that far.

Nothing. No footprints, no hair left behind, nothing to tell him that's where she was hiding.

Who the hell was she? And how was she figuring out who all these criminals were?

Pryce didn't have the answers, but he was going to find them. And she was going to go to jail for her crimes.

EDIE SIPPED her coffee and stared into the pie case. Her mouth watered at the options. Chocolate, lemon meringue, apple, cherry, peach. She didn't really need to think about which one she wanted, but she was warring with herself.

"They all look good, don't they?" a voice said from right behind her.

Edie jumped, her coffee spilling over the side of the mug.

"Crap, I'm sorry. I didn't mean to startle you."

Edie set the coffee on the counter and grabbed for napkins.

"Let me help you, please. And let me buy your pie."

Edie forced her lips to lift and glanced back at the man speaking. When she saw him, she froze.

He noticed the reaction and took a step back. "I apologize. I know a lot of people are uncomfortable around police officers. My name is Pryce Murphy. I don't think we've met."

"Hi, Officer," Jenny said. "Here, hun, let me clean that up for you. Did you get it on you, Edie?"

Edie shook her head. "I'm good, Jenny. Thanks."

Jenny worked the night shift at Bob's Diner. Edie went in there the first night she brought someone to justice. Her first was a man involved in moving drugs through the city. Most of them were. Because the drugs were what kept Edie captive. What hurt her the most. If they hadn't filled her with drugs, she would have escaped long before she did.

That first night, Edie felt a new kind of high. A high that said she was finally helping. After months as a prisoner, and more months terrified and nearly catatonic with fear, Edie was helping people. Jenny made her feel like she belonged in that diner. Like she had a safe space to be. Edie wouldn't say they were friends, but she liked Jenny and loved the pie.

"Put her coffee and pie on my bill, Jenny," the officer said. "It was my fault it spilled."

Jenny raised an eyebrow at Edie for confirmation. Edie just shrugged. She wasn't really going to argue about a two-dollar cup of coffee and a four-dollar piece of pie. Especially with the man who helped her bring in so many criminals. Even if he didn't know she was the one who delivered them.

"Sounds good. Anything I can get you, Officer?" Jenny held the coffee-stained towel in her fingertips and smiled at the officer.

"Same as she's having. Coffee and pie."

"What kind can I get you two?"

"Peach," they said at the same time.

Edie gasped and looked up at him. He smiled sheepishly and shrugged.

"It's always been my favorite."

"Mine, too," Edie admitted.

Jenny plated two slices of pie and pushed them across the counter. Edie grabbed hers and her coffee and nodded her thanks to the officer. She headed for the back corner where she could sit alone. Far away from the cop she didn't know.

Edie tucked into her pie and savored the first bite. It was perfect, like it always was. She had no idea where the peaches came from, but she knew the pie was homemade. Jenny confessed once that she was the pie master, and Edie bought a slice every time she went into the diner since.

"Mind if I join you?" Officer Murphy asked.

Edie nodded, chewing her overly large bite slowly.

He still stood there. "Does that mean you do mind or that I'm welcome to join you?"

Edie breathed a laugh around her food and waved her hand at the other side of her booth. She wasn't looking for company, and definitely didn't want it from a cop, but she couldn't deny the man who bought her pie. Or who unknowingly helped her so many times.

Or who was so attractive she wondered if the pie was really what made her mouth water.

Officer Murphy took a bite of the pie and groaned, his hazel eyes falling closed. Dark lashes brushed his cheeks, a sharp contrast to his dark blond hair and pink-tinted skin. His uniform stretched tight over a well-defined chest and bulging biceps.

Edie had never understood the appeal of a man in uniform before. But this man was different. She knew he was on the same side as her. It had taken Edie a while to trust the police again after having disappeared and learning no one bothered to look for her, but the police captain convinced her there were good people on the force.

She couldn't help but wonder if Officer Murphy was one of them.

"This pie is amazing," he said, meeting her gaze in a conspiratorial way. "Why did we only get one slice each?"

Edie chuckled. "Well, unlike you, I'm going home and going to bed after this. Too much sugar and I won't be able to sleep."

"Were you working? Is that why you're up?" The question was casual enough, but Edie knew it was not an innocent question.

Edie shook her head. "I saw you take that man away."

He looked at her more closely, then nodded. "I thought you looked familiar. I did see you there."

"You saw me?" Edie breathed. She did her best to be invisible. Blend in with the crowd. If he noticed her in it, he could figure out she'd been in more of the crowds. All the crowds.

Officer Murphy nodded, stabbing another piece of his

pie. "Yeah. We're trying to figure out who's capturing these people."

"Does it matter? She's helping."

The officer grimaced. "She might be helping catch these people, but we don't always have evidence that keeps them behind bars. And if she's hurting them, it's assault, and she should be charged. Plus, some of these people are dangerous. She could get hurt."

Edie wasn't worried about getting hurt. Pain was minor compared to what she'd been through. Getting caught would be a problem, but she was careful. And wasn't catching these people helping? Wasn't it worth a minor crime now and then?

Edie knew it was possible she could get in trouble for what she was doing, but she always assumed the police would be happy she was helping. She hid who she was so she didn't have to answer questions. So she could keep helping.

"Did you see anything tonight?" the officer pushed. "Anything that could help me find the woman who's doing this? I'd really like to have a conversation with her."

Well, shit. He already was. But Edie couldn't admit that. "Uh, no," she lied. "I didn't see anything."

2

———————

PRYCE LOOKED AT THE WOMAN ACROSS THE BOOTH FROM HIM. Something told him she was lying, but he had no reason to think she would be. Even if she agreed with what this vigilante was doing, people had no reason to protect her.

Pryce nodded, focusing on his pie so he'd stop staring at Edie's mouth as she ate. Her lips wrapped around her fork, and her tongue darted out to lick off the last bit of deliciousness. He should not be getting hard from a woman eating pie, for fuck's sake.

But he totally was.

Pryce cleared his throat. "So, uh, do you live around here?"

She looked up at him, startled, like he caught her. "Why?"

Pryce shrugged. "You said you saw me take that guy away. I figured the sirens woke you up."

She shook her head, hiding her eyes by focusing on her coffee. She took a healthy sip. Must be decaf if she was going home to bed. Unless she lied about that.

"I was on my way here."

"Here?" Pryce asked, more than a little shocked.

He looked more closely at Edie. She wore black jeans and a purple sweater. Her face had traces of makeup from earlier in the day. She was stunning, but she looked a little more pulled together than the diner they were sitting in.

"Can you really tell me the pie isn't worth it?" she asked.

Pryce chuckled. "You got me there."

She smiled at him, and Pryce was momentarily speechless. She was beautiful before, but when she smiled, she was downright stunning. Her eyes lit up with humor, and her full cheeks plumped up. Her skin glowed, the brown tones highlighted like she was a work of art instead of real. Her lips had a sheen on them, like she'd licked them right before she looked at him.

He wasn't sure he could survive the rest of the night. Not without kissing her. And that was a very bad idea.

"So, what—"

Her question was interrupted by the squawk of Pryce's radio. He kept it turned down when he was inside, but the screech was loud and drew the attention of half the people in the diner.

"This is Officer Murphy," Pryce said into the radio, pressing his lips into a smile for Edie.

"Vehicle accident. Are you available?"

Pryce looked down at the crumbs left on his plate and back up at Edie. She was watching him closely. He wanted to know what she was thinking. If she wanted him to stay. He couldn't, but he wanted to.

"Ten-four. On my way out now. I'll call right back for the address."

"Copy."

Pryce put his radio back on his belt and slid to the edge of the booth. "Thank you for letting me share your booth.

And for letting me buy you a slice of pie. I apologize for running off."

Edie smiled. "Understood. Duty calls. I need to get home, anyway."

"Can I walk you out?"

Edie's smile faltered but only for a second. She shook her head. "I don't want to hold you up. I need to use the restroom before I go." She held up her hands. "Sticky."

"Understood. Well, hopefully I'll see you again sometime, Edie."

"You know my name?" she gasped.

Pryce looked at the counter. "I thought that was what Jenny called you. I apologize if I heard wrong."

She shook her head. "No, that's right. I just didn't realize. It was nice meeting you, Officer."

"Pryce Murphy," he said. "Call me Pryce."

She looked him up and down, then nodded. "Pryce."

"Be careful going home, Edie."

"You be careful, too."

He nodded, then hurried to the door. He stopped when he got to the door, then looked back at her. Edie lifted her hand in a wave. Pryce returned her wave, then went to his car, reluctant to go back to work for the first time in a very long time.

EDIE PUSHED her way into the bathroom and drew a deep breath. She couldn't remember being attracted to a man since she walked away from the hell that motivated her to take down men who thought they could do whatever they wanted to others.

Pryce was... different. She'd thought that before, so just

the thought sent a shiver down her spine. The last man she had that thought about was Damon Street. A man who said he was going to help her, then held her captive as a toy to mess with.

Street deserved the bullet he got to the chest. More than almost anyone else Edie had ever known.

And any similarities to him and Pryce made her more than a little anxious about the man she'd found herself attracted to as they shared a table and a love for peach pie.

Edie waited until she was sure Pryce would be gone, then walked out of the bathroom with clean hands and an empty bladder. She stopped by the counter to say goodnight to Jenny and was surprised when the woman grinned conspiratorially at her.

"Officer Murphy seemed pretty smitten with you."

Edie laughed it off. "He was just being kind."

Jenny shook her head. "I'm not so sure about that. I've never seen him buy pie for anyone else. He's in here almost as much as you are, too."

"Really? I've never seen him here."

Jenny shrugged. "Guess you've just missed each other. He's good to the neighborhood. I think it's because he doesn't have a partner. He talks to the people who live around here. Makes sure no one will go after him."

"Why would anyone go after him?"

Jenny shrugged. "Not everyone likes the police."

"Don't blame them," Edie mumbled.

"Officer Murphy is good, though. He's always watching out for this neighborhood. He was probably hoping to find out something about that vigilante that's been on the news lately." Jenny's words held an edge.

"That's what he said," Edie replied, not willing to get into more of a discussion about her alter-ego.

"Well, I think anyone who's looking to take criminals off the street is doing us a favor." Her pointed look made Edie wonder if the sweet diner employee knew more than she was letting on. "But I also think if everyone was just a little nicer to each other, the world would be a better place."

"Not everyone is willing to do that," Edie said without thinking.

Jenny nodded. "I agree. Which is why that woman is a gift to us."

Edie nodded slowly, wondering if there were more people who agreed with Jenny or more who agreed with Pryce. Edie had never cared a lot about what others thought, but hearing two opposing views in one night made her think.

"Well, have a good night, Edie. Be careful."

"You, too, Jenny."

Jenny nodded, then went back to wiping down the counter, working her way over to the booth where Edie and Pryce had been.

Edie let herself out of the diner, relieved when there was no police car outside. She walked across the well-lit parking lot to where she parked her borrowed van and let herself in. The engine cranked up without a second of hesitation, and Edie pulled out onto the street.

The streets were quiet at quarter-to-eleven on a Tuesday night. Most people were asleep in preparation for the next day of work and school. Edie liked the quiet of the night, almost as much as she liked knowing she was doing something to help. Something she never felt like she had the power to do before.

Edie parked the van in the lot behind Shelter in the Storm. She locked it and pocketed the keys Frannie let her have. The house was mostly dark, but the lights all around the outside were bright, erasing all shadows between the parking lot and the door.

Edie let herself in the side door. She locked it behind her, doing her best to stay quiet so she didn't wake anyone up. Frannie and Marcus were doing her a favor by letting her stay there. Frannie was wonderful. She owned Shelter in the Storm, a dream she created after she witnessed a woman murdered in an alley. Frannie wanted to give women a place to go when they had nowhere else to turn. And she'd done that. Marcus was the police captain, and Frannie's husband. The two of them protected the women who stayed in the shelter, helping them to heal and rebuild their lives.

Edie thought of herself as lucky to call them friends. Even though she felt like their generosity was so much more than just a roof over her head. Edie needed Frannie and Marcus's help just as much as every other woman who called the place home, for however long they were there.

Edie turned to the door that led up the stairs to the rest of the shelter. Frannie and Marcus lived in the basement, and the others lived upstairs. There was almost always someone awake, but curfew was eleven, so Edie was careful to be quiet in case others were sleeping.

"Hey," someone said as Edie stepped onto the bottom step to go up to her room.

She stopped and turned, spotting the young woman on the living room couch. Charlotte was barely a legal adult, but she'd already witnessed the worst a person could see. Her boyfriend tried to kill her, and she was lucky enough to escape from him. When she got to the police station, Marcus called Frannie and had Charlotte whisked away before the boyfriend could figure out where she was.

Not that he didn't try. But Charlotte was safe. If safe

meant hiding from a man who vowed to finish the job if he ever found her.

"Hi," Edie said, changing direction to speak to Charlotte.

"Where were you?"

"Visiting a friend," Edie said. Her standard lie. She told everyone she was visiting a friend whenever she went anywhere. Most people didn't ask for more.

Charlotte wasn't most people.

"Who's your friend?"

Edie shrugged. "Jenny. What are you doing up?"

Charlotte picked at her nailbed, the pink skin turning red before she made her way through the layers of skin to the blood beneath.

"Are you okay?"

Charlotte shrugged and laughed mirthlessly. "Are any of us okay? I mean, really?"

Edie sighed and sank to a seat on the couch across from Charlotte. Charlotte was curled up on a chair, looking younger than eighteen. Edie was so full of hope and excitement when she was Charlotte's age. On her way to college on a scholarship to play tennis. Surrounded by new friends and fun. Her whole life was ahead of her.

Sixteen years later, nothing had turned out the way Edie was foolish enough to hope for back then.

"Have you talked to Stacey?" Edie asked.

Charlotte shared one night that she didn't like talking to Stacey. The counselor for the women in the shelter, Stacey, was kind and understanding and compassionate. But Charlotte couldn't relate to her, according to her excuses.

Edie was fairly sure she was not willing to face the shit in her head. If that wasn't the pot calling the kettle black, Edie didn't know what was.

"Why? Talking isn't going to change anything." It was Charlotte's default answer.

One Edie didn't have a good response to. "Maybe it'll help."

"Are you talking to her?"

Edie eyed the younger woman. Stacey was a friend. Even if Edie didn't like the idea of talking to her as a therapist, Stacey was a wonderful person and someone Edie thought of as a friend. "I'll go if you go," Edie said.

Charlotte narrowed her eyes at Edie. "Why?"

Edie shrugged. "Maybe it's time for both of us."

Charlotte rolled her eyes and went back to picking at her nails. It was a good sign, even as more blood oozed from the wounds. It meant she was actually thinking about it.

"Fine. But you go first."

Edie nodded. Busted. She was planning to make Charlotte go, then never get an appointment. It was a shitty plan, but it was all she had.

"Agreed. But you have to go."

"I will if you do."

Edie examined Charlotte and nodded once, an agreement.

"You going to bed?" Edie asked.

Charlotte shrugged but unfolded herself from the chair. Edie knew the only sleep Charlotte got was fitful and usually resulted in being woken by a nightmare. Their rooms were next door, but Charlotte never woke Edie up. Edie didn't sleep any better than Charlotte. She'd just learned not to scream when the nightmares woke her.

At the top of the stairs, they turned down the hallway. They didn't touch, neither was okay with touching, but Edie waited until Charlotte reached her door and waved. When Charlotte went inside her room and locked the door, Edie followed suit, hoping sleep would be nicer to her than it usually was.

EDIE SAT in the chair in the corner of her room, staring at the door. She'd spent the night alternating between dreams she couldn't remember but knew were terrifying and remembering the look of delight in Pryce's eyes when he took a bite of pie.

The world outside was waking up, and it wouldn't be long before the world inside the house would follow. Charlotte was up. Her nightmare came just after five, which was a little more sleep than she'd gotten the night before. Edie heard Charlotte moving around in her room, changing positions and staying busy. Probably so she didn't fall asleep again.

Edie was restless and felt the need for coffee. Her stomach rumbled, telling her breakfast was a good idea, too. Her slice of peach pie was digested and gone, and even though the house was quiet, she hoped she'd be able to find something in the kitchen.

Edie let herself out of her room and closed her door silently, not wanting to disturb the others, and secretly not wanting to let Charlotte know she was awake. Edie liked Charlotte a lot, but the nightmares made Edie felt like her skin was too tight. When she felt that way, being around others was a challenge.

Well, more of a challenge.

No one was in the hallway, but the lights were on downstairs. Edie hugged the wall, having learned months ago that the right side of the stairwell didn't creak. She made it to the front hallway before she heard voices.

"I can't do anything," Marcus said. His voice was rough, broken. Like he'd given up.

But on what?

"There's nothing you can do? A man like that is going to go back out onto the streets?" Frannie hissed.

Marcus grunted. "You know I wish I could change that, but the system works that way. He made bail, so he's going to get out."

"And you know what he's going to do." Frannie was not happy.

Marcus sighed heavily. "Yeah. He's going to sell more drugs and probably kill more teenagers."

Edie sucked in a silent breath. No. It wasn't possible. The man she gift wrapped last night was getting out of jail? After a handful of hours? A teenager died. Because of him. He all but admitted it, even though Edie couldn't tell them that without also confessing she was the one who tied him up. What was wrong with their justice system?

"I thought you said he confessed," Frannie said.

That was news to Edie, good news. She tiptoed closer to make sure she didn't miss a word.

"Officer Murphy tricked him into saying the girl's name. Murphy called the girl Sara, but the guy corrected him to Tara."

"That's good. Why is he being let out?"

"You know why," Marcus barked. He drew a breath and let it out slowly, the sound of it audible in the otherwise silent house. "Tara's name was on the news. Reports of her death were all over the place. The guy said he heard it somewhere. Not that he knew her. Not that he had any contact with her. Just that he heard it."

"You know that's utter bullshit, right?"

"Of course I do." Marcus laughed sourly. "But I can't do

anything. What am I supposed to tell them? The vigilante is only capturing bad guys, so this guy must be bad. The justice system doesn't know as much as she does?"

"Sure, you could start with that," Frannie said. Her tone was soothing and kind.

A sharp contrast to the anger and pain Edie felt. She wanted to rush in there and tell Marcus she was the vigilante. That she was the one bringing all those guys down. She could share all the information she used to find them.

But she knew the system. She'd learned a lot when she was living in safe houses. She'd learned how evidence needed to be discovered, how it needed to be handled, and who could turn it over. If any of that was messed up, the guilty party walked free.

Which was so fucking ridiculous. Because most of these criminals were smarter than the cops investigating them. They knew how to manipulate the system. They knew what to say and do in order to get out.

As evidence by the fact that the guy she had in cuffs less than twelve hours earlier was already about to walk free.

"If there's something out there to find on this guy, we will find it," Marcus said. His tone was firm, a promise.

Unfortunately, it wasn't the first promise Edie had heard from law enforcement. So far, few promises were kept. Which was why she decided to take matters into her own hands two months ago. She refused to sit around and wait for them to find something. To let these people walk free when others were being held captive for the enjoyment of the sick fucks who decided they were in power.

No. Edie wasn't going to sit back and let it happen like that. She was going to stop the evil that was ruining Niagara Falls. She was going to help make it beautiful again.

Even if she had to do it alone.

3

———————

PRYCE CLIMBED OUT OF HIS BEAT-UP SUV AND LIFTED THE door, holding it up while he slammed it closed. He paused, making sure the door stayed closed before turning away from the POS to go into the diner.

It'd been a week since he met Edie there. A week that he hadn't been able to get her out of his head. He told himself she knew something, that she could help him, but when he wrapped his hand around his hard length every night and groaned her name while he came in his shower, alone, he knew whatever he told himself was lies. All fucking lies.

He liked her. Like a teenage boy who'd never seen boobs before. He was fucking pathetic. But he was still walking into the diner in hopes of catching her.

"Hi, Officer," Jenny said, giving him a smile as he walked to the counter. "How are you doing tonight?"

"Good, Jenny. How are you?"

Jenny nodded, her tight gray bun not moving an inch. "Not too bad. Quiet night so far. It'll get busier in a little while."

"I'm sure it will." Pryce looked around the diner, trying

to hide that he was looking for Edie. He returned his gaze to Jenny, her smirk telling him he wasn't successful.

"Edie's not here," Jenny said without a hint of judgement. "Can I get you a slice of peach pie?"

Pryce nodded as Jenny lifted the pie from the case. She retrieved a large knife from under the counter and sliced into the crust, a crack audible when it pierced through the resistant outer shell.

Pryce's mouth watered as he stared at the knife, almost as transfixed on the pie as he'd been on Edie when she ate hers a week ago.

Pie should not make a man horny. Pryce told himself it wasn't the pie but his companion last time he had the pie that had his cock swelling behind his zipper.

Jenny added a generous scoop of vanilla ice cream and set a fork on the side of the plate before sliding it across the counter to Pryce. When she went back at the pie with the knife, Pryce paused his impending attack on the pastry.

"Are you joining me?" he teased, knowing Jenny never would. She didn't eat in front of customers. Ever.

"I was trying to help you out. Figured you wouldn't mind paying for an extra slice, so you had an excuse." Jenny kept her gaze focused on the pie, but Pryce knew exactly what she was saying.

The door opened behind Pryce, the soft whoosh the only thing that alerted Pryce to Edie's presence. That and his fully hard cock. And Jenny's knowing smirk.

"Hey, Edie," Jenny said. She lifted the second piece of pie, complete with another scoop of vanilla ice cream, and waved it around. "Peach?"

Edie groaned. "I don't know if I love you or hate you, Jenny."

Jenny chuckled as she set the plate down in front of the

stool next to Pryce. She barely glanced at him, but Pryce had no doubt Jenny was either a mind-reader or he was a lot more obvious than he was trying to let on.

Probably the second one.

"I keep you in pie, so I'm hoping you love me," Jenny said.

Edie slid onto the stool, her scent floating around her and settling on Pryce as she ignored him completely and focused on Jenny and the pie. Coconut, Pryce realized. That was what she smelled like. Like a piña colada.

That would taste really good with peach pie. Edie would taste really good with peach pie.

Pryce groaned, his dick throbbing as his mind conjured an image of Edie as his dinner plate, licking the sticky peach filling from her body before he tasted her.

"Oh!" Edie gasped, finally realizing he was there. "Officer. I, um." She made a move to get up, but Pryce put a hand on her arm.

"Don't go," he growled, the words coming out more strained and rough than he intended. "Please."

Edie stared at him for a long moment, then nodded and returned to her seat.

Jenny drifted away, leaving the two of them to their pie and silence.

Pryce needed to say something, something that would tell her he wasn't the asshole he sounded like. But also something that didn't scare the woman off. Telling her the real reason for his tone, and his visit, would send her running for the door.

Edie groaned, sinking into her seat like she'd just experienced the height of pleasure.

So much for getting his erection under control.

"Good?" Pryce choked out.

Edie nodded, licking the filling from her lips. "It's my treat to myself. I don't let myself have it often, but when I have a good night, I always come here."

Pryce smiled. "Well, I'm happy I could be here for your good night."

Edie grinned back at him, her dark brown eyes sparkling with mischief. "You're not working tonight?"

Pryce shook his head. "I work tomorrow night."

"I guess even heroes need a night off."

Pryce chuckled. "I'm hardly a hero. Just a guy doing his best to help others."

"Do you?" she whispered.

"Do I what?"

"Do you help people? It seems like the police have had more problems than positives these days."

Pryce sucked in a breath. Even though he wasn't a decision-maker in the department, he felt an obligation to the reputation his fellow officers had created. Bernard was involved with a criminal organization and murdered by one of the men in charge. Others were working with Bernard, destroying evidence or tampering with it so it was inadmissible. Pryce hated that they'd sworn to protect and serve and only protected and served themselves.

"I can't speak for the others, but I signed up to be a police officer because I wanted to help people."

"Who did you want to help?"

"Excuse me?"

Edie turned to face him, setting her fork on the side of her plate. She focused on Pryce completely, folding her hands in front of her. "Who did you want to help? Friend, family? Who put you here?"

"I'm not sure what you mean." Pryce's throat tingled with the lie.

Edie narrowed her eyes at him. "Yes, you do. You just don't want to tell me." She spun in her seat again, lifting her plate with the slice of pie on it. She spun the other way, lowering herself off the stool and retreating to the booth in the back corner alone, ignoring Pryce entirely.

Pryce turned back to his dessert, the sweet suddenly not as appealing. She knew he was lying, and instead of calling him on it, she just walked away. She wasn't wrong. And that truth was unsettling.

Pryce's job depended on him being able to read others and not be read by them. It required him to understand people, what made them tick and what drove them to do the things they did, and to figure it out in a few seconds.

The drug dealer he picked up a week ago? That guy wanted to feel smart. He wanted to be the one who got one over on the police. He would mess up again. He would keep selling drugs to kids. Pryce just hoped the guy either stopped selling drugs laced with fentanyl or that no one else died. He doubted either would happen, which would mean back to jail for the drug dealer. One day.

Edie was harder for Pryce to figure out. She wasn't a criminal he was taking in for questioning. She was a woman. A woman who intrigued him, and had his number.

Dammit.

Pryce grabbed his slice of pie and left a twenty on the counter for Jenny, then made his way across the diner to Edie.

She watched as he approached, her stare not wavering as he moved closer. She tilted her head back as Pryce grew closer, keeping her eyes locked on his.

When he stopped next to her table, she raised an eyebrow and waited.

"My sister," Pryce admitted.

Both of Edie's brows jumped up in shock, whether that he actually answered or that it was his sister who drove him into the force, Pryce wasn't sure. Edie nodded to the other side of the booth, an invitation for Pryce to sit.

He slid onto the bench and set his pie down, staring at it as he searched for the words.

"My grandfather was in World War Two. He enlisted when he was seventeen, lied about his age. He ended up overseas in Germany. Met my grandmother there. After the war, he brought her back here to live. They were so in love. He was always checking in with her. Said she was the only bright spot in the middle of hell for him. He never talked about the war unless he was talking about her. Refused to tell us anything. At the time, I didn't get it, but now, seeing the things I've seen, I understand."

Edie lifted her fork and speared a bite of her pie, engrossed in Pryce's story as she ate.

"Grandma died when I was in high school. Grandpa didn't know how to function without her and followed a few months later. The last time I saw him, he told me to always protect the ones you love. That's all that matters."

Edie set her fork down. She looked up at him with something frighteningly close to understanding in her gaze.

"I was already planning to study criminal justice, but I decided I wanted to be a cop when I was in college. My sister... she got into some trouble and was arrested on a possessions charge."

Edie sucked in a sharp breath.

"Katherine insisted the drugs weren't hers and she got off with a warning. I saw it all happen and decided I wanted to be like that. I wanted to be able to see the whole story about a person, see beyond the one thing that put them in my path. It wasn't just about the drugs, it was the person.

She'd never even had a parking ticket. She was pulled over for a busted taillight, and the cop happened to see a baggie on the floor of the backseat. Katherine let a friend borrow the car not long before then and had no idea who'd been in the car. She was scared, and her whole future was at risk, and the cop went to bat for her."

"Wow," Edie whispered. She chewed on her lower lip, lost in thought or the story or something.

"Two years later, I was out of school and a rookie on the force. Katherine was a junior in college. There was a party. Cops showed up, not me, but there was a tip about drugs flowing at the party. Heavy drugs. With big time dealers and weapons and God knew what else. Everyone took off when the cops showed up. They were ready for it and had teams out through the area, waiting to grab people who were running away."

"Oh, no," Edie whispered.

Pryce nodded, confirming what Edie had already figured out, but it was so much worse. "Katherine was trashed. She got out of the house, but she was slow because of the drugs and alcohol in her system. She was with her boyfriend," Pryce spat the word.

Edie's brows jumped at his tone.

"The cops found them. First, he tried to ditch her. Tossed her into a bush and ran off."

"What?"

"Then he blamed me."

"Whoa. Seriously?"

"Katherine was dating a friend of mine from high school. He knew I was a cop and thought if he told the officers they were with me it would get them out of the charges."

"I'm guessing it doesn't work that way."

"Nope. All it did was bring me into the mess. I was brought in for questioning, had to prove where I was and that I wasn't with them. Since it was technically Katherine's second offense, she was ordered into rehab."

"And the boyfriend?"

"He was flipped as a confidential informant."

"Meaning he was let off."

"Yep."

"Wow." She shook her head, looking as dejected as Pryce felt the night it all happened. "And yet you're still a cop? After seeing the way they operate?"

"Not everyone is bad. The cops that arrested my sister were doing their job."

"What about the ones who let the boyfriend go?"

"Trust me, I don't love that. The cop who works with him is now a detective and makes sure to remind me regularly that he brought me in for questioning."

"What an asshole."

Pryce chuckled and nodded. "Yeah, he is. But it happened. That cop has brought down other people. He's helped. He's a detective, and he's trying to figure out who this vigilante is and bring her down."

"Why would he do that?"

Pryce froze. It was the second time Edie had questioned the vigilante's actions and the police involvement.

"She's a criminal."

"She's helping. Same as you."

"But she's not doing it with evidence. Our justice system is—"

"Flawed. At best. A complete fucking disaster at worst. Trust me, I know."

"You know? How do you know?"

Edie exhaled roughly and shook her head. "It doesn't

matter. Thanks for the pie, Officer." She stood, stepping away from the booth.

"Edie, wait."

She paused, not looking at him. "It won't be hard for you to find the answer to your question. For you to figure out who I am."

"What...?"

She left. Waved to Jenny and walked out the door like she hadn't just told him he should know who she was.

So why didn't he?

THE COP PARKED in front of the restaurant and turned off his car. He stuck his phone in the glove compartment, not wanting anyone to be able to reach him when he went inside.

Showing up in uniform got attention. People would see him there, which was a risk even without his name on his shirt, but it was a risk that was outweighed by the benefit of showing off his power.

"Good evening," the woman at the stand said. "Table for one?"

"I need to see Trevor," he told her.

Her brown eyes widened for a second before she schooled her red painted lips to an anxious smile. Her fake-blonde ponytail was too tight, pulling her face back and making her look like an ad for plastic surgery gone wrong. The boobs, though, those were an ad for plastic surgery gone right.

Wonder if she's on the menu?

"Follow me, please." Her hips swayed as she led him away from the front and to the door hidden on the side. A curtain separated the main dining room from the back of the house.

He licked his lips, his cock hardening as he watched the pretty blonde. He could hold that ponytail while he plunged into her red lips. Take her—

"Just through there, sir," she said, all breathy like she was imaging the same thing he was.

He nodded curtly to her, turning to watch her disappear through the curtain again before raising a hand to knock on the door.

A few seconds later, the locks disengaged, letting him in. He was immediately met by a man twice the size of the biggest professional football player with an abundance of weapons strapped to his body. The man blocked the path farther into the sanctuary, waiting.

With an eye-roll, he straightened his arms to allow the football player sized man to pat him down. Satisfied he hadn't brought any weapons inside, the guy nodded for the cop to pass.

Another door, another lock, all watched by cameras hidden in the darkened space. He finally made it to the back, where Trevor sat at a table for two, one woman in a g-string waiting for instructions, another on her knees under the table.

"You're interrupting my night," Trevor growled at his visitor.

"I'm here for a trade. I have some information you might want."

"What kind of information?"

"About what Bernard knew." He smirked, knowing the information was valuable.

Trevor scoffed. "Fuck Bernard. He's dead. And so's Street.

All I care about is this woman going around picking off my suppliers. This vigilante."

The cop scowled. He didn't know anything about the vigilante. Didn't even have any suspects. She was smart. Too smart.

"Until you bring me something about her, I don't have anything for you."

"We don't know who she is."

Trevor raised a brow. He waited a long minute, then shook his head and tsked like he was chastising a child. "You're not as smart as I thought you were."

"Fuck you."

Trevor snorted. "I'm not the one here begging for a favor."

"You need the information."

"Not useless information. I need something that will help me. Edie Warren is a threat to what we do. She knows too much."

"Edie Warren? That woman who showed up in the snowstorm last year?"

Trevor raised an eyebrow. "She was one of mine. Street knew it. Took her from me, then waited too long to re-fuel her and she got out."

"You make her sound like a dog."

"She is! They all are. Expendable." He gestured to the woman between his legs. "This one is doing such a piss-poor job that I can have a fucking conversation. I should have blown down her throat by now, but she's useless." He shoved her to the side, his half-hard dick flopping uselessly to rest on his pants. Trevor shoved it back in his fly and yanked the zipper up, kicking at the woman to get her out of his way. "Edie Warren is your vigilante."

The cop shook his head. "There's no way. She lives with the police captain. He would know if she was the vigilante."

"You're making it sound like he would care. She's doing his dirty work."

"I just can't see it. He's too by the book."

"Find me proof. If you find me something that says she's definitely not the vigilante, or bring her to me, I'll let you have whatever you want."

"The blonde?" the cop blurted before he could think.

"Maya?" Trevor asked, a twisted grin lifting his lips. "From up front?"

The cop nodded curtly, hating that he'd shown a weakness.

"She's yours. If you bring me something solid."

"Consider it done."

Trevor smiled, then nodded to someone. He turned to the woman who'd been standing behind him, putting a hand on her shoulder and shoving her to her knees.

The cop hardened as he watched the woman's breasts bounce. Before it got good, someone grabbed his arm. "Time for you to go."

He cast a glance back, but he couldn't see anything else before the door closed in his face.

Fucking asshole.

4

————

EDIE SLID THE BURNER PHONE OUT OF HER POCKET AND swiped through the pictures she'd taken over the last few days. One after another, she gathered the evidence the police were too useless to collect on their own.

Yeah, she was angry. Angry enough that she was hiding in the same fucking alley she'd hidden in weeks ago when she brought the scumbag down the first time. Except he got out. No proof of what he'd done.

Well, Edie got their damn proof. And she intended to leave it with the man when she tied him up again.

See if the police could ignore it this time.

Fury tore through her as she looked at the pictures. Big H, as he was known, was selling to kids again. Teenagers. Edie learned he offered them a freebie if they brought a friend. Getting more and more teenagers to try the garbage he pushed out into the streets. Teenagers who had no clue how dangerous what they were doing was. Teenagers who were foolish enough to think he was a decent guy who just happened to sell them drugs.

Drug dealers weren't nice. They were manipulative and

would turn on a kid in a minute. And Big H was smart enough to know most cops didn't look young enough to go undercover as teenagers. That's why they were his target market.

Fucking asshole.

Edie was done waiting for him to fuck up and for the police to catch him. She was going to catch him herself. Again.

The dumpster provided her with cover once more. A spot to crouch and wait for Big H to walk out of the club where he likely got his supply. Edie had been following him enough to know he was there every other night, and the days in between, he was hanging around where the teenagers were.

Supply and demand, the perfect economic cycle.

The door opened with a loud squeak, almost startling Edie into making noise and giving away her presence. She tucked the phone into her pocket, knowing she'd need both hands to take this guy down again.

Edie watched as Big H lit a cigarette and leaned against the brick wall next to the door. He looked relaxed. Like he didn't have a care in the world. He probably didn't. He was arrested and released, free to continue his business without the police giving a shit about the kids he was endangering.

Edie waited a few more seconds, then eased out of her hiding spot. She tiptoed down the alley, sticking to the shadows and keeping her gaze locked on Big H. She almost made it to him before she felt a tingle at the base of her throat.

They weren't alone.

"Think you can outsmart me again, bitch?" Big H growled, lunging for her.

Edie caught a glimpse of something shiny in his hand

right. She moved to the side, the blade missing her by inches.

"You're a stupid whore, aren't you? Coming at me again. I know exactly who you are, Edie Warren."

Fear gripped her. The way he said her name sent ice down her spine.

"What?"

Big H laughed. The booming sound was loud enough to almost hide the sound of someone sneaking up from behind Edie. Almost.

She spun just before the man behind her looped his arms around her body. He squeezed her tight, shocking her with his size and strength, but overwhelming her with his scent.

A scent she knew.

"No," Edie breathed.

"Nice to see you again, Edie," the man whispered. His voice was deep and smooth, appealing if it weren't for the fact that he was a rapist.

Big H laughed again, finding humor in her predicament.

"Shut the fuck up," the other man growled. "Someone will hear you. And then I'll have to kill you."

Big H choked on his laughter, slinking back against the building once more.

"I've missed you, Edie. When I heard you were out paying visits to dealers, I volunteered to say hi. Make sure you know not to keep doing it."

The man let go of her, opting to wrap a hand around Edie's throat instead of keeping her immobile in his massive arms.

"What are you doing, dude?" Big H hissed as Edie's head slammed into the brick wall next to Big H. "You're going to kill her."

The man cast his dark eyes at Big H. The hard glare was enough to silence Big H. "Should I kill you, Edie?"

Edie tried to shake her head, the move barely noticeable under his thick hand. She tried to remember him, but she couldn't place his name or his face. He was careful to stay in the shadows so she couldn't identify him. Her memory only went so far as to recall his scent.

He pressed his large body against her, letting her feel his thick erection. "Maybe I should take you back to Trevor and have another turn. The ones he has now are useless. Your tight cunt always got me off in a hurry. And you never once complained."

"It was rape, you fucker," Edie whispered.

The man chuckled softly. "You never said no."

"What the fuck?" Big H breathed.

The man spared him a glance. "Are you going to be a problem?"

"You raped her?"

The man leveled Big H with a steady glare, one intended to scare him into silence.

Big H didn't get the message and pushed off the wall and moved toward the man. "You can't do that. What the fuck, dude?"

"You were offered assistance to eliminate the threat against you. Are you telling me you no longer want that help? You're an employee."

Big H shoved the guy, surprising him into loosening his grip on Edie's throat. "Leave her alone."

The guy dropped Edie, removing his hand and turning on Big H. He swung at Big H, the big man going down like a tower of stacked bricks.

Edie gasped, drawing back against the wall and hoping the man would ignore her and leave. No such luck.

He checked to make sure Big H wasn't getting up, then turned to Edie again. His hand went right back to her throat and squeezed, hard.

Panic filled her. She fought to suck in a breath, but there was no air moving past his fist. She clawed at him, trying to pull his hand from her throat.

He lifted her, squeezing tighter as he suspended her against the brick wall.

The rough brick against her back dug in, scratching her body. Black filtered in around the edges of her vision. The only sound was the rush of blood through her ears, her entire body panicking as death raced for her.

Then she was on the ground. Pain radiated from her knees where she was dropped. Her hands hit the dirty ground, squishing into some unknown substance.

She sucked in a breath, her lungs greedy for air, even if it was air tinged with urine, vomit, and shit.

A hand grabbed her shoulder, and she spun, swinging out at the person.

"Are you okay?" a man asked. Not the man who'd held her against the wall. "I didn't mean to scare you."

A woman crouched in front of her. "We saw that man choking you and shouted. We rushed down here, and he took off. Are you okay?"

Edie shook her head, rubbing a hand on her aching throat. It was wet, which brought a whole new level of terror. He cut her throat.

She lifted her hands to the light, but she didn't see blood. It was wet. She was crying.

"We called the police," the woman said. "Is there someone else we can call for you?"

The woman's words sank in just before the first siren pierced the night. A whole different kind of panic gripped

Edie. She knew the young couple in front of her wouldn't be able to tell the police who she was, but if she was there when they showed up, they would find out. They'd know why she was in that alley and that she was the vigilante.

Edie pushed to her feet, ignoring the advice from the young couple to stay there until the paramedics arrived. Edie adjusted her mask, making sure it was in place, then turned toward the alley entrance. A small crowd had gathered.

"What are you doing?" the woman asked as Edie started toward the crowd.

"I have to get out of here."

The woman grabbed Edie's arm, but she shook her off roughly. "You could have some serious damage to your throat. And anything else."

Edie shook her head, moving away from the woman again. She slid her hands down her side and felt the phone in her pocket. Edie pulled it out and went back to where Big H was still knocked out.

For half a second, she hesitated. He tried to help her. To save her. It was ironic that a man who was responsible for the death of a teenager drew the line at rape, but apparently everyone had their morals.

Edie turned the phone over in her gloved hand. Leaving it there would mean he'd go away. Taking it would mean he was out again. Selling more drugs.

But he helped her.

Edie knew that wasn't enough to make up for a teenager dying. One life was not more important than another. Every single person mattered. Maybe Big H would be more willing to talk with the evidence on the phone. Trade his sentence for information on his bosses. The man said he was an employee. Big H knew something.

Edie dropped the phone next to him and turned back to the street. The young couple stared after her, yelling at her to stay and get checked out, but Edie couldn't. Not if she was going to keep helping people. Saving people.

And she had to. Until they were all free, she had to. Tonya died looking for Edie. No one else was going to die if she had anything to say about it.

PRYCE CLOSED the doors on the back of the ambulance and patted the back twice, letting the paramedics know they could pull away. The siren whooped in the night, the lights flashing on the surrounding buildings as the ambulance slowly pulled away with Big H, and Officer Dempsey guarding him, inside.

Big H woke up shortly after Pryce arrived, groaning about the vigilante showing up. When Pryce asked if she was the one who knocked him out, Big H got quiet in a hurry.

The two witnesses had already spewed their version of the story, so Pryce knew there was a third person in the alley, but the young couple said he took off when they showed up, disappearing before the crowd formed and vanishing into the night.

Big H pretended to pass out again, but he woke up in a hurry when the couple mentioned the vigilante tossing a phone toward him before she ran.

Pryce whistled as he flipped through the photos on the burner phone without a password. Photos that would help keep Big H behind bars. Once he was out of the hospital.

"You need me here, sir?" Officer Maxwell asked Detective Drake Foster.

When Pryce realized everything that was going on, he called for backup and a detective, knowing someone would need an official statement from the witnesses. Maxwell and Dempsey showed up first, securing the scene with Pryce before the detective arrived to take control.

Of course, it was Foster.

Foster looked at Maxwell and shook his head. "You can go pick up your partner from the hospital. We have a unit already on the way there to stand guard until the suspect is ready to transport to holding."

Maxwell nodded at Foster, then turned to go back to his car.

Pryce wasn't sure if he was still needed, but until he was dismissed, he was sticking around.

"She got away from you again, Murphy?" Foster asked.

Pryce swallowed his groan. "She was gone when I arrived, sir."

"So I heard. Those two kids were pretty shaken up."

"Understandable."

Foster nodded. "Sounds like she was lucky they were paying attention and said something. Whoever the guy was that had her against the wall would have killed her."

"Do we have any idea who he could have been?"

Foster chuckled. "A man as big as they described who could pin a woman to the wall and knock Big H out with one punch? I would think we would have noticed a guy like that."

Pryce nodded. Witness statements were rarely completely accurate, but the two of them were in agreement about the size of the man. The man had to be well over six feet. The bruising on Big H's face said he'd only been hit once, and the size of the mark suggested a very large fist.

If they were lucky, traffic cameras and security

cameras in the area might give them something, but Pryce learned a while ago not to hold out too much hope for that.

"You gonna work your magic and canvas the neighborhood?" Foster asked.

Pryce was a little taken aback at the quiet encouragement he thought he heard in Foster's voice. "I was planning to. Is there something else you need from me, sir?"

Foster shook his head. "I wish we could nail this woman. Makes me crazy that she's out here and doing all of this and we can't get close to her."

"She's smart."

"Yes, but I'm also wondering if she has help."

"I don't know her, sir. I'm not helping her," Pryce growled.

Foster glared at Pryce. "Someone is. Maybe it isn't you, but there's no way she's doing all of this alone. No one knows who she is, so we don't know anything. We don't even know for sure it's just one woman. Could it be more than one? Could the one on the streets be getting information from someone else? Could they have a network of some sort?"

"That's a scary thought," Pryce mumbled.

Foster nodded. "Especially considering how close she came to getting seriously hurt tonight. I'm thinking we might want to put the local hospitals on alert for any woman who comes in with strangulation bruising."

Pryce had never considered that option. Or that Foster could be a decent human being without an audience. "That's a really good idea."

"I know it is," Foster spat. "That's why I said it."

And there was the dickbag Pryce knew.

"I don't have time to waste here with you. Let me know

what you learn talking to the locals. I'll be at the precinct after a quick trip to the hospital."

Pryce nodded, but Foster was already walking away, assuming his instructions were going to be followed.

Asshole.

By the time Pryce made it to his car, the crowd had disappeared. The excitement was over, and they were back to their normal lives.

Pryce wondered if someone else was back to her normal life.

Edie Warren. He couldn't believe he didn't make the connection when Jenny first said her name. Edie was a common enough name that Pryce wouldn't have thought of her, but it was recent enough that he should have remembered the story about the woman who survived kidnapping, and God knew what else, only to escape during one of the worst snowstorms in local history and land on the doorstep of an emergency call center.

Pryce read every article he could find about Edie Warren, and her cousin Tonya, and the police reports about Edie's disappearance and her eventual reappearance. Bernard did the initial investigation. Knowing what they knew now, Pryce had to believe Bernard knew what happened to Edie when she was first taken. He was working for Damon Street, who ran the organization that held Edie captive for months.

Which didn't help Edie, then or now, and didn't help Pryce when he was trying to get to know the woman who'd captivated him for some unknown reason.

That wasn't true. Saying Pryce didn't know why he was drawn to her was an insult to Edie. She was beautiful. Her brown skin glowed, even in the crappy lighting in the diner, she glowed. Her eyes lit up the room. And her smile made

Pryce feel like he didn't need oxygen. And all of that was after her curvy figure pulled him in like a damn magnet when he walked in that first night and saw her sitting at the counter and staring at the pie case like it held the answers to life's most interesting questions.

Pryce was hooked. And knowing her story didn't do anything to slow that train.

He parked outside the diner and glanced around. There was still foot traffic as it was only ten, and a Friday night. The area would be busy for hours. The diner was well lit and a little more than half-full. And in the corner booth was Edie.

Pryce opened the door, his gaze going to her immediately. She looked up from her phone, her chest rising with the breath he couldn't hear from so far away. Her eyes widened. She pulled her lip between her teeth, then turned back to her phone.

"Good evening, Officer," Jenny said loudly, catching his attention.

Pryce looked over at her, a smile ready for her. She jerked her head for him to come closer. Pryce's smile slipped. Jenny never beckoned him.

"Everything okay, Jenny?" Pryce asked quietly.

Jenny opened the pie case and removed the peach pie. "She hasn't said much since she got here, Officer. Seems scared. I asked her what's going on and if there was anyone I could call, but she was quick to say no."

"What do you know about her personal situation?"

Jenny shook her head and cut a second slice of pie. "Nothing. She doesn't talk much. Keeps it real vague. Mentioned a cousin once, but I get the feeling she's passed."

"She has," Pryce said without thinking.

Jenny's brows shot up. "Then you know more than me."

Pryce glanced at Edie again, finding her focused on her phone, but something told him she wasn't paying as close attention to her phone as she wanted people to think. "Not really."

"Well, I thought it might be nice for her to have someone to sit with. Maybe she'll talk to you a bit. You've talked to her more than anyone else I've ever known. She's a really sweet girl, but she's got some demons. Breaks my heart to imagine anyone laying a hand on her."

"Me, too," Pryce admitted, the thought of what she went through turning his stomach.

Jenny added ice cream to both slices of pie and pushed them toward Pryce. "Decaf or caffeine tonight?"

"Night shift. Caffeine for me."

"I'll bring it right over. Good luck, Officer."

"Thanks for the head's up, Jenny."

"Any time."

Pryce picked up the two slices of pie and walked across the diner. Everyone watched him, dressed in full uniform, including his gun and taser. If any of them wanted to try something, it wouldn't have been nearly as challenging as it should be, but Pryce was focused on Edie and the pie he was hoping would help her to open up to him.

He stopped next to her table, knowing she knew he was there. "Hey."

She finally looked up at him. The pain and fear in her gaze nearly sent him to his knees. Pryce's gut twisted.

Anger swamped him so fast his knees buckled. He fell to the bench seat across from her, the pie clattering to the table as he growled, "Who do I have to kill for hurting you?"

5

———

Edie looked at the man across the booth and wasn't sure if she was going to laugh, cry, or admit the truth. Maybe all three.

"Talk to me, Edie. What happened?"

Her throat burned. From holding back her tears and the hand that cut off all her air a few hours earlier. When she left that alley, the only place she wanted to be was in the corner booth at Bob's Diner. She felt safe there. No one wanted anything from her there. She was nobody there.

But as soon as she sat down, she knew why she went there. She was hoping Pryce would show up.

"Are you okay?" Pryce asked, his voice softer, gentler.

Edie nodded, the move jerky and stilted. She wasn't okay, and they both knew it, but she wasn't so not-okay that he needed to do something about it. Or could.

Telling him everything would not happen. Even as she wished she could.

"Just a rough night," she finally whispered. Her throat was raw, aching from the man who would have killed her if not for the couple who intervened.

"Did someone hurt you?" Pryce asked softly. His voice held an edge of danger, a hint of who he could be.

It was a tone that should have scared her. A tone that told her he could be deadly if provoked.

Edie held his gaze, debating. He would want to know who. He would ask more questions. He would get the truth out of her if she gave him anything.

Her hold on her emotions was tentative at best. She ached to let it all out. To cry and admit she was still scared. To give in to the fear that had raced through her the minute the man pinned her to that wall.

The fear that had kept her in hiding for months. The fear that nearly crippled her. The fear she told herself she wasn't going to let control her any longer.

Edie shook her head.

Pryce's lips pursed into a thin line. He knew she was lying. The disappointment in his gaze said he'd hoped she would trust him. Let him help her. Let him in.

But he had no idea what he was asking.

"I'm sorry about Tonya," he said, instead of pushing her to confess. "And I'm sorry for everything you've been through."

Tears filled Edie's eyes. Tonya was why Edie dressed in black and went after the people she stalked. Tonya was innocent. She was loved and valued. She was a wonderful person. But she was in the wrong place at the wrong time and an evil soul stole her from the world.

Tonya's death took a piece of Edie. The moments she was aware of what was happening to her, which were few and far between, she thought of her family. Tonya was the first person she wanted to call when she got free. Her cousin who was more like a sister, Tonya was her best friend in the world. They hadn't been in touch as much in the last few years, and Edie would live with that regret forever.

Her chest ached for the loss of her cousin, and she let her tears fall, unable to withhold the emotions that swarmed her like bees. One sting after another weakened her defenses, and before long, Edie was sobbing in the booth.

Pryce slid in next to her, his warm body startling her when his arm moved around the back of her neck.

They both froze, panic threatening to drag Edie under.

"It's me, Edie. Lean on me. Let me be here for you." Pryce's voice was soft, emotional, and soothing.

Edie turned into him, burying her face in his chest and not letting herself think about why she was willing to let him comfort her when she hadn't been able to lean on anyone else since she escaped hell.

Pryce's hand rubbed up and down her back, a touch that had her quieting even as he encouraged her to let it all out. He never once shushed her or asked her to stop the outpouring of emotion that had her crying in a public place.

Edie finally cried enough to wrangle her emotions back into control and drew a shaky breath, inhaling the scent of his uniform and the scent of the man holding her. It wasn't familiar. Something that brought her a bone-deep sense of relief she didn't know she needed until it was there.

Edie inhaled again, enjoying the unfamiliar smell of him and let herself be comforted another minute. She finally lifted her head from his chest and looked at the man.

His eyes held sympathy, but no pity. His face was open and understanding. His hand remained on her back, his fingertips trailing over her shoulder and keeping them connected.

"I'm sorry," Edie whispered.

Pryce shook his head. "Never apologize for emotions. They're what make us human. If we stop expressing them, we stop living. And after what you've been through... I'm sorry, but I'm happy I was here to offer a shoulder for you."

Edie smiled up at him. "Thank you."

Pryce nodded once, then eased the pie in front of them. He speared a bite of his, settling into the seat next to Edie as though it was perfectly normal for them to share one side of a booth.

Edie focused on her pie, enjoying the simple task of eating it. She chewed carefully, the crust scratching down her throat as she swallowed. She tried not to wince, but with Pryce next to her, he didn't miss it.

"Are you sure you're okay?"

Edie smiled at him, not saying a word.

He held her gaze for a long minute, studying her face as though it would tell him all he needed to know. "Go on a date with me."

It wasn't a question. It wasn't an order. It was a request, one he seemed as surprised by as Edie was.

"A date?" she rasped.

"Please. I'd like to get to know you better. I'd like to spend more time with you than I have. We can come here one night. Meet here. Or somewhere else. Where you can wear a dress and I can kiss you good night and maybe hold your hand."

"Yeah?"

"Was that an agreement or a question?" He smiled, his eyes lighting up at her response.

Edie grinned. "Both."

Pryce smiled. "Good. You choose where. Somewhere you feel comfortable. Somewhere you feel safe."

"Safe?" Edie asked.

Pryce scowled and looked away. "I love Niagara Falls, but the city isn't always safe. And the vigilante isn't helping."

"What do you mean?"

"She almost got herself killed tonight. She was lucky. But others are following her lead. We had a woman who attacked her ex-boyfriend a few nights ago. Said he'd been abusive, and she wasn't going to sit around and take it. Almost killed him. She's going to end up in jail for assault instead of him going to jail. Another woman fought back against a would-be carjacker. Maced the guy and drove off, hitting a pedestrian."

"What's wrong with women protecting themselves? Defending themselves? A victim of domestic violence was only doing what the police never did. Same with the other woman, it sounds like."

"People are getting hurt. The ex-boyfriend could have died. The pedestrian the second woman hit could have been, too."

"Are you seriously telling me she should have let the carjacker take her car? Or hurt her?"

"No, I'm not. But that pedestrian was innocent. The vigilante, a young couple helped her tonight. They saw what was going on and shouted for the man to stop. But what if he'd turned on them? Or if his partner hadn't been knocked out?"

"People just need to let others get hurt? Ignore the bad and trust the system?"

"Yes! That's what the system is there for. To handle criminals and get justice for victims."

"Who's getting justice for my cousin? Or for me? Or the other women who are still being held captive in that house where I was held? Who's doing something about that? Or taking down the drug dealer who supposedly sold drugs to that kid? People are dying, disappearing, lives destroyed. Tell me what the police are doing to stop it? Because as far as I know, they're letting all the bad things happen."

"Edie, that's not—"

"True? Fair? I was missing for months, Pryce. Months. And no one thought anything of it. Said it looked like I just left. I'd be willing to bet the same thing happened with all the other women I was kept with. Meet a man at a bar, or a diner, think he's nice, and the next thing you know, you've been drugged, raped, and you're chained to a wall. Tell me again how the police are doing so much to help."

"Edie." There was the pity missing before. The pity that said she was both unhinged and flipping his savior switch.

"Let me out, Pryce," she growled, shoving at him to move from the edge of the booth. "I can't sit here with you."

"Edie, let's talk about this," he said, even as he moved.

The second he was out of the booth, she shoved to her feet. "I think I've heard all you have to say. And if it wasn't obvious, I think a date is not such a great idea. Have a good night, Officer."

"Edie. Edie!"

She ignored his shouts and hurried out of the diner, catching Jenny's scowl and glare in his direction.

Edie jumped in the van and sat there. She wasn't sure if he was going to follow her out of the diner and didn't want to risk Pryce following her back to Shelter in the Storm, so she sat in the dark of the van.

A minute later, he walked out. He looked at the parking lot, scanning the cars. Edie was low in the seat, barely visible and even better hidden with the shadows she parked under.

Pryce paused, looking around again, then lifted his radio to answer a call. He listened, then replied to whoever was talking to him. He glanced around once more, then went to his car and pulled out. As soon as he was on the street, lights and sirens went on and he was gone.

It was better that way. Edie wasn't ready to let go of her quest for vengeance. Not yet. And a man like Pryce would challenge that.

It was better to be done with him before they even got started.

EDIE SAT at the kitchen table and sipped her tea, letting the honey and lemon calm her and soothe her throat from the inside. It was still sore, and would be for a while. There was bruising in a telltale ring around her neck, but her dark sweater, brown skin, and an extra layer of foundation disguised the color enough that someone would have to look very closely to notice it.

Thank God for small favors.

"Good morning, Edie," Stacey said, walking into the kitchen with a smile.

"Morning," Edie said, forcing the word out past her aches and pains, knowing Stacey would pick up on even the slightest change and call it out.

As predicted, Stacey looked at Edie twice, once before pouring her coffee and once after. The second look was careful, calculating, evaluating. Knowing in a way that felt supernatural at times and comforting others.

"How are you today?"

"Good, how are you?" Edie said with a smile. Distraction and turning it back on others was her favorite way to get through a day. After years of working as a video editor for a large company, Edie was used to going long periods of time without talking to others in person. She'd learned she preferred her own company to that of others most of the time. Living alone had been easy. She could go out into the world when she wanted companionship and be alone when she didn't.

Living at the shelter meant living in the world Frannie had constructed. One intended to heal women who had nowhere else to turn. One Edie desperately needed even as she fought against the tools available to her to actually help her heal.

"I'm doing well," Stacey said. She settled across from Edie at the table. "The boys are in the middle of baseball season. Wray is the coach for both of their teams, which means I'm the team mom for two groups of little boys. It's been fun, though. Evan has taken to playing really well. Better than Joey when he was this age. Our lives are so different than they were a year ago."

"Mine, too," Edie said, her anger catching her off-guard.

"It's coming up on a year since you were taken, isn't it?" Stacey asked.

Edie sucked in a breath. Yes, it was getting close. And no, she didn't want to think about it. Or talk about it. No matter what she promised Charlotte. Edie nodded.

"Is there something you want to do?"

"Like what? Celebrate?" Edie snarled. She wasn't being fair to Stacey, but she slept like shit, even worse than usual, and was sore and scared and angry. She'd almost ended up a victim all over again, dead in an alley next to a man who poisoned kids. And in that moment, she wondered if that was what she deserved. To be lost and forgotten, abandoned.

It was better than what the man could have done to her. What he did do to her.

"How was your night?" Stacey asked with expert precision, like a surgeon skilled at cutting out the dead parts of a person's soul and lifting them to the light.

"Fabulous," Edie said with a fake smile and an ache in her chest.

Stacey didn't reply, just waited. It was her favorite tactic.

Edie wasn't technically a guest in the house, so she wasn't required to attend regular therapy sessions with Stacey, but she'd shared some of what she'd been through with Stacey. Stacey was exceptional at her job. She never once judged or criticized. She made Edie feel heard and valued instead of guilty and shameful.

Things Edie felt constantly. Guilt. Shame. Blame. For Tonya's death. For leaving others behind. For not fighting back more. For being dumb enough to think the man she met in the bar was decent.

"You know my door is always open for you, Edie. If you need something, I'm happy to talk to you."

"Why?" Edie asked. When she made the deal with Charlotte that she would talk to Stacey, Edie was in a different place. After facing death once more, Edie wasn't sure she could do it. Even for Charlotte.

Stacey lifted her mug to her lips and drank her coffee. She took her time, not in a hurry to answer. Another one of those things she did that drove Edie crazy. Edie hated the silence. She hated waiting for someone else to speak.

"I'm just in a shitty mood," Edie said, as if that explained everything away.

"It has nothing to do with what happened last night?"

"What?" Edie gasped.

Stacey raised a brow.

"What do you know?"

Stacey shrugged. "Nothing more than you want me to."

"I don't want you to know anything."

"Edie, I know you have the mask. You know that. Raina told us. When there are reports on the news of a vigilante running around the city and tying up bad guys for the cops, I have to assume it's you. And before last night, I was worried but would never have asked. Now, after you were attacked, I need to ask if you're okay."

"Because you're a therapist."

"Because I'm your friend, Edie."

Edie stared at the woman across from her. Stacey had everything Edie always thought she wanted. A husband, two kids, a job she enjoyed. A full life.

A part of Edie wanted to hate Stacey for making it all look easy, but it hadn't actually been easy for Stacey. She'd been through her struggles, from her marriage nearly ending to the lives of herself and her family being threatened. She got through it, but it wasn't without a few scars.

Edie couldn't see a way through what she was dealing with. Maybe that was what she needed to talk to Stacey about.

"He knew I was coming. Big H. He's the drug dealer who sold to that teenager who died. He got out twelve hours after I delivered him to the police, so I followed him this time. I took pictures of him selling to other kids. Then I went to get him again, but he knew I was coming. He had backup."

Stacey leaned back in her seat, sipping her coffee while she listened.

"I knew the other man. Not... Like I knew Damon."

Stacey nodded, understanding what Edie wasn't saying. What she couldn't bring herself to say.

"When he wrapped his arm around me, I froze. I was so scared, Stacey. I just... I couldn't..."

The tears started again, racing down Edie's cheeks.

Stacey reached across the table for Edie's hand. She left

hers palm up, giving Edie the option to squeeze her hand or not.

Edie put her hand in Stacey's and borrowed the other woman's strength while she finished her story.

"Big H tried to defend me. The guy made it clear he knew who I was. Wrapped his hand around my neck. He was going to kill me, and Big H... The guy punched him, knocked him out with one hit. I couldn't breathe. I couldn't... He would have killed me. Which was only good because he threatened to bring me back to Trevor. I would have rather died than go back there."

"You're safe now," Stacey said.

Edie laughed mirthlessly and shook her head. "For now, maybe. But there are other threats out there. Others who wouldn't hesitate to kill me or attack me. Or others. Trevor has clearly taken over, and there's nothing I can do. Because they can still get to me. And when they do, I'm too fucking scared to stop them. I'm weak, Stacey. Just like I was the first time."

Stacey pursed her lips, the rebuttal fighting against her. It was clear in her eyes.

But she didn't say the words. The words Edie hoped she'd say. The words Edie needed to hear.

You're brave. You're strong. You can do anything.

Stacey didn't say those words.

6

———

"LET'S GO TO MY OFFICE," STACEY SAID.

Edie sighed. She didn't want to go to Stacey's office. She wanted to go back to bed and actually sleep. But that wouldn't happen, so she followed Stacey down the hallway to her office.

Stacey closed the door and took her seat on the other side of her desk. She sipped her tea and watched Edie.

Edie fidgeted. She didn't like being appraised. She knew Stacey saw something, but until the other woman opened her mouth, Edie didn't know what it was.

"I don't think you'll believe me since I've said it before and you keep refuting it, but you were not to blame for what happened. For what happened to you, what happened to Tonya, or what happened and is happening to those other women."

Edie let out a breath, her exhale a relief and a physical blow. Her body recoiled against Stacey's words, doubting them even before she finished saying them.

"We tell ourselves stories, from the time we have independent thoughts, we tell ourselves stories. Our brains are wired to protect us. To keep us safe. The problem is those stories aren't always accurate. Your brain has decided that you were to blame. That's one of the most common things we tell ourselves, especially as women. We are taught if we aren't perfect, bad things happen. And a bad thing happened. Many bad things. So, your brain has decided you're to blame."

"Tonya would still be alive if I hadn't been taken. She never would have come here looking for me," Edie whispered. Emotion overwhelmed her, adding to the tightness in her sore throat.

"That's true. But that still goes back to the belief that you're to blame for being kidnapped. That you did something wrong by flirting with a man in a bar. By thinking he was nice. By agreeing to leave with him."

Edie swallowed roughly. The night was partly a blur, but she remembered the man she'd spoken to. He was attractive and funny. She never suspected a thing.

"You shouldn't have to be watching for a man to drug you anymore than Raina should have been worried her boyfriend was going to turn abusive."

Stacey leveled Edie with a look that dared her to argue about Raina. They both knew Edie wouldn't. Edie and Raina had become friends, and Edie's quest for justice was almost as much for Raina as Tonya and the others still missing.

"How can I trust another man?" Edie whispered.

"You know it isn't about a man."

Edie didn't know that. Clearly, the look on her face said it all.

Stacey smiled. "It's about trusting yourself. It's about making what you think is the right decision. It's about you, not him. Whoever he is."

Edie chewed her lip, thinking about Pryce and the man

who almost killed her the night before. She felt like she could trust Pryce. She didn't know why, but she wasn't afraid of him. Not when he held her and let her cry, and not when she pushed him out of the booth and he moved.

Was it because she was in a public place? Or was it because of the man himself?

The man in the alley... He was obviously not someone she could trust, but she wondered if she would know that in any other situation. Would she think he was attractive if he didn't have her pinned to the wall with his hand around her throat? Would she consider going home with him if his scent didn't trigger a memory she couldn't access but could feel?

"What if I don't know how to trust myself?" Edie finally asked.

"What makes you think you can't trust yourself?"

"Aside from the obvious?" Edie asked wryly.

Stacey laughed. "Yes, aside from the obvious. Why are you unsure?"

Edie drew a breath. "I don't know what the man who attacked me last night looks like. I can't see his face. He was careful, staying in shadows last night so I wouldn't be able to see him. He was big, but that doesn't describe a person. I don't even know what color his skin was because the thing exposed was his hands and I was trying to breathe when his hands were close to me."

"And you were in shadows," Stacey added.

Edie nodded.

"So, what are you wondering? Do you think if you saw this man you'd be attracted to him?"

"I don't know! How do I know? I recognized his scent, which meant I knew him, but what if I didn't recognize his scent? What if he changed his cologne or something? What if he never forced himself on me and he's just a psycho I haven't met yet? What if—"

"Edie, Edie. Take a breath." Stacey moved around her desk to sit in the chair next to Edie, taking Edie's hands and inhaling with her until Edie's lungs stopped screaming for air.

"I have so many blank spots in my memory. So many things that are just gone. And I'm grateful for that because I don't want those memories, but it…"

"It catches you off-guard when one slaps you in the face like that."

Edie nodded. "I don't want to have this fear inside of me. I don't want to have it swamp me and make me feel like I'm not in control."

"What do you want to be in control of?"

"My body. My life."

"Is that it?"

Edie looked at Stacey, knowing Stacey was right. There was more. "I want to end Trevor and the company he works for. Or runs or whatever. I want to dismantle it piece by piece."

Stacey nodded slowly. "What did the man say to you last night?"

"What?"

"You said he made it clear he knew you. What did he say?"

"He said he heard I was out there trying to stop them and wanted to make sure I got the message to stop."

"Are you going to stop?"

Edie stared at Stacey. There was no judgement on her face, just understanding and curiosity.

"About a year ago, a woman named Holly came here. She was running from her husband. Her daughter came with her. Oscar was a violent man, and Holly knew he would kill her if she didn't get away from him. She was here for five months. Five months of rebuilding her confidence and learning to trust herself. Five months of doing the same for her teenage daughter. I encouraged them to go back to their life. To move on from here."

Edie was surprised. Stacey always recommended people leave the area when their abuser was still local.

"I know," Stacey said. "Holly is the reason I tell people to leave. I told her to leave, too, but Vera wanted to stay in school here. Close to her friends."

"What happened?"

Stacey shook her head sadly. "Oscar knew Holly's route. He knew when Vera had to be at school. He's her father, and he had access to information. He made it look like a random act, but it was him."

"How do you know?"

"He told me. When I went after him."

"You did what?"

"Holly was an amazing woman. She was kind and sweet and talented. She wanted to live. But she didn't want to deprive her child of a life. I was angry, and I started following Oscar."

"And you got him arrested?"

Stacey shook her head. "I got him killed. A teenage girl lost both of her parents, and it's because of me."

"You can't blame yourself," Edie said, repeating the words Stacey told Edie many times.

Stacey smiled, making Edie laugh and shake her head.

"Okay, fine. You got me to admit that," Edie said.

"Good, but that wasn't why I told you about them. I told you because from the time Holly died to the time Oscar died, I refused to stop chasing him. To stop trying to prove what he did. It almost cost me everything, including my life, as I've shared before. But I didn't care. I wanted justice for Holly."

"That's how I feel," Edie whispered, realizing this was the story Stacey had hinted at before.

Stacey nodded. "I thought you might. And I can't tell you to stop. I know I wouldn't if I were you. I didn't. We all understand. We've all been there. I'm not sure if going back out there makes you crazy or brave or both, but the last word I'd ever use to describe you is weak, Edie. You're one of the strongest women I know."

Edie couldn't hold back the tears at Stacey's words. They calmed something she'd been doubting. Blame, weakness, and fear all came together for Edie. If one wasn't pounding on her, another one was. When all three jumped on together, it was the worst.

"So, how do I handle my fear?"

Stacey smiled. "You're not going to like my answer."

"What is it?"

"You can't. Fear is there to protect you, and until you get rid of the danger, fear will always be there. All women worry about what had you paralyzed with fear. About someone bigger and stronger surprising them and hurting them. For you, and for all victims of abuse or assault, it's worse because you've experienced it. You know what it is. It's not hypothetical for you. It's very real. Even though you don't remember everything you went through, your body does."

"Which is just a mind-fuck for me."

Stacey chuckled. "I can only imagine. Are there any men you trust? Any you aren't afraid of?"

Edie's mind immediately went to Pryce. Before she could dismiss the thought, Stacey grinned.

"Who are you thinking about right now? There's this little smile on your face I haven't seen before."

"It's no one. He's just..."

Stacey's brows shot up. "So there is someone."

Edie shook her head. "He's a cop."

"It's not Marcus, is it?" Stacey hissed.

"No! Of course not. I mean, I trust him, but he's not the man I was thinking about."

"Okay, then, who is the man you were thinking about?"

Edie groaned, knowing she'd walked right into that one. "His name is Pryce Murphy. He's the one who usually picks up the guys I tie up."

"Interesting. I didn't realize you waited around to talk to the cops."

"Oh, no, I don't."

"Then how do you know him? Because that smile is not the smile of a woman who's seen a guy a few times. There's more to it."

"After a night out, I go to Bob's Diner. He came in one night a few weeks ago."

"Okay. And?"

"He bought me pie. And we've talked a few times. He was there last night."

Stacey took a minute to process everything Edie said, then held up her hands. "Okay, first things first. What kind of pie?"

Edie laughed. "Peach."

"Ooh, nice choice. Is he cute?"

Edie chuckled, her cheeks warming.

"That's a clear yes. And he's nice?"

Edie nodded.

"Have you asked Marcus about him?"

"No. I... No. That's crossing a line."

"I don't think it is. You're asking as a woman who's been through a lot and you met a man and think he's nice and cute. You said you trust Marcus. Why not ask him if he ever had any suspicions about Officer Murphy?"

"I don't know. It feels unfair."

"Does he know who you are?"

Edie knew what Stacey was asking and nodded. "I told him."

Again, surprise showed on Stacey's face. "Really. Wow. You definitely trust him."

"His scent isn't familiar."

Stacey cocked her head. "And how do you know that?"

Edie fought a laugh and lost at the curious and suggestive look in Stacey's eyes. "Not because of that. He showed up last night. After... He brought me pie, and I sort of cried all over him. He smelled good. Not familiar."

"That's a good thing, Edie."

Edie nodded. "I know. But I can't just trust that if I don't know their smell that they're decent."

"No, you can't. But it sounds like you trusted Officer Murphy before you cried all over him. That you'd already been talking and had a bit of a friendship going on."

"He asked me out."

"Whoa, what? You're dripping all this out here like diamonds. He asked you out?"

Edie laughed, really laughed. She couldn't remember the last time she laughed like that and didn't feel fake doing it.

"What did you say?"

"I said yes at first, but then he started talking about the vigilante and how she was putting others at risk. How other women were taking matters into their own hands and people were getting hurt."

"It's a tricky line," Stacey said diplomatically.

"You agree with him?"

Stacey shook her head. "No, I don't. Because just like I don't think you were to blame for getting taken, I also know these others weren't to blame for their situations. Marcus reached out to a lawyer friend to be in touch with the girl-friend who attacked her boyfriend. The history of abuse is not well documented, but there is some history. Gage Stevens usually focuses on estates, but he takes a pro-bono case here and there. He was going to help Jessica when she was arrested, but she ended up not needing him."

"What about the woman who hit the pedestrian?"

"That's a bit trickier because they're both victims. But you can't expect a woman who thinks her life is in danger to be rational and careful. I think that one will go away, too. But regardless, none of that is your fault. It's the fault of the people who put those women in those positions."

"Do you really believe that?"

"Yes," Stacey said without hesitation. "People use threats to induce fear and they use fear to control people. When someone is being controlled by another, I don't feel they should be accountable for their actions. Not when they're acting from a place of survival."

"Isn't that what I'm doing? Using threats and fear to control people? I'm scaring these people and trapping them. I'm not sure I'm any better than they are."

Stacey shook her head slowly. "I know there's a line. Officer Murphy isn't completely wrong that what you're doing is a risk. What I did was a risk. What we've all done was a risk. You're trying to do the work the police should be doing. Marcus is frustrated that things have gotten as bad as they are under his command. After he learned about Bernard, he personally went through the record of every single person on the force, from administration up to the top and had Internal Affairs investigate people he thought might be involved in something illicit. They got rid of a few people. He thinks there still might be more, but he has no proof and no suspects."

"Maybe I should ask him about Pryce."

Stacey nodded. "I think you should. If for no other reason than Marcus will keep a closer eye on him. Especially if he's always the first one to your scenes."

"Mackenzie wouldn't call him directly unless she trusted him," Edie said, trying to figure out how Pryce was always there before anyone else.

"Does she know him? Do you think she's calling him specifically?"

Edie shook her head. "I don't know. She's never mentioned him, but that doesn't mean she doesn't know him."

"Sounds like you have two people to talk to. But Edie?"
"Yeah?"

"Be careful. And if you ever need someone to go with you, or want someone to know where you are, reach out."

"I've never wanted to implicate the rest of you."

Stacey snorted. "We have connections. I think we'll be okay. Plus, that's nowhere near as important as making sure you come home every night."

"Thanks, Stacey," Edie whispered.

"You're welcome."

They both stood, and Edie reached over to hug a very surprised Stacey. It was the first time she'd ever done that.

Stacey returned the hug easily, holding on to Edie until she let go.

"Thank you for pushing me to talk. And for the advice."

"You're welcome. And make sure you talk to Marcus," Stacey said as she opened the door.

"Talk to me about what?" Marcus asked, a few feet away.

Edie sucked in a breath. She gave Stacey a scared look.

Stacey smiled and stepped forward. "Edie met a police officer at Bob's Diner one night. He seems nice, but Edie's a little apprehensive and wondered if you'd give her your thoughts on him."

Marcus looked at Edie and nodded. "Yeah, of course. Who is it?"

"Pryce Murphy."

Marcus rocked back on his heels and looked at the ceiling. "Murphy had some trouble as a rookie. His sister and her boyfriend—"

"Got caught at a party and said they were with him. Yeah, he told me," Edie said.

Marcus tilted his head and laughed softly. "Impressive. He keeps to himself. A lot of the other cops are reluctant to work with him. He changed partners a lot the first few years. Usually it was just a bad fit, but Murphy seems like a good officer. From what I've seen, he never crosses a line. Any line. He's a real stickler. Which I can't say I disagree with."

Edie nodded, wondering if Marcus was trying to tell her something else.

"He works alone, electing not to have a partner anymore. He's built a network of CIs that are invaluable to him and the rest of the force. I think he's a man who can be trusted."

Stacey nodded, looking between the two of them, her brows high in question as she met Edie's gaze.

Edie considered Marcus's words. If the police captain would trust Pryce, Edie had no reason not to. How relieved that made her feel was not something she was willing to think about at the moment. "Thank you, Marcus. I appreciate your assessment."

"Any time, Edie. Have a good day, ladies." Marcus continued down the hallway and turned into the dining room.

"Do you feel better?" Stacey asked.

Edie nodded. "Yeah, I do."

"Good enough to agree to that date he asked you out on?"

Edie chuckled. "We'll see."

7

Pryce handed a woman over to booking and went to his desk to finish the paperwork. The woman was charged with public intoxication and disorderly conduct after she flipped a table and broke a barstool. When Pryce arrived, she tried to dry-hump his leg and propositioned him if he didn't arrest her.

She didn't know who she was dealing with.

Pryce hated calls like that. It made him uncomfortable, but these days, it also made him think about Edie and everything she went through. The woman was going to wake up with a hell of a headache and a few charges against her, but she was safe. Which was how it should be.

She was lucky. Which sucked to even think, but Pryce knew it was the truth. Any random person could have taken advantage of the woman in the state she was in. It pissed Pryce off that a woman couldn't go out and get as drunk as she wanted and be safe, but that was the unfortunate reality of the world. And the unfortunate reality of his job. He'd seen more than his fair share of shitty situations where a person wasn't safe at a time when they should have been.

All the more reason Pryce was determined to stop the vigilante. She got lucky when she was rescued by the young couple, but luck had a tendency to run out. Pryce did not want to find her body on the side of the road one night.

There hadn't been a call about the vigilante since the night she was attacked, which did not help Pryce to sleep better. He thought it would, that knowing she was off the streets would be a good thing, but he found it worried him. That not knowing if she was still out there or if something happened to her weighed on him heavily. He didn't expect that to be the case, but it was.

Pryce finished his paperwork for the woman he brought in, then went through notes from the last week. No one had any reported incidents with the vigilante. No one had seen her and received any gifts from her.

Which meant she was either in hiding, injured, or missing.

But without knowing her identity, Pryce couldn't do anything about it. He had to wait.

And hope he would be able to find her one day and convince her to put her mask away and stop chasing bad guys. Or maybe join the police force and fight with them to stop criminals.

Pryce went back to his cruiser, marking himself as available for calls before he pulled out of the police department parking lot.

Pryce went into the city, heading toward Bob's Diner even though he hadn't been able to bring himself to stop in there since the night Edie ran out on him. The night she defended the vigilante and refused Pryce's request for a date.

But that area was known for rough nights and criminal activity. When Pryce brought in Big H, thanks to the vigilante he admitted to himself, they learned where he'd been selling drugs to teenagers. Where he met them. How he connected with them.

It only made sense to go back to that area.

A call came through the radio as Pryce turned down a side street.

"Bee-one-eleven, call in your area. Are you available?"

Pryce grabbed the radio from his dash. "Ten-four. Where am I headed?"

Dispatch gave Pryce the address, then said, "It's a gift."

Pryce hit the sirens and pushed the gas a little harder. He knew what it meant. The vigilante was out again. And leaving packages.

"On my way," Pryce told dispatch, hoping he made it there before the vigilante disappeared.

EDIE RETRIEVED the red wig from her bag and secured it into place. She checked her reflection. The wig was new. An online purchase that couldn't be traced back to her. She hoped. Plus, it was one more thing to give her confidence.

She took time after her talk with Stacey to decide what she wanted to do. Stacey was right, Edie finally decided. She wasn't going to ever get over her fear of being taken again, and putting herself at risk wasn't going to help that.

But Edie also knew she couldn't sit back and hide either. She could help. She was helping. And not getting back out there would only mean more women would be taken, raped, killed.

Edie couldn't stop all of it. No one could. But if everyone tried to do their part, she had hope things could change.

So, she was ready. All black clothes with a colorful top to

change into after her victory. And she would be victorious this time. She would bring down the bad guy and make sure he didn't hurt anyone again.

Snooping through Marcus's files was probably not the best thing to do to someone who'd been nothing but kind to her, but Edie couldn't help herself when she saw the folder on the table one morning. She didn't realize what it was until she'd already read it.

No, that was a lie. She knew what it was a lot sooner, but she didn't care. It was a new lead. Big H's supplier was a person of interest, thanks to Big H. He was singing like a canary and telling the police everything. Thanks to the pictures Edie provided and him hearing what she'd been through.

By some miracle, Big H hadn't told them her name. He knew it, which scared her almost as much as his friend, but Big H was keeping that information a secret. If Edie was going to make a difference, she needed to do it while her identity was still a secret.

Which was exactly what she was doing. She'd been following Big H's supplier and knew he parked his car in the garage Edie was in. She left her vehicle on the first floor and walked to the fourth floor, where James Hampton parked his vehicle.

He was a cocky son-of-a-bitch. Thought he was untouchable. Never bothered to carry a weapon or to employ a bodyguard. He'd been brought in for questioning more than a few times, but the man was smart. He always got away with whatever he was accused of. And probably more.

Edie positioned herself where she could see the stairwells and Hampton's vehicle. She knew it wouldn't be long before he arrived. The garage was dark and mostly empty. The people who worked in the area had gone home hours ago. The people left were there for other reasons. Reasons Edie didn't want to think about.

Footsteps echoed off the concrete stairs, alerting Edie to his presence before the man stepped out on the pathway toward his SUV. He was dressed like any other businessman in a gray suit and black dress shoes that clicked on the floor. His walk was brisk but not in a rushed way. More like a man who had places he needed to be.

Like processing more drugs that would kill kids.

Edie stepped out from the vehicle next to his, surprising him. "Your reign is over, James Hampton."

He looked her up and down, his gaze assessing.

Edie's skin crawled at the look in his eyes. A look that said he was not only not done but he was going to enjoy forcing himself on her.

She wasn't showing up unprepared again.

"You sure? Because I'd be happy to share with you. If you share with me."

"I'm good, thanks. But it's time for you to pay for your crimes."

He shook his head and took a step toward Edie. "I'm good, thanks."

Edie wasn't expecting him to lunge at her, but she was ready for him to fight back. She lifted her new bottle of pepper spray and pressed the trigger.

"Fuck! What the fucking hell, bitch? Aw, fuck!" He sputtered and shouted, trying to wipe the spray from his face.

Edie grabbed one of his arms. He shoved at her, but he was still swearing and in pain, giving Edie the opportunity she needed to zip-tie him to his own vehicle. She tightened the plastic over his wrist and the handle of the SUV, cinching it down until his wrist turned white.

"What the fuck is wrong with you?"

She glared at him. "I'm not the one making and selling drugs to kids. Getting them hooked now? Taking a book from the playbook of others. I get it. Great plan. Except, fucking hell, dude. They're kids. They're innocent. And you're manipulating them. You're killing them."

"One dead teenager is worth the risk," Hampton snarled.

Edie swung, punching him in the face. She didn't mean to, but she couldn't hold back.

Hampton's head hit the side of the SUV with a thud, but unfortunately, it didn't knock him out. Just made him louder.

Edie dialed nine-one-one and reported her present to the person who answered. Not Mackenzie, but another woman who supported Edie's mission to make the city safer. She told Edie to be careful, then hung up.

"I'm going to hunt you down and kill you, whore. I have powerful friends. I'll find out who you are."

"Good luck with that," Edie said, rolling her eyes.

She walked away, knowing she didn't have long before an officer would arrive. She hated that she hoped it might be Pryce.

Edie got halfway to the stairwell before she heard the door open. She stopped, turning around in time to see Hampton pull a knife from somewhere inside the vehicle.

Fear washed over her, like standing under the faucet before the shower turns on and getting doused with ice cold water. For a second, Edie froze, watching in horror as Hampton sliced the zip-tie and tugged his wrist free of the door.

"Thought I wasn't prepared? That I didn't know your preferred tool? I don't usually like the stupid ones, but I'll make an exception for you."

He advanced on her, the knife glinting in the shitty garage lighting.

Edie spun, ready to make a run for it, when the whoop of the police siren stopped her in her tracks.

Pryce. She nearly collapsed in relief.

Until she realized he was wholly focused on her. Not the drug dealer she'd packaged for him.

Edie pointed at the man retreating toward his vehicle. The knife was mysteriously missing, but the man himself was still there. And if the paperwork Edie read the other day was correct, the police wanted to bring him in.

"He's going to get away!" she shouted, hoping she was loud enough for Pryce to hear through the windows. And hoping she disguised her voice enough for him to not recognize it.

Pryce's gaze flickered between them. Recognition lit when he saw Hampton, but Pryce carefully climbed from his vehicle, his gun pointed at Edie while his eyes followed Hampton.

"James Hampton, don't move!" Pryce shouted.

"I didn't do anything wrong. She attacked me!"

"You're a person of interest. I need to bring you in for questioning."

"What about her?"

"She needs to come with us," Pryce said.

"Fuck that. I'm outta here." Hampton made a move toward his SUV, drawing all of Pryce's attention. He raced over to where Hampton circled his vehicle, giving Edie time to get away.

As soon as Pryce's back was to her, she ran for the stairs. Her sneakers were quiet on the concrete, and she was on the ground floor before he shouted above her.

Edie avoided the few cameras in the garage, cameras she

knew didn't work but didn't want to take any chances, then let herself into the shelter van. She eased out of the garage, not wanting to draw any attention to herself as she left from the entrance on the opposite side from the stairs she ran down.

Her heart pounded. Palms were slick with sweat. Her wig was hot and heavy. Everything felt too much.

But she did it. She brought down another bad guy. Someone the police were looking for. Someone who helped hurt others.

Edie drove to a residential street and parked along the curb with dozens of other vehicles. She cut the engine, hopeful there weren't any doorbell cameras that could see her.

She took a deep breath, her hands gripping the steering wheel. Then another. And another. Slowly, her heart slid back to a normal rhythm. A rhythm that wasn't dangerous. Edie unbuckled her seatbelt and moved between the front seats to the back of the van. She removed the wig and stuffed it into the bag she brought with her. She unzipped the black hoodie she wore. And last, she took off her mask. Everything went into the bag, then she pulled her sweater over her head and fluffed her hair. She added a few sprays of dry shampoo to hide the scent of her sweat more than anything else. Edie swiped on another coating of deodorant, then changed her shoes.

Completely transformed, she returned to the front seat of the van and started the engine again. She pulled out onto the quiet street and navigated her way through the neighborhood, smiling the whole way.

She needed pie. It was a night to celebrate. A night when a bad guy was put away and Edie escaped with her identity concealed. Pie was definitely in order.

PRYCE SEETHED the entire way to the police station. Yeah, he got the bad guy, but he only got one of them. Something James Hampton reminded him of every minute of the drive.

"She attacked me. My lawyer will have me out in ten minutes. You're a disgrace."

Pryce ignored the man in the backseat, knowing all of it was true, sort of. Hampton was not an innocent man. He was deceitful and manipulative. Big H named him as his supplier.

But Pryce let the vigilante go. He made a choice. A choice that could cost him. A choice he might regret forever.

Pryce pulled into the police station and unloaded his passenger, walking him through booking to where he was processed. Pryce reported the situation and signed the paperwork to allow Hampton to be moved to a cell before being given his phone call and questioned by detectives.

"Another gift?"

Speaking of detectives.

Fuck. "Detective Foster," Pryce growled.

Foster shook his head. His brown hair didn't move. Laugh lines on his face sprung to life when he looked at Pryce. "This time, your friend was still there when you arrived."

"How the hell do you know that?"

Foster moved fast, getting in Pryce's face before he could step back. "I'm a fucking detective. It's my job to know what happened. You let one criminal go so you could bring in another. Even though you knew the entire department was looking for your friend. Do you really think you're not going to get into some serious shit for this?"

"Hampton is on the board," Pryce seethed. "He's a known drug supplier."

"And your girlfriend is a known assailant. She's going to be charged with assault, many times over, not to mention kidnapping and obstruction of justice."

"What? Why?" Pryce barked.

Foster rocked back on his heels. "I didn't realize your job description included being kept up to date with active investigations. I thought you were just supposed to bring in the bad guys, Murphy."

Pryce swallowed the retort on his lips. Knowing what was going on gave him ammunition to do his job the way he needed to do it. He saw Hampton as the bigger threat, as the one he should have brought in. They had a witness who could testify against him. A witness who was willing to cut a deal.

The vigilante was a ghost. Even though they knew what she'd been doing, everything about her was circumstantial. Unless there was a witness who could confirm her identity, every single charge was built on guesses and estimations. They had no idea if there was more than one, which would give alibis to whoever was caught. They also had no witnesses who could say without a doubt who the vigilante was.

Even Pryce. He'd seen her, but all he knew was she was a Black woman. Her red hair could have been a wig or a weave. She could change it and he'd never be able to pick her out. Even the way she moved and her figure were a mystery to him and wouldn't prove anything.

Which was why he chose to stop Hampton instead.

"If I had the opportunity to bring them both in, I would have. I made a judgement call based on the information I had at the time."

"A judgement call that might cost you your job." Foster shook his head like he couldn't believe what Pryce had done. "Can't say I'm surprised, though. It was only a matter of time."

Foster walked away before Pryce could say anything else. He squeezed his hands into fists and fought the urge to chase after the other man.

"Murphy," Pryce heard from behind him.

Pryce spun, finding Captain Marcus Patrick a few feet away.

"We need to talk," Patrick said.

As if the night wasn't bad enough, Pryce was about to be fired.

Fuck.

8

———

Pryce followed Captain Patrick to his office, swallowing hard when the captain closed the door behind them.

"Sir, if I may explain myself—"

"Sit down, Officer Murphy," Captain Patrick said.

Pryce gulped and lowered himself to the seat across the desk from the menacing captain. Pryce believed Captain Patrick to be a fair man, one who would listen to the evidence before making any assumptions.

But maybe not.

"I understand you had an encounter with the vigilante tonight," Captain Patrick said. His voice was low, like a father trying to get a child to confess to wrongdoing.

"Yes, sir."

"Did you get a good look at her?"

Pryce shook his head and dropped his gaze. "No, sir."

Captain Patrick was silent for a long moment. "I know you've been working hard to prove yourself lately."

"Sir?" Pryce's head snapped up to meet the captain's gaze.

"The vigilante has not made life easy for any of us. She's helped put away some pretty nasty criminals, though."

"Yes, but she's a criminal, too, sir."

"Is she?"

"Yes. She's assaulting people, and Detective Foster just told me she'll be charged with kidnapping and obstruction of justice. She's not innocent."

Captain Patrick shrugged. "Detective Foster is a little misguided. He also seems to think you have a connection to this vigilante."

"I've never seen her before tonight, sir."

Captain Patrick raised one dark eyebrow. The man had hints of gray at his temples, but otherwise, there was no indication of how old he was. His career was long and distinguished, which was what earned him the command of the precinct. That and his ability to know when someone was lying.

Pryce squirmed under his boss's appraisal. "I don't know her, sir. I've never met her. She's not tipping me off. I assure you, I'm not breaking any laws."

Captain Patrick shook his head. "I never said you were. Just that Foster has his own beliefs."

"You believe me?"

"Officer Murphy, a lot of shit has happened in this precinct recently. Right under my fucking nose. Trust me when I tell you that's not something I ever want to have happen again. I've personally looked into every single officer here. There are some I'm still looking into. But I have no choice but to trust the team we have. If I can't trust the people I send out every single day to do their job and to keep this city safe, then why the hell am I here?"

"Uh, I don't know, sir."

Captain Patrick didn't look too pleased with Pryce's

answer. He scowled and jerked his head to the side like he was shaking off the response. "Officer Murphy, did you lie when you were brought in years ago? Were you actually at that party and partaking in the drugs there?"

"No, sir," Pryce answered forcefully. He didn't appreciate his character being called into question, even by his boss.

"Do you know the vigilante? Are you helping hide her identity so she can evade charges?"

"No. Sir."

"Would you admit to either of these things if they were true?"

Pryce definitely was not expecting that question. He hesitated, drawing back just enough to show his reluctance to answer.

"Officer?" Captain Patrick growled.

Pryce pulled the dog-tags from under his uniform. He looked at the name stamped into the metal, then met the eyes of his captain.

"My grandfather fought in World War Two. Growing up, he told me stories about being there, vague and mostly focused on my grandmother, but it was enough to know he was proud of what he did. He enlisted when he was only seventeen because he couldn't bring himself to sit back and do nothing. He met my grandmother there and brought her back here. My grandfather was my hero, sir. He taught me the value of service and the pride that comes with doing something others won't do. He also taught me to protect those I love, and more importantly, that sometimes protecting the ones we love means leaving them to face the consequences of their actions."

Captain Patrick leaned back in his seat, studying Pryce carefully.

Pryce continued his story. "My sister was dating my best friend from high school. When we were teenagers, we did stupid shit. I'd like to think all teenagers do, but I don't know. I went to college, and I straightened myself out. I became the person my grandfather saw in me. The night my sister and her boyfriend were arrested, the night he said I was with him, I was nowhere near that party. I didn't know they were dating. I didn't know anything about any of it until the officers showed up at my door and dragged me here out of bed for questioning."

Captain Patrick nodded, his brows raised in understanding as he considered Pryce's story. "It's not an easy decision to make people live up to their actions. To refuse to step in and help. What do you think would have happened if you'd said you were with them that night?"

Pryce shook his head. "I don't know. I'm assuming I'd have lost my job. They might have gotten away with it at the time, but I'm sure eventually they would have been caught."

"And you wouldn't have been there for them to drag down."

Pryce nodded slowly, agreeing and understanding.

"Is that why you're so interested in the vigilante? Because you believe she should face what she's done?"

"Do you not, sir?"

Captain Patrick shook his head. "I didn't say that. I think we all have a responsibility to abide by the laws. But I also know the laws don't always do what they were intended to do. The man you brought in tonight?"

Pryce nodded.

"He's a dangerous man. He's been questioned many times before. He always gets away with whatever he's done. We all know he's guilty, but his lawyer knows the law almost better than we do and uses every trick in the book to make sure the work we do to bring him in is questioned and he's released."

"So you're saying it was a waste of my time to bring him in and let the vigilante go?"

Captain Patrick chuckled. "No. Not at all. I would have done the same thing as you. He's dangerous. He's killed people. I'd bet my career on it. The vigilante is helping. She might not be doing it the way we would, but she's helping."

"We don't always have enough for a case."

"True, but getting the people she leaves for us into the station can sometimes do things we didn't expect."

"Like Big H flipping?"

Captain Patrick nodded. "Exactly. He's still going to jail, but he'll get an easier sentence and he'll be in a minimum security prison instead. He'll have a chance at a future one day. And thanks to him, James Hampton is going away."

"Do you really believe that?"

"I do. And we have the vigilante to thank. If I knew who she was, I'd definitely tell her that."

Pryce nodded, trying to piece together everything Captain Patrick was saying. Pryce didn't like crossing lines. It meant going against what he'd been trained, both by his grandfather and in the academy.

But there were limits to what the cops could do. And none when someone worked outside the law.

Maybe Pryce needed a new perspective. The kind of one Edie seemed to have.

EDIE FINISHED her pie and coffee. She was more than a little disappointed Pryce hadn't shown up, but she didn't have any reason to think he would. It wasn't like they had an agreement. And it wasn't like she could reach out and ask him to meet her there.

It was still disappointing.

She waved to Jenny on her way to the door. Her adrenaline had dissipated, and she was ready to go to bed. With any luck, she might actually get some sleep.

Edie reached to push the door open as it was pulled out by someone on the other side. "Officer," Edie gasped.

"You're here," he breathed. "But you're leaving."

"Oh, um, I don't have to," Edie stammered. Her lips lifted in a smile. She felt like a teenager with a crush on the quarterback. Like she was special because he was paying attention to her.

"I don't want to hold you up."

"I don't mind."

They stood there, staring at each other, both wearing dopey grins, until a man cleared his throat behind Edie.

"Mind letting me out?" he asked gruffly.

"Sorry," Edie mumbled as she stepped back. Into the diner.

Pryce held the door for the man, then followed Edie into the diner. He stood in front of her, looking her over.

Was he looking for red braids? Or black clothes? Edie's mind raced as she wondered if he recognized her. He hadn't said her name but that didn't mean—

"Should we get a table?"

Edie nodded, willing her racing heart to slow. Pryce held his hand out for Edie to go first. She returned to the booth she'd just left, reclaiming her seat facing the door.

Pryce sat across from her, smiling at her like he couldn't believe she was there.

She felt the same way.

"Can I get you two anything?" Jenny said, smirking at Edie.

Edie's cheeks warmed under the older woman's assessment. Edie didn't like people knowing her business. Not anymore. And knowing that Jenny was not only aware of the two of them sitting together but also had an opinion made Edie a lot uncomfortable.

"Pie?" Pryce asked.

Edie shook her head. "I already had a slice. But I'll take a water."

Jenny nodded, then turned back to Pryce.

"Peach pie and a coffee, please."

"Coming right up," Jenny said, walking away without another word.

"How are you?" Pryce asked as soon as Jenny was a few feet away.

Edie nodded. "I'm good."

"Yeah? Last time I saw you..."

Edie fought the urge to cup her neck. Pryce knew something happened, but revealing exactly what happened could be a clue she didn't want him to have. "I'm better. Thank you."

Jenny delivered Pryce's coffee and pie and Edie's water, then left them alone again.

"I haven't seen you here since then," Edie said. She hadn't been back much, but when she was, he wasn't.

Pryce shook his head. "I didn't want to risk upsetting you more than I did."

"But you're not worried about that tonight?" Edie teased.

Pryce chuckled. "Not entirely. I came looking for perspective."

"About?"

"The vigilante."

Edie choked on the sip of water she'd just taken. Of all things, that was the last one she thought he was going to say.

Pryce stared at her with alarm while Edie struggled to drag air in and shove water out of her lungs. "Are you okay?"

Edie shook her head and coughed out the last of the water, sucking in a full breath of air and finally feeling like she wasn't going to die. "Sorry. Just didn't expect that."

"I didn't mean to startle you."

"Startle is a bit of an understatement. You were pretty clear how you felt the last time we talked."

Pryce nodded. "I was. And I... I saw her tonight."

"You did?" Edie gasped, hoping the reaction was appropriate and convincing.

Pryce nodded again. "I let her get away."

"Why?"

"Because the man she was after was going to get away if I chased her. And he was... not someone who needed to be on the streets."

"But you think you did the wrong thing?"

"I thought I was going to get fired."

"Marcus wouldn't fire you," Edie said.

"Marcus? You know my boss?" Pryce asked.

"Shit." Edie didn't think about what she was saying. It wasn't a big secret that she was living at Shelter in the Storm, but it wasn't something she went around talking about either.

"How do you know Captain Patrick? Unless you're talking about another Marcus who has the power to fire me."

Edie sighed heavily. "I live at his house."

Pryce tilted his head. "His house? He lives... at Shelter in the Storm."

Edie nodded. "My apartment was rented to someone

else when I came back. I went to rehab, because they gave me lots of drugs. When I got out, I had nowhere to go and couldn't really function. It's been..."

Pryce reached across the table and put his hand over Edie's. "I'm sorry, Edie. I'm such an idiot. I never thought about what things could be like for you. About what happens after. During was bad enough, but now you're rebuilding your entire life."

Edie nodded. "Marcus and his wife, Frannie, have been amazing. They let me stay at the shelter when I got out of rehab, but I had a lot to work through and every sound set me off. I ended up in a safe house for a while—"

"Raina London," Pryce breathed.

Edie nodded again.

"You were there when Damon Street... Jesus, Edie. And I'm the asshole who asked you out on a date. Like you'd ever want anything like that. I'm so sorry. I—"

"I wanted that, too," Edie interrupted. "A date. I..." She inhaled and swallowed roughly. "I feel like my life's been on hold. My old job was filled, so I'm having to start from scratch with that. I'm living at the shelter because I have nowhere else to go. I couldn't afford a place anywhere. I have no furniture or clothes or anything. Just what I've gotten in the last few months. I'm... I'm trying to figure out who I am now. What I want. And Marcus and Frannie have given me the space to do that."

"Edie, I..." Pryce looked as though he didn't know what to say. Where to go with the conversation.

"So, what perspective were you looking for?" Edie asked, choosing to move forward with the conversation he started instead of getting sucked into the conversation she created.

Pryce smiled at her. His hazel eyes sparkled, grateful and

open. Honest. Trustworthy, like Marcus said. "Captain Patrick pulled me aside tonight."

Edie was a little surprised by that, but she tried not to react. She hoped Marcus wouldn't betray her confidence, and Pryce's surprise that they knew each other was too natural to be faked. Especially if he was just going to tell her they were talking.

"Some of the others in the department think I'm working with the vigilante. That I know where she's going to be. That it's how I'm usually the first on the scene."

"But that's not true."

Pryce shook his head, thinking she asked a question. "It's not. I swear. I have no idea who she is. Even after seeing her tonight, she's not familiar to me. But I let her go, so the rumors are going to be even more rampant."

"What did Marcus say?"

"I think he believes me. But he also told me he would have done the same I did."

"Letting her go?"

Pryce's face twisted with pain as he nodded. "Captain Patrick said she's helping. That if he knew her, he would thank her for what she's done to help."

"He said that?" Edie gasped. She never expected Marcus to be on her side. Or that he would agree with what she was doing. Stacey knew, and she made it seem as though they all knew. Did that include Frannie and Marcus? Was he telling her something?

Did he leave that file out on purpose?

Did she care?

"When my sister was arrested, I knew she needed to feel the bottom. That she wouldn't get her life back together unless she was forced to face what she'd done. Some people don't do the work, but Katherine did. It wasn't easy, but she did it. She turned her life around."

"You're proud of her."

"Extremely."

"And you think the vigilante needs to do the same? Accept what she's done and face the consequences?"

"I did. But Captain Patrick... I think he sees a bigger picture. There's more to it than I know. And I feel like you can see the same thing. That you understand more than I do. I wondered if you could share some of your thoughts with me."

"I did before, and you got mad."

Pryce nodded. "I'm sorry about that. I wasn't ready to listen. But I am now. Why do you think the vigilante is doing the right thing?"

Edie drew a breath and thought back to her first night of freedom. The first night she remembered. "Damon Street rescued me from the house where I was kept for months. He promised me drugs and got me to follow him. Then he locked me up. The drugs wore off enough that I knew I had to get out of there. I climbed out a window and disappeared into the snowstorm last winter. I ended up at the rescue center and was fortunate to find two people who were able to protect me, keep me alive, and make sure I was safe. They got me to Marcus, who got me to rehab."

Pryce sipped his coffee and started to eat his pie, settling in and open. For the first time, Edie felt like someone was listening to her.

"My first night in rehab was painful. I wasn't there because I wanted to be. I needed to be there, but it was hard. I screamed at the nurses to give me drugs. I pounded on the door until my fists were bloody. I wanted to die. I prayed I would."

"But you didn't."

Edie shook her head slowly. "Someone sat down outside my door. It was after hours and we were locked in our rooms for the night. The only way they were allowed to open the doors was if there was a medical emergency. She sat there and told me she was sorry and that I had to be stronger than the drugs. Stronger than the people who gave me the drugs. That I had to fight back. She said it wasn't easy, but she kept telling me I was strong and I could do it. I laid on the floor on the other side of my door and listened to her voice until I fell asleep."

"Wow."

Edie swallowed roughly. "I believed her. I knew she was telling me the truth. I decided when I woke up the next morning that I was going to do what she said. I was going to be strong. I was going to fight back. I was going to overcome the forced addiction and help others. Tell my story so the men who took me would go away for the rest of their lives."

"Good for you. And what a gift that woman gave you."

Edie breathed a laugh. "That's what I thought. I asked the next day if I could meet her. They told me no one was there. The nurses walked past my door many times overnight, and there was never someone who sat there."

"What? Then who was it?"

"I think it was my cousin. Tonya. Maybe it was my imagination, maybe it was the drugs, maybe she was a spirit, but I dedicated my recovery to her, and every day, I wake up and I tell myself I'm going to do whatever I have to that day to make sure no one else is ever in the position Tonya was in. That no one else is going to die because of men like Damon Street and the others in his organization. And the vigilante, she's out there doing it. She's out there making that happen.

So, yeah, I'm a fan. I'm a supporter. And I'd definitely tell her thank you, too."

Pryce was quiet for a long moment. He studied his empty pie plate and spun his fork in his hand. Then he looked up and met Edie's gaze. "Are you the vigilante?"

9

———————

THE LOOK OF SHOCK ON EDIE'S FACE WAS ALMOST ENOUGH TO make Pryce laugh. He was amazed he managed to ask her with a straight face, but the horror on her face was even better than he expected.

"Are you kidding?"

Pryce let out the laugh he was holding back and nodded. "Yes, I am."

Edie sighed, her entire body sagging with relief. "You had me worried."

Pryce shook his head. "The way you were talking about Tonya and your recovery and everything, you made me think you might be the kind of person we're looking for. Obviously not you."

"Obviously."

Pryce chuckled, reaching across to grab her hand. "I'm sorry. I didn't mean to upset you."

She shook her head, the shock wearing off before she met his gaze with her regular sassy one. "I'm a little uneasy about cops in general, and the idea of being questioned was kind of scary."

"Shit, Edie. I'm sorry. I really didn't mean anything by it. I've been trying to figure out what could drive a person to do what she's doing. She's putting herself in danger, but she's also out there trying to help."

Edie raised a dark eyebrow. "You're a fan now?" she teased.

Pryce exhaled a laugh. "I'm not sure I'd go so far as to say I'm a fan. More like I'm trying to understand her perspective."

"Don't you cop-types call that profiling?"

Pryce nodded. "Yes, but that's not my job. I'm not a detective, nor am I expected to have any opinion on a suspect. I'm supposed to bring in the people I pick up and let my superiors figure out the rest."

"You sound a little bitter about that," Edie said.

Pryce leaned back, sliding his hand from hers. He missed her touch almost immediately, but he wouldn't reach for her again. Not when he wasn't sure where things stood with them.

"I wanted to be a detective. It was a goal when I started. I liked the idea of not just bringing people in, but helping them. Obviously, part of the job is putting away the people who commit crimes, but there are a lot of programs where cops work with the community and give back. Detectives are expected to participate in some of those, but they're also the ones who do the investigations. Look beyond the obvious to figure out what actually happened."

"So people don't slip through the cracks," Edie snarled.

"Exactly. Honest, real police work would have brought you home sooner and saved your cousin from coming here."

Edie looked up at him with tears shining in her dark eyes.

Pryce hated that he put that look there. That he brought up the worst piece of her life. "I'm sorry about Tonya."

Edie nodded slowly, wiping the tears from her lashes before they fell. "Thank you."

"What the vigilante is doing is still not okay. She's hurting people, but after talking to you, and Captain Patrick, I can see where she thinks she's doing the right thing. Protecting people. Trying to give back in her way."

"We all have to do what we can. If too many people look the other way, nothing changes."

Pryce nodded. "That's very true. That's why I've created a network of confidential informants. I know people see things. If they aren't willing to tell us what they see, we can't eliminate threats. The vigilante knows things most people don't know. She's finding people that are on our radar, but we either can't find or don't know we should be looking into in the same way. She would be a good detective."

"Really?" Edie gasped.

Pryce laughed. "Yeah. Obviously, she'd have to follow the rules, but I think she would be. I'm not sure I'm ready to thank her for what she's doing, but I guess her getting away tonight wasn't the worst thing in the world."

Edie grinned. Her brown eyes lit up with joy. "I think you should ask me out again."

"Why is that?" Pryce asked.

"Because I'll say yes this time."

Pryce's heart jumped. His dick did, too, but he ignored that one. "Oh, yeah?"

Edie nodded slowly.

Pryce tilted his head to the side. "Maybe I should wait for you to ask me out."

"Okay. I will. Pryce, will you go on a date with me?"

Pryce grinned so wide he felt like a fool. A fool for her. He nodded. "Hell, yes."

"Good. Maybe someplace with tablecloths?"

"I think that's a good idea. Although, I think this might be my favorite place in the city these days."

"Really?" She wrinkled her nose in an adorable way.

Pryce nodded. "It's where I met you."

Edie ducked her chin and smiled like she was more than a little pleased by his words. "I think I agree."

"Are you willing to give me your number, or do you want to set something up now so we can meet?"

Edie studied him closely. "I think I can trust you. After all, Marcus vouched for you."

Pryce could not have been more shocked to hear that. "What? You asked him about me?"

Edie shrugged. "I haven't dated since... And I..."

"You don't have to explain, Edie. Thank you. For trusting me and for saying yes."

"I think you're the one who said yes. I had to ask you."

Pryce laughed. "You're right, I did. So I guess I should say thank you for asking me out."

"You're welcome."

Pryce grinned as he handed over his phone. She keyed in her number and handed it back. Pryce sent her a text so she'd have his number in her phone. He was about to ask when she was free when he got a call on his radio.

"I'm sorry, but I have to go."

"Good luck. Be safe."

Pryce stood and looked at her. No one had said that to him in years. It was touching, and told him he wasn't the only one who cared. "Thank you, Edie. I'll see you soon."

"I hope so."

Pryce stopped before he walked out the door and looked back, finding her watching him. He definitely liked that.

TAKING down a bad guy and having a date lined up with a good guy made Edie confident. She wasn't sure she was ready for the night she had planned, but she wanted to be. She'd been thinking about it for months. She needed to do it.

Even if she couldn't go through with her plan.

It had been almost a year since she walked into Bottom's Up. It had been her regular hangout before she was kidnapped from the place and lost months of her life to drugs and assault.

The outside was shockingly familiar with the gravel lot and poor lighting. Neon lit up the area more than street-lights and led the way to the bar. Edie pulled the handle, memories assailing her as she stepped inside.

She'd been happy going there before. Excited. She met old friends and new at the bar that had become her favorite place to spend an evening. Nearly a year after stepping foot in the place, she expected it to look different, or at least feel different, but it was like stepping back in time.

Music played through speakers positioned throughout the space. Tables lined the outside walls, with the bar front and center in the middle. The scent of greasy food dragged Edie back to the night she was last there and the fries she shared with the man she remembered talking to.

"Ketchup or mayo?" he asked.

"Who dips their fries in mayo?" Edie asked, flirting with the man as she swiped a fry through her puddle of ketchup. "Gross."

He laughed, the sound deep and rumbly. Appealing. Every-

thing about him was appealing. Dark brown hair and light brown eyes with an easy smile and a caring demeanor.

He stepped in when another man tried to get handsy with her. Told the guy to back off when Edie tried to stop him from dragging her to the dance floor. She invited the guy to sit down.

Jason? She thought that was his name.

Now she wondered if Jason and the other guy were in on it. Probably. It was an opening. An excuse. And it worked like a fucking charm.

Someone bumped into Edie from behind, jostling her back to the present. They apologized and kept going, moving toward the bar.

Edie fell into step behind the person, warring internally. She wanted to leave. Turn around and walk out the door and never step foot in there again.

But it was where she was taken. It was definitely a place others were taken from. It was possible a bartender or server was in on the scheme. If not, whoever was taking women from there was even sneakier than Edie suspected.

She grabbed a stool toward the edge of the bar, where she had a good view of the entire place. It wasn't long before a bartender was in front of her, asking what she wanted to drink.

The old habit was strong, one that had Edie opening her mouth and asking him for a Long Island Iced Tea.

The guy grinned at her and nodded, clearly approving of her choice. It was an expensive drink, and bartenders knew you were either there to get drunk or didn't know how strong it was.

"Want to open a tab?" he asked as he set the drink in front of Edie with a flourish.

"No. I know better than to think I can handle more than

one of these." She handed over enough cash to cover the drink and a good tip.

He grinned and nodded. "Let me know if you need anything else. I'm Scott."

"Thanks, Scott."

He nodded again, then walked away. He was friendly, but not creepy. Then again, Edie didn't trust her instincts, so what the hell did she know?

Cheers went up from a table behind Edie, a group of men who looked barely old enough to be in a bar celebrating something on one of the TVs. On the other side of the bar, a glass smashed, causing the patrons nearby to boo whoever was to blame.

The sounds and smells threatened to drag Edie under. She worked so hard to fight off her fear, but being back there, in the last place she remembered being, was a lot.

She looked at the drink and debated. She hadn't had a drink since she got free. Drugs were never her thing and staying away from them would be easy, but alcohol? Edie liked a drink once in a while. She enjoyed relaxing with friends and taking the edge off.

Could she still handle it?

She closed her eyes and wrapped her lips around the straw, sucking gently.

The flavor washed over her tongue, bringing back more and more memories. Tears welled behind her closed lids. For the life she used to have, the woman she used to be.

Edie knew she would never be the same, but being there was another slap in the face that proved it.

She couldn't stay there. She was wrong to think she was strong enough to do it. She wanted to, but being there was more than she could handle.

Edie set her drink down on the bar and turned to slide

off her stool. She looked up as her feet hit the floor and spotted Jason. The man who talked to her that night. The man who was so nice to her.

She blinked a few times, thinking the past and present were merging and she was wrong, but no, he was there. And he was helping a woman to the door. A woman who could barely stand on her own. A woman who was likely drugged and was never going to be seen again unless Edie could get to them.

A man stepped in Edie's path, talking to another man at the bar.

Edie sidestepped him and found Jason and the woman closer to the door. She pushed her way past the man, then weaved around another group of people.

She felt like she was in a pool, where every step felt slow and sluggish. She kept losing sight of Jason and the woman, but she knew they were heading for the door.

One step after another, Edie pushed herself forward. She couldn't stop. She couldn't let the woman disappear. She had to keep going.

She finally made it to the door, but Jason and the woman were nowhere to be seen. Edie burst outside into the cool night air. She swung her gaze left, then right. No cars left the lot. No one screamed. No one made a noise.

"Where are they?" she whispered into the dark.

"You okay?" two women asked, appearing from the darkness even though they'd only been a few feet away.

"Did you see a man and a woman leaving? He was almost carrying her."

The women exchanged a glance and shook their heads. "Sorry, no. Were they your friends? Did they ditch you?"

Edie shook her head. "No. I... I used to know him. Wanted to say hi."

"Sorry you missed them." The women moved past Edie and went into the bar, the noise deafening when they opened the door.

It closed again, sealing the sounds inside with Edie in the parking lot. Wondering what happened to the woman she saw with Jason.

Edie pulled out her phone and hesitated. If she called Mackenzie, there would be a record of the call. And Edie had nothing to report. Not really.

She scrolled past Mackenzie to Raina's number. Edie stood near the door, stepping to the side when people walked out, and waited for Raina to answer.

"Edie? Are you okay?"

"Yeah, I just... Can I come see you?"

"Of course. Do you need us to pick you up?"

"No. I'm okay."

"Are you sure?"

Edie chuckled. "Stacey told you where I was going, didn't she?"

"Um, maybe?" Raina was a shitty liar.

"I'm fine. I just need to talk to someone."

"We're here. I'll be waiting. Adam will watch the door and open it as soon as you get here."

"Thanks, Raina."

"Be safe."

Edie nodded and hung up, making her way to where she parked the van. She checked the inside and cranked it up, pulling away from the bar and hoping she was wrong about the woman she saw being led out of the bar.

ADAM WAVED to Edie as she parked the van in front of their condo. When he and Raina decided to move in together, they opted for a condo in a secured building instead of a house. Adam was new to the area, and Raina still had trouble sleeping even after Damon was gone.

Edie was happy for her friend and the new romance Raina had, but she was a little jealous. She and Raina talked about moving in together, but Edie didn't want to feel like a third wheel. Neither Adam nor Raina ever made her feel that way, but she wanted them to have the freedom to get to know each other and start a life together without Edie in their space.

Edie turned off the van and climbed out, locking the doors behind her and sliding the keys into her handbag before she walked up the path to the front door.

"Hey," Adam said, pulling her in for a hug as he let her into the building. "You doing okay?"

Edie shook her head as she hugged him, almost laughing as she realized she didn't hesitate to hug Adam. Adam was a nice guy, cute and kind. He was perfect for Raina. Hell, he'd be perfect for just about anyone, but Edie was happy he and Raina were together.

"I've been better."

Adam held out his hand for Edie to go ahead of him toward their unit. "I would have gone with you if you'd told us where you were going. Raina would have, too."

Edie nodded, even though it never occurred to her to do that. She wasn't sure if Adam was aware of her extracurricular activities, or if he approved, but she felt like she had to do things herself. Especially when she wasn't always on the legal side of things.

"Thanks."

"You're incredibly brave to go there. And to be working

with us to try to dismantle the rest of the organization Damon built." Adam was an FBI Agent on the team taking down Damon's organization. Adam and Raina met when he was brought in to protect her from Damon.

"I definitely didn't feel brave tonight."

"You are brave," Raina said, catching the end of their conversation from her spot at their door. "I don't think I could have ever done what you did."

Edie shrugged, feeling the emotions of the night welling up inside her. She bit her lip, trying to keep things inside, but Raina caught the move.

Raina's eyes widened. "Oh, my God, what happened?" She reached out for Edie, pulling her in for a hug and inside the condo in one move.

Edie fought to control her emotions as she heard the door close and lock behind them. She hugged her friend and knew she was safe and everything came out.

"I think the man who took me was there, and he left with someone else. I tried to chase them, but it was busy and I didn't get there before they were gone. She's gone. She's never coming back. And it's all my fault. I should have—"

"No," Adam growled. "It is not your fault. He went there with the intention of taking someone else, if that's what happened. It had nothing to do with you. You couldn't have stopped it."

"But—"

"He's right, Edie," Raina said. She led Edie to the couch and pulled her down, handing Edie a box of tissues. "If that was him, you probably weren't the first, and you definitely won't be the last. But you are not to blame."

"I saw them! I didn't do anything. I followed them, but I was too slow. And she's gone. Disappeared, just like I did.

Like so many others. How can I sit here and not blame myself?"

"Because you're not the bad guy here. You're not the one who took that woman, or any of the others. But you might be able to help us get her back. If you're willing to tell me what you saw."

Edie looked up at Adam in full on law enforcement mode. His blue eyes were sharp and searching, waiting for Edie to decide.

"Of course. Anything that could help. I can't just sit here and wonder."

"Start at the beginning," Adam said. "And tell me everything you can remember about tonight."

10

EDIE'S HANDS SHOOK AS SHE TOLD ADAM THE ENTIRE STORY.
She hated the weakness she felt. She let Jason get away with
that woman. She didn't do anything.

"It's not your fault," Raina whispered when Edie was
done. "You chased after them, but he was already gone."

"I could have yelled out, pushed through the crowd,
something. I just froze when I first saw him."

"Which is completely normal," Adam said. "Even going
there was a brave thing you did. And it's going to give us a
direction. If they're using it as a home base, someone there
is likely involved."

"That's what I thought, too," Edie said. "It can't be a coincidence, right?"

Adam shook his head. "It's not likely. Maybe a coincidence you were there the same night, but not a coincidence
the same man is still going there. We're going to stop this,
Edie."

Edie nodded as Adam stood. He squeezed her shoulder
as he walked past her, then lifted his phone to call someone.
Probably his partner, Lorelei Sloane. After Adam met Raina,

he decided to move to Niagara Falls and transfer his assignment to the local FBI office. Lorelei was still bouncing between Niagara Falls and Boston, where they were located before.

"Are you okay?" Raina whispered when Adam was out of the room.

Edie shrugged, shaking her head in a noncommittal way. "I don't know if I'll ever be okay again."

"Because of Jason? Or just in general?"

"Both? I don't know what I expected when I went there, but it wasn't to see him leading someone else out the door like he did to me that night." Edie wrapped her arms around her body. She wanted to curl up in the fetal position and pull a blanket over her head, blocking out the world outside and pretending there was nothing wrong with it.

"Why did you go there?" Raina asked.

Edie laughed mirthlessly, a flat sound that felt as foreign as it sounded. "I thought I could handle it. That I was strong enough to do all of this, so of course I could go there."

"You are strong," Raina said, reaching out for Edie's hand.

Raina's fingers were warm, welcoming. Inviting. That contact was why Edie went there. She still shied away from most contact, but Raina didn't bother her. Raina understood.

Edie stared at their joined hands, and her mind went back to Pryce gripping her hand. When he touched her, it was the same as Raina. Comforting. She didn't get the twitchy, uncomfortable feeling she had from many others when Pryce touched her.

Which was why she agreed to a date.

"I have a date," Edie blurted.

"What? With who?" Raina asked, a smile breaking out on her face.

"He's a cop. Marcus said he's a good guy."

Raina's brows went up. Her eyes crinkled at the edges. Her smile was bright and full of joy. "You asked Marcus about him?"

"Stacey did, technically."

"How did you meet this cop?" Raina asked.

"He's the one chasing the vigilante," Edie said with a smirk.

"No." Raina laughed, understanding Edie's smirk and shaking her head. "I take it he doesn't know?"

Edie shook her head. "It seems as though he doesn't. He asked me the other night if it was me, but he was joking."

"He asked you?"

"I was talking about Tonya. How I don't want anyone else to ever go through what she went through. Looking for me, getting no answers, then being killed for being in the wrong place at the wrong time."

"Because she was looking for me. She knew I had a connection to Damon," Raina said, her previously happy voice full of regret.

"Tonya never handled being told no. It doesn't surprise me at all that she went looking for you, even though Cade told her not to. You didn't do anything wrong. The man who killed her did."

"And Damon," Raina said.

Edie nodded. "And that's why I'm doing what I'm doing. Because Trevor is just as bad. And anyone working with him is just as bad. They're not going to stop, so I'm going to stop them."

Adam walked back into the room, picking up on the tension immediately. "What did I miss?"

Raina looked at Edie, letting her answer the question.

Edie turned her attention to Adam and forced a smile. Just like Marcus, she wasn't sure if Adam knew what she was doing, but she wasn't going to take a risk and tell him. "I was telling Raina she's not to blame for Tonya's death. That Damon and Silver were the only ones who were responsible."

"I've been telling her that for months. I have a feeling coming from you it has a much bigger impact," Adam said.

"I still feel guilty. Damon caused so much pain to so many people," Raina whispered.

"And none of it was your fault," Adam told her, taking a seat next to her on the couch.

"If I'd never left him, he wouldn't have killed Tonya. He wouldn't have known anything about Karli or Jessica or Stacey. Lives would have been so different."

"I'd still be with Trevor," Edie said softly.

Raina and Adam looked at her.

Edie shrugged, fighting the emotion rising inside her. "Damon knew people were looking for me. He knew it would piss Trevor off to take me. I'm not saying I'm glad it all worked out the way it did, but I'm not disappointed to be out of there. To be able to go and do what I please."

Raina nodded as she leaned over and pulled Edie in for a hug. "You're right. And for that, I'm grateful."

"Me, too."

Edie warred with that gratitude and regret every day. She wondered if it would ever go away. Stacey told her once that she couldn't change the past, so accepting blame for it wouldn't do any good, but Edie knew it was more complicated than that. Remembering the past meant not repeating her mistakes.

"I should go. I need to get back to the shelter."

"Are you sure you're okay?" Raina asked. "You can stay here if you want."

Edie shook her head. "Frannie needs the van back, just in case there's a call overnight."

"Do you want us to follow you?" Adam offered.

Edie hesitated on that offer. She hadn't needed to be followed home since she was a teenager. Since she got lost at a party one night and her friend led her out of the woods where the party was, then made sure she got home after a deer ran in front of Edie and spooked her.

Jason wasn't a deer, but he was more than enough to spook her.

"Raina, why don't you ride with Edie? I'll follow behind," Adam said, standing and taking the decision from Edie.

She was grateful. She'd felt weak too many times already. One more might break her.

Raina happily rode back with Edie, keeping up the conversation the whole way with talk about life with Adam. Edie was thrilled for her friend. For how she'd moved on and built a life she enjoyed. How she'd found love again, in the middle of her own personal hell.

Edie wasn't confident she'd do the same, but she was excited about her date with Pryce. More than she'd been since she saw Jason in Bottom's Up.

"When's your date?" Raina asked as Edie pulled into the driveway that led behind the shelter.

"Friday night. He's off this weekend."

"Have you been in touch? Or do you just see him at the diner?"

"How do you know about that?" Edie asked.

Raina grinned.

Edie shook her head. "Nothing is secret with this group."

"You need to read your texts more often. Especially if there might be some from your cop in there."

"There aren't," Edie admitted before she thought twice about what she was saying.

"So you check for his texts but ignore ours?" Raina teased.

Edie shook her head. "I usually don't have anything to add. I must have missed the ones where you were all talking about my dating life."

"We're all happy for you, Edie."

Edie smiled at her friend. It had been a while since she felt like she had someone she could count on. Raina, Mackenzie, Stacey, Frannie, Karli, and Jessica were all people who'd become friends. Even Lorelei, despite being law enforcement, was someone Edie thought she could trust. It was a nice change from how things had been the last few years.

"Thanks," Edie said.

"Have fun on your date," Raina said.

Edie nodded as they both climbed out of the van. She locked the doors and moved to the back of the van with Raina, where Adam waited. "I hope I will. He wanted to go to the diner, but I suggested we go somewhere else."

"The diner? Why would he want to go there?" Raina asked.

Edie shrugged. "Because it's where we met."

Raina's face morphed to a sappy grin. "That's so cute."

Edie wrinkled her nose. "Maybe."

"Oh, you know it's cute. It's sweet."

Edie rolled her eyes. "Fine. It is."

Raina chuckled at Edie's reaction. "So, where are you going instead?"

"I suggested Mario's."

"Nice. Not too fancy but nicer than Bob's Diner."

Edie nodded. "That was my thought, too. I don't want him to think he has to spend a fortune, or that he should expect something else to happen."

"Edie," Raina said in a voice that put Edie on guard again.

"I want to be ready for sex, but I'm not sure how I'll handle it."

"And if he's decent, he'll not only understand that, but be okay with it."

"I think he's decent."

"Good. Then stop worrying about all the things you think are going to go wrong and enjoy a night out with a man you like."

Edie drew a breath and nodded. "I'll try."

"And be careful," Raina said. "You can always call me, before or after you do something. We will always be there for you."

Edie hugged her friend and nodded. "Thank you."

"We'll wait until you're inside," Raina said when Edie pulled back.

Edie nodded and waved to Adam, who'd stayed in his SUV while they were talking. He waved back, his gaze following Raina as she moved to climb in the passenger side.

When she was in the vehicle, Edie walked to the door and let herself in. She waved to them, then locked the door and went upstairs to her room, where she could finally curl up and hide and pretend the world didn't exist.

PRYCE FELT like a teenager picking up a girl for their first date. When Edie said she used the shelter van to go out, Pryce volunteered to pick her up and bring her back for their date.

As he stood on the porch of Shelter in the Storm getting stared down by his boss, he wasn't so sure it was a good idea.

"Edie's been through a lot," Captain Patrick said. "What are your intentions?"

"Sir?" Pryce had to have heard him wrong.

"Your intentions, Officer. Edie is important to my wife, and to me."

"I enjoy talking to her, sir. I think she's beautiful and smart and funny. I admire her strength and bravery, but also her courage to keep moving forward."

"If she says stop, what do you do?"

"Excuse me?" Heat rushed to Pryce's cheeks. Was he really having a conversation about sex with his boss? Was that really what was going on?

"I'm assuming you've read the case file. All the reports about what she went through. She's been living here for a few months, and she was in a safe house and rehab before that. Don't fuck with her, Officer."

"Sir, forgive me, but what happens between Edie and me is between Edie and me. I don't owe you an explanation, nor do I owe you any promises. I do owe those to Edie, and I intend to deliver them to her. As for what she's been through, I'm aware. The fact that it happened at all sickens me, but that it happened to a woman like Edie makes me want to dig up Bernard and kill him all over again for not bothering to investigate her case. How a person can knowingly and intentionally harm others is beyond me, sir. And as for my intentions? Those are my own, but I assure you, sir, the only intention I have toward Edie is one of care."

Pryce exhaled his breath heavily, panting with his speech and fear that he was going to lose his job and his date all at once for the way he spoke to his boss.

Captain Patrick leaned back, arms crossed over his chest. He dropped his hands to his side and took a step toward Pryce.

Pryce resisted the urge to retreat, standing his ground against the man who could ruin his night and the rest of his life if he so chose.

"Good," Captain Patrick said. "Edie deserves someone who will treat her well and not take shit." He tilted his head to the side and nodded sharply. "And I agree about Bernard. And Street, for that matter. The world is better without them in it."

"Much better," Pryce said, relief coursing through him that he managed to survive the interrogation.

"We have strict rules about men being inside the building, so I apologize for keeping you out here. The women inside need to be protected. No one knows who's there, and no one can know. You understand?"

Pryce nodded. "Of course, sir. I would never want to jeopardize the safety of someone who's here to escape a situation they couldn't otherwise get free from. What you and your wife do is sadly needed."

"Yes, it is," Captain Patrick said, rubbing his jaw and looking more thoughtful than Pryce had ever seen him. "That also means you won't be able to come back here with Edie. Ever, Officer."

Pryce nodded. "I have no intention of things going that far on our first date, sir, but when Edie is comfortable with anything that would require privacy, I have my own place."

"And you know I have access to your personnel file and know where that place is, right?"

"Yes, sir," Pryce said, once more feeling like he was being interrogated. There was a reason Captain Patrick was the captain. He could get the truth out of anyone, and Pryce learned very quickly why.

Because the captain was damn good at putting the fear of God in a person. Damn good.

"Good," Captain Patrick said as the front door to the building opened behind him. He took a step back and turned to Edie with a wide grin. "Don't you look nice."

The change in the man was almost jarring. From the dangerous, threatening, overprotective man to the kind, caring one who focused his attention on the woman they were talking about.

"Thanks, Marcus," Edie said.

Her gaze skittered past Marcus to Pryce, which made him endlessly happy. He returned her smile, until he caught sight of Captain Patrick glaring at him.

"Are you ready to go?" Edie asked.

Pryce nodded, reaching for her hand as she walked toward him. She slid her hand into his, her skin soft and warm. The boots she wore had heels high enough to do some damage if set on the right target. Her jeans were fit to her curvy legs. Her top draped low on her chest and hung off one bare shoulder, telling Pryce she either wasn't wearing a bra or she was wearing one of the complicated ones that men never had a chance of understanding.

All Pryce cared about was the smile on her face and how her eyes lit up when she looked at him.

"You look beautiful," Pryce said.

"Thanks." Red tinged her brown cheeks, only visible because of how close he was. He'd never seen her blush before, but it was charming and gorgeous.

Pryce stopped when they reached the bottom of the

stairs and turned back to Captain Patrick. "Is there a time the house needs to be locked up? A curfew or anything?"

Captain Patrick opened his mouth, but the woman who hadn't been there before stepped up and put her hand on his chest. "Not for Edie. She's welcome to come and go as she pleases. If it's late, she can direct you to the parking lot behind the building. She has a key."

"Thank you," Pryce said to her. He assumed she was Captain Patrick's wife, Francesca, but he was not going to get too friendly with the woman.

"Have fun," Francesca said brightly.

"Thanks, Frannie. Have a good night. You, too, Marcus," Edie said. She waved to the two of them.

Pryce opened her door for her, which earned him a smile. When she sat down, he closed the door gently behind her, thankful that one still worked as designed. He nodded to the watchful couple on the porch as he jogged around his SUV and climbed in behind the wheel. Pryce lifted his door from the inside to pull it closed. It only took two attempts before it latched.

"I wasn't sure I was going to actually get you out of there," Pryce said when they were closed in the vehicle.

"What? Why not?" She didn't comment on his messed up door.

Pryce nodded to his boss, still staring at them. "He's scarier than the father of a teenage daughter with a gun behind the door. Probably because he doesn't have to go as far as the door to get to his gun and he's even more protective of you."

"Marcus?" Edie asked, looking out the window and laughing. "He's a softie."

Pryce shook his head. "Not even a little bit. He asked what my intentions are, and said he knows where I live."

Edie threw her head back and laughed, exposing the long line of her thick neck. Her eyes squeezed shut with her humor. She was the most beautiful woman in the world when she laughed.

And he put that look on her face.

He was a lucky son-of-a-bitch, even if he was going to have to face his boss when he dropped off the most beautiful woman in the world after their date.

Totally worth it.

11

———

THE RESTAURANT WAS PERFECT, IN PRYCE'S OPINION. QUIET enough for conversation but not so intimate it felt like there were expectations. He had none for the night other than getting to know Edie better, and the restaurant delivered on that front.

She laughed at something he said and pushed her dinner away from her. "If I eat another bite, I'll be sick. Especially when you keep making me laugh."

"Does that mean I can't talk you into dessert?" Pryce asked, nodding to the dessert menu the server left on the table when he refilled their drinks a minute ago.

"Oh, I never said that," Edie said, reaching for the menu.

Pryce chuckled as she studied the menu. He couldn't remember the last time he felt so comfortable with another person. They'd talked about their childhoods and growing up in families they were no longer close to and the pain of that loss. They talked about who they thought they'd be and how things changed as they became adults. And they talked about her experiences and how she was building her life from scratch and including people she wanted in it.

She continued to amaze him. Not only had she escaped her captor, but she fought back by providing information to the FBI to help bring down the organization Damon Street ran. The organization that was still under investigation.

And through it all, she was trying to give back and help others. She was trying to remember who she used to be, but also who she believed she could be. Pryce knew cops who weren't as strong as Edie, who'd been trained to move on from the horrible things they saw daily and still couldn't manage to put other people's horrors behind them.

"It's been far too long since I've had tiramisu. I keep coming back to that," Edie said, breaking into Pryce's thoughts.

"That's always a good choice."

"It was my favorite dessert growing up. It was something I got as a treat, but I haven't thought to have it since I've been back."

Pryce understood *since I've been back* was Edie's way of saying since she escaped Damon and Trevor. To be able to give her a small bit of happiness made him feel like he'd done something right. "You should get two," he blurted.

Edie shook her head. "It's not as special if I can have it all the time. It's like sex, you know? You can pretty much always get okay sex, but great sex is special. It's different and makes you appreciate it that much more."

Pryce couldn't speak for a long moment. He stared at Edie. Her eyes were closed, a blissful look on her face. His cock took notice and thickened, devouring every word she said as if she was praising him instead of speaking in generalities.

"Sorry," she said, sucking in a sharp breath and ducking her chin in embarrassment. "I shouldn't have said that."

Pryce reached across the table for her hand. "Never apologize for telling me how you feel. And never apologize for talking about great sex. It is special."

Her gaze snapped to his. Her eyes softened, like she was feeling the same need as he was. She licked her lips, leaving behind a sheen that sparkled in the dim restaurant lighting.

"Do you want to skip dessert?" she whispered.

Pryce shook his head slowly, not breaking eye contact. "I want you to have everything you want tonight, and that includes tiramisu."

Her smile plumped her cheeks to the point she nibbled on her lip to stop the grin from getting bigger.

"Dessert, guys?" the server asked, stacking their empty plates and waiting for a reply.

"Tiramisu and chocolate lava cake," Pryce said without looking away from Edie.

Her eyes widened again, like she was surprised he knew that was the other dessert she'd considered.

"Excellent choices. I'll be right back," the server said. He carried their dinner plates away, disappearing as quickly as he'd appeared.

"I was thinking about the chocolate lava cake, too."

Pryce nodded. "I know. I saw you pointing at both. I was going to order whichever one you decided against and see if I could talk you into sharing."

Edie pursed her lips. "I'm not sure. I don't share very well."

Pryce grinned at her displeasure. "Does that mean you don't want to try my chocolate lava cake?"

"Don't get too crazy."

Pryce laughed, delighting when Edie joined him.

She sipped her water and studied him. "I wasn't sure about you when we met."

He nodded. "I know. I get that a lot, but once you told me

who you were, it made even more sense."

"I wish you'd been the one who'd investigated when I disappeared."

"So do I."

Edie smiled sadly, then seemed to shake it off and drew herself to her full height. "I can't go there. It doesn't do me any good. All I can do is move forward."

"You seem like you're doing a pretty good job of that."

Edie laughed mirthlessly. "I don't know about that. I'm thirty-four and still single. I haven't been on a date since I've been back, until tonight. I live in a shelter and have no job. I don't feel like I'm moving anywhere."

"It hasn't been that long, Edie."

She sighed. "Almost six months. I don't have a lot to show for it."

"You're here. You're trying to move on. No one faults you for that."

"I do," she confessed. "I was so easy-going before. I thought nothing could hurt me. I was fearless. Since then, all I feel is fear. For the women who are still there, the ones who could be taken, to be back there again." She fell silent, her thoughts on her distraught face. "When we met, I didn't trust you because of your job, but I let you in because you don't smell familiar to me."

"Smell familiar?" Pryce asked, unsure why she would use that phrase or why he would have been familiar in any way since they'd never met.

The server delivered their desserts and asked if they needed anything else. When Pryce assured him they were good, he told them to enjoy and left.

Pryce waited. He wanted Edie to finish what she was telling him before. There was pain in her gaze, but he wouldn't push.

"I am lucky because I don't remember a lot of what happened. Bits and pieces at most, and more toward the end. Usually, I was too high for anything to sink in. The therapists I've seen said it was also my brain's defense mechanism, blocking everything out so I didn't remember it. But I remember scents of them. Men I've never seen before, men I don't know, are familiar to me because of the way they smell."

Pryce's stomach turned as he understood what Edie was telling him. He wanted to find each and every one of them and pummel them. Then lock them up and never let them see the light of day. It made him ashamed of humanity that there were people out there raping women who couldn't say no, who didn't know what was happening. People who thought that was okay.

Pryce had no words, but he couldn't sit there and say or do nothing. He stood from his side of the table and pulled her from her chair into his arms, holding her tightly and hugging her to his chest. His hand went to her neck, needing to reassure himself she was there and she was okay.

She wrapped her arms around him, leaning on him as she shook.

He didn't know if it was tears, fear, shock, or something else, but Pryce didn't care. He wanted to be the one she turned to. The one she talked to. The one she leaned on when she felt alone and afraid.

"I'm so sorry for everything that happened to you," he whispered in her ear. "So sorry, Edie."

She nodded, holding him tighter as the trembling slowed. She eased back just enough to let him know she needed him to let go.

Pryce released her but didn't let her go far. He leaned

down, meeting her gaze and holding it for a long moment. "Edie, I want to kiss you. Is that okay?"

She nodded and tipped her lips up to meet his.

Pryce didn't hesitate, but he didn't rush. Kissing Edie was like having your last meal. It was meant to be savored and cherished. He was never going to get to kiss her for the first time again, and he knew he would remember the moment their lips touched for the first time for the rest of his life.

They came together slowly. Her lips brushed his gently, a little off-center, but the jolt that hit him was not off center. She gasped, the sound barely audible in the public place, but Pryce heard it.

And he needed more of it.

He stepped closer to her, their bodies meeting like their lips. He wrapped his arm around her back once more, his fingertips sliding over the smooth fabric of her shirt to feel the heat of her body beneath. He angled his head and licked her lips.

She made that noise again and opened her lips for him.

Pryce groaned, the first brush of her tongue to his enough to make him forget where they were. She was better than the forgotten dessert, better than okay sex, better than any other moment he'd previously experienced.

She was alive and passionate and so damn exciting that he couldn't stop with just one taste of her.

Pryce licked against her tongue, tasting her and delving deep for more. He hardened between them, not bothering to hide the effect she was having on him.

Her hands slid up his chest, circling his neck tentatively. Her nails scraped along the tender hairs on the back of his neck, and he wondered how bad it was for him to take her back to his place.

"Excuse me." The humor-filled words said right next to

them had Pryce taking a step back.

He shielded Edie from the person trying to get past them, making sure a stranger had neither access to touch her nor access to see her.

When the person was past their table, Pryce released his grip on Edie, smiling when she stumbled to her seat and sat down hard.

"Thank you," he whispered, leaning down to kiss her once more, a quick kiss that still lit him up. He returned to his seat and smiled at the dazed look on her face. "You okay?"

She shook her head slowly. "That was definitely not okay."

Pryce's heart sank. His erection shriveled. His confidence and joy withered. He hated himself for pushing her too far. "I apologize. I didn't mean to overstep."

She looked up at him, fog clearing her gaze as she tilted her head to the side. "What are you talking about?"

"You said that was not okay. I didn't mean to make you uncomfortable. If you'd like to call Marcus, or someone else, for a ride home, I will not push myself on you again."

She chuckled, the sound counter to the words she'd used. Her chuckle turned to full-blown laughter as she fought to contain herself.

Pryce sat there, watching her, unsure what he did that was so funny, but knowing if those were the last few minutes he would spend with her, he was going to enjoy them, and enjoy her laughter. Even if it was at his expense.

"I'm sorry. I didn't mean to laugh at you. And I didn't mean to confuse you. I meant not okay like okay sex. I meant that was... I don't know if there are words for how good that kiss was."

Pryce deflated with relief. "Yeah?"

She nodded, closing her eyes and licking her lips. "Oh, yeah. I don't think I've ever been kissed like that. I definitely haven't had a kiss that made me want to go home with someone. Usually that was the result of lots of alcohol and not a lot of concern for what could happen to me. But with you? Pryce, I..."

"I didn't plan for that," Pryce said quickly. "I promise you, I wasn't trying to get you to come home with me."

Edie nodded. "That's part of what I like about you, Pryce. You don't push. You seem too good to be true. And you might be, but my friend is your boss, and he knows where you live. If something happens to me, you won't get away with it."

Pryce wasn't sure if he should be more afraid of Captain Patrick or Edie at that moment. Both were intimidating.

"I would never hurt you, or anyone, Edie. I need you to know that before I take you home. I don't want you to sleep with me because you know if something happened, I wouldn't get away with it. I want you to sleep with me because you want me so badly you can't imagine not being with me."

She shifted in her seat. "I passed that a few weeks ago."

Pryce's grin was slow and satisfied. "Is that so?"

"You know you're sexy."

He shrugged. "I really don't. I think you should tell me."

She chuckled. "I'm eating my dessert now."

Pryce smiled at her and lifted his spoon, following her lead.

EDIE COULD NOT BELIEVE she admitted that to Pryce. It didn't matter that she'd thought about him more than once when she was alone. It didn't matter that the only time she felt any inkling of desire was when she brought his image to mind. It didn't matter that the only orgasms she'd had since she'd been back were inspired by him.

But it did matter.

It mattered to her. Because now the man himself was aware of how much she wanted him. And he was a good enough guy to turn her down because he wanted her to trust him instead of just want to fuck him.

Edie wasn't sure trust would ever happen. Not the way he wanted it to. She was there. She agreed to a date. That was huge for her.

She wanted more, too. She wanted more of what that kiss promised. She wanted to feel his hands on her without the barrier of her clothes, without the presence of a room full of strangers.

She wanted to trust him. Completely. With her body and her soul. If she could trust anyone, it would be him.

But the big question she hadn't managed to answer yet was if she could trust anyone that way ever again.

The first time she made herself orgasm, she cried. In relief and shame. It felt wrong to enjoy something that had been a source of punishment for so long. To be able to find pleasure in sex again. To know so many others were still being punished for that same thing.

She cried herself to sleep and didn't touch herself again for a week. Until the next time she saw Pryce at Bob's Diner.

Sitting there across from him on a date, her panties were soaked. She felt the now-familiar need building inside her through their date. Edie wanted him. More than just the imaginary experience she created for herself, the real thing. She wanted the man who made her feel like she wasn't completely broken.

"How's your tiramisu?" he asked.

Edie looked down and realized she hadn't taken one bite yet. It was there, on her fork, but she'd been dreaming about sex with Pryce instead of eating her dessert.

She glared at him, to which he chuckled and ate a bite of his lava cake.

"How's your lava cake?" she asked.

"Delicious," he said right before he shoveled another bite into his mouth.

Edie ate the first bite of her tiramisu and groaned. Her eyes closed without thought, the richness of the dessert overwhelming all of her senses. Sweet and savory with the mascarpone and espresso balancing each other out. The dusting of chocolate hit a minute later, adding another layer to the deliciousness and eliciting another groan from Edie.

"Fucking hell," Pryce grunted, dropping his spoon.

Edie opened her eyes, finding him staring at her with pure, raw lust in his gaze. She inhaled sharply, nearly choking herself on the powdered chocolate topping.

When she could breathe again and swallowed her bite, she asked, "Are you okay?"

Pryce shook his head. "Not even a little bit. You're stunning, Edie. I am trying so hard to be a decent man right now, but the way you sound when you're enjoying yourself, the way you look when you laugh, how honest and real you are... It's all making it really hard for me to be decent."

"Who said you have to be decent?" she asked.

"I did," he said, almost to himself. "I'm not the kind of man who will take advantage of a woman. I'm not going to use my badge or anything else to get a woman into bed. It's been a while since I've brought a woman home. I don't like casual sex and I don't want something temporary. I want someone in my life who's going to be honest with me and share her life with me, just like I want to do the same."

"Okay," Edie whispered, her palms sweating at the thought of being honest with Pryce about her extracurricular activities and the real reason he always found her at the diner.

"I like you, Edie. A lot. I've liked you from the moment I saw you in that crappy diner salivating over the pie case, and I've liked you more and more every time I've spoken to you since. If you want me to take you back to the shelter as soon as we leave here, I will do it without questioning you. I will respect whatever it is you want from here on out, but I need you to know I'm not looking for a quick fuck. I'm looking for someone I can possibly share my life with. So, yeah, it kills me to be a decent man, but that's who I am. It's who I'm always going to be. If that's not what you want, that's okay, but I'm not going to change."

Edie swallowed roughly. She didn't think men like him existed, let alone put it all out there to explain why he wasn't going to bend her over the table and have his way with her right then and there.

Edie had given up on forever, but Pryce made her wonder if maybe she gave up too soon.

"I like you, too," she said.

"And?"

"And does being a decent guy mean you're not ever going to fuck me or just not tonight?"

Pryce choked on the breath he sucked in, coughing as he reached for his water. He shook his head and met her gaze with a lust-filled one. "That depends on you, Edie. Because I'll do whatever you want, as long as you know I'm not a one and done kind of man."

Edie smiled. "Good."

12

___

"Where are we going, Edie," Pryce asked. He was not going to push or encourage. He was going to let her decide. If she asked him to take her home, he would, without a second thought. If she asked him to take her to his place, he would do everything in his power to not lose his damn mind on the way there.

"Do you have a roommate?" she whispered.

Pryce shook his head. "I do not."

"Then I think you should show me your place."

Pryce nodded once, then shifted the SUV into gear. He pulled out of the parking lot with far more patience than he felt inside. He wanted to speed down the street and get her into his place as soon as possible, but he was not going to rush. He wasn't going to rush anything with her.

The drive was quiet, both of them in their thoughts. Pryce wondered if she was second guessing her decision, but when he parked and looked at her, the excitement in her gaze erased all his doubts.

He fought to close his door and by the time he made it around to open her door, she was already out. Pryce reached for her hand, needing her touch. She squeezed his hand, hurrying beside him to the front door to his building.

He led the way up the two flights of stairs to his apartment. It wasn't fancy, and it wasn't great, but it was well below what he could safely afford. He put most of his income into savings, just in case he needed it one day.

"My place isn't great," he said in apology as he unlocked his door. It was an understatement, one he never cared to explain before Edie. "It's kind of a dump."

He unlocked the door and opened it wide, letting her go in ahead of him. She looked around, taking in the space while he watched her, and wondered if his crappy apartment was enough to send her running.

"How long have you lived here?" she asked.

"Since I joined the police force. At first it was because I knew I could afford it without worrying about stretching myself too thin."

"And now?" she asked, picking up on what he wasn't saying.

Pryce shrugged. "After my sister, and being brought in for questioning, I never felt secure enough to spend more of my income on a place to live."

"You're still waiting for the other shoe to drop," Edie said. Not a question, more like an understanding of what he was doing.

Pryce nodded. "I think I've always been that way. Something bad always happens. A major repair or debt, an accident or illness, someone in need. I don't like the idea of needing something and not being able to get it."

"I get that. Tonya spent the last of her money hiring Cade to find me. She tried to get someone to look into what happened, and he was the only one who would help her. She spent everything she had."

"Wow."

Edie nodded. "Cade insisted on giving the money back to me, but it doesn't feel like mine."

"What did you do with it?"

Edie looked around the apartment and was silent for a minute. "Nothing. I thought about donating it to Frannie for the shelter, but I don't think she'd accept it. I know there are places that need the help, but there's a part of me that thinks I should keep it for when I decide I'm ready to find a place."

"What would she have wanted you to do with it?"

Edie laughed softly. "She would have wanted me to have fun. Enjoy it. Tonya was funny and friendly. She was always saying we should enjoy our lives. If she knew how little I'd enjoyed things since I've been back, she would drag me by the hair to a club and make me dance until I stopped feeling sorry for myself."

Pryce pulled out his phone and tapped the screen, opening his music app. He tapped a few buttons, then music filled the apartment, soft and soothing. He set his phone on the coffee table and reached a hand out to Edie. "Dance?"

She grinned and moved into his arms, letting him wrap an arm around her and pull her in close.

They swayed together, shuffling their feet and shifting their bodies in tune to the music. Pryce closed his eyes and enjoyed the moment with Edie.

"I haven't been alone with a man since before," Edie whispered.

Pryce inhaled deeply. "Nothing has to happen, Edie. And if you want to leave, I'll—"

"No," she blurted. "I just... I didn't see you coming."

Pryce chuckled. "Trust me, beautiful, I didn't see you coming either. Not at all."

THE CASUAL TERM caught Edie off-guard. Not that it should have, but she liked the way he said her name. And hated the endearment.

"What?"

She shook her head.

"Please tell me," he pressed.

"I like when you say my name. When I was gone... they didn't use names. Even though I don't remember much, I know they never called me by my name. My name didn't matter. None of ours did."

"I'm sorry, Edie."

She forced a smile. "I didn't mean to bring things down."

"You're not bringing things down. You're being honest. That matters to me. You matter to me."

"Thank you."

They fell silent again, dancing to the soft music. It was a new experience for Edie. She'd dated men before, but usually they would get to the main event quickly, like it was the goal of the evening. Sex was the date, instead of a part of the date.

Pryce wasn't in a hurry. He was content to dance and talk and get to know each other instead of jumping into bed.

"I had a nice apartment before. It was exactly what I wanted. I worked hard to get to where I could afford it. It felt like such a victory when I was able to move in there," she whispered.

"Have you thought about going back?"

She shook her head. "I'm not that person anymore. All my stuff was sold, and the income used to pay for the rent I didn't pay, but I can't imagine going backward. I also can't imagine fitting into my old life."

"What did you do for work?"

"I'm a video editor. I worked for a local company that had contracts with people all over. We'd edit videos for anyone from social media influencers to major media outlets. I mostly worked from home, but we had an office to go into if we wanted to."

"That's different. I don't think I've ever met a video editor."

Edie chuckled. "I have a degree in communications with a focus in film. I always loved how it all worked. How a video could go from something rough and unfocused to something beautiful and creative and expressive of the creator."

"And the editor, apparently."

Edie laughed. "I helped to bring their vision to life. It was fun."

"Have you thought about going back to that job?"

She nodded. "A few times. I've been in touch with my old boss. He's supportive of me coming back when I'm ready. I don't really have other skills, unless you count playing tennis, so—"

"Tennis?"

"I had a full ride to college on a tennis scholarship."

"Whoa. That's impressive."

"I started playing when I was really young. I loved it. It was a passion for me. In school, I decided I didn't want to travel forever. I loved playing, but when it got more and more competitive, I wanted out. I loved the game, but playing at a higher level required a competitiveness I never had."

"There's nothing wrong with that."

"Thanks. It was hard for a lot of people to understand. Especially my coaches."

"No one else gets to call the shots in your life."

"I agree."

Edie looked up at Pryce, her breath catching at the look in his eyes. She was taking her life back little-by-little, and being there with him was one more step.

Another step was making the first move. She wanted to kiss him. She wanted to touch him and feel him inside her. She wanted him.

And she wanted to move things forward.

She lifted up on her toes, bringing them closer and closer until her lips were a breath away from his. She waited for a second, curious if he would eliminate the gap between them.

"I'm following your lead, Edie," he whispered, giving her the answer she was looking for.

She sealed her lips to his, pulling on his neck to bring him closer to her.

He tightened the grip he had on her waist. He stopped swaying, letting the music fade into the background as the entire room changed.

Edie vibrated with need. She worried she would feel trapped, but she felt free. Like she could do anything.

She slid her hands into his short hair, enjoying the soft feel of it against her fingers. She gripped the strands, tugging slightly.

Pryce groaned and stepped closer, letting her feel the effect their kiss was having on him.

Again, Edie felt free. Beautiful and strong and empowered. He wasn't there because he was paying to be with her. Because she wouldn't put up a fight or argue. He was there because he liked her. Because he was as interested in her as she was in him.

Edie removed her hands from his hair and moved them

down to his waist, tugging his shirt free so she could feel his bare skin.

He broke free from her and pulled his shirt off.

Edie froze, and Pryce froze. His hands were halfway between them, like he was reaching for her and time stopped.

Edie reached up, splaying her hands on his chest. His heart thumped against her palm, his skin warm and sprinkled with soft blond hair. Her eyes devoured him, soaking in every inch she could see while he stayed frozen for her to peruse.

After a minute of her touching him, he reached for her slowly, his hands going to her hips. He didn't move her or try to hurry her along or anything, just held her, connecting them.

Edie leaned forward and put her lips on his neck, kissing his skin. He exhaled roughly, shaking with her touch. She kissed his collarbone, then licked her way to his nipple. She teased the tip and felt him shudder.

Edie looked up at him and found him watching her. "Is this okay?"

"Anything you want to do to me is okay, Edie. Anything. Like I said, I'm following your lead."

"Will you... will you touch me?"

"I'd love to. Where do you want me to touch you?"

"Everywhere," she said with a laugh.

Pryce exhaled a shaky laugh with her. "We'll go slow."

Edie nodded.

Pryce took her hand in his and lifted them together. He started at her hip, easing his way under the edge of her shirt. She couldn't see their hands on her skin, but she felt his touch. Warm and soft. Good.

He moved their hands up, his gaze bouncing between

hers and where their hands were. He stopped when he reached the band of her bra, looking up at her for direction.

Edie drew a breath and closed her eyes. She took his other hand in hers and moved it to the same spot on her other side. She let go of his hands and lifted her top up and off. The strapless bra she wore lifted her breasts, like they were being presented to Pryce on a platter.

"My God, you're beautiful, Edie," he rasped.

She took his hands and nudged them over the band of her bra, encouraging him to keep touching her.

"Edie?"

"Please, Pryce."

He stepped forward and cupped her breasts, the reinforced fabric of her bra preventing her from feeling the warmth of his skin. His thumbs brushed over the exposed tops of each, his eyes lustily watching her.

"Pryce," she whispered, her needy tone foreign to her ears. She couldn't remember the last time she was so turned on by a man at all, let alone one who hadn't even gotten her clothes off, but she wanted Pryce. More than almost anything in the world.

"Do you want me to tell you what I'm going to do or do you just want me to do it?" he asked, still not moving his hands from where they held her breasts and rubbed her sensitive skin.

"I... I don't know."

"How about I tell you, and you can stop me before, during, or after anything you're not okay with? Is that okay?"

Edie nodded.

"Okay, Edie. I want to see your breasts. I'm going to move your bra down so I can look at them and touch them."

"Okay," she whispered.

His hands moved slowly, giving her plenty of time to

stop him as he eased the cups down and exposed her nipples to the cool air. They both gasped.

Pryce held her breasts again, this time bare skin to bare skin. His rough palms rubbed over her nipples and added to the moisture pooling between her thighs.

"I'm going to lick your nipple, Edie. First one, then the other."

"Okay."

He lifted one to his mouth, holding her gaze until the last second. His tongue flicked out and brushed the edge of her nipple.

She moaned greedily, feeling pleasure with another person for the first time in what felt like forever.

Everything she went through threatened her. It hung at the edges, trying to break into the moment and steal the joy she felt, but Edie pushed it back. She wasn't going to let Trevor, Damon, or any of the others take anything else from her.

She wanted this. She wanted Pryce. She had done the work. She remembered pleasure. And she wanted it in that moment with Pryce.

He switched to her other nipple before bringing them together and sucking both into his mouth. He licked over them, alternating quickly enough to make Edie dizzy with want.

"Can I take your bra off, Edie?"

She nodded as she reached back to remove it herself.

He didn't push her out of the way or urge her to hurry as her fingers fumbled over the clasps. He held her breasts up, easing the tension on the band while she fought to release herself.

When she finally freed her breasts, she dropped the bra on top of her shirt. She fought the urge to cover herself, even though she was no more exposed than a minute ago.

"I will always stop, Edie. Without question. Do you understand me?"

Edie nodded, his words bringing her relief she didn't realize she needed in that moment. She moved closer to him, pulling him to her for a kiss.

He dove in eagerly, groaning when her bare chest pressed against his. The sound was full of pleasure and desire and made Edie feel so damn good she could barely keep herself from climbing him and using him to get herself off right then and there.

"What do you need, Edie?" he asked against her lips, as though he read her mind.

"I need an orgasm," she blurted. Her cheeks burned as soon as the words were out, hating how needy she sounded.

"How do you want to come? Clothes on or off?"

"On," she whispered.

"Do you want to ride me on the couch? My leg against the wall? What do you want, Edie?"

"Couch," she breathed.

He pulled her with him, sitting in the center of the couch and guiding her on top of him. "What do you need from me?"

"What you were just doing."

"Playing with your breasts?"

Edie nodded.

"You need something else, you tell me, Edie."

She nodded again, then shifted. And groaned. His erection was firm and thick. She rubbed herself against him shamelessly, the friction of him rolling her eyes back in her head.

Then he licked her. His mouth closed over one nipple,

and she rocked her hips faster. He was hot and thick beneath her. The pull was just right. Faster, more.

She threaded her hands into his hair, and he bit her nipple, sending another jolt through her.

"Pryce," she moaned.

She looked down at him, watching his pink tongue lick her other nipple.

"Oh, fuck," she breathed.

"You taste so good," he rasped. "So good."

He flicked her nipple, then closed his pink lips over her dark skin. Her hips rocked, faster and faster, reaching for the orgasm that was just barely out of reach.

She moaned frustratingly, wanting to come so badly and not getting there.

"What do you need, Edie? Anything. You tell me," he said around her nipple. He released it and kissed his way across her chest.

"I..."

"Anything, Edie. I want you to feel good. Anything."

"Touch me."

"Where?"

"I need you to rub my clit."

He stopped, completely frozen with his lips against her breast. Slowly, he eased back, looking up at her with a blend of lust and unease in his gaze. "Are you sure, Edie?"

"I want to feel your hands on me. And I usually come by rubbing my clit."

"Are you sure you want me to? If you want to touch yourself, I understand. I can leave, too. If you—"

"No. I... I think about you. I want to feel you."

His cock twitched beneath her. "Fuck, Edie. I am so... thank you." He moved his hands from her breasts, one sliding around her back and the other going to her waistband. "I'm going to unbutton your jeans, Edie."

She nodded, leaning back to give him access.

The button popped free. The zipper was loud even over the music. His breath heaved in and out of him, like he was struggling to control himself.

"I'm going to touch you, Edie."

She nodded, sucking in a breath when his hand brushed her belly. She shook as he moved lower, pulling the band of her panties away so he could reach beneath.

His hand moved lower, his palm sliding against her belly. When his fingertips brushed her curls, then moved lower to her clit, they both moaned.

"You're so wet, Edie."

"I've been thinking about this for a while."

"About me touching you?"

She bit her lip and nodded.

"Can I go lower? Feel how soaked you are?"

She nodded.

He held her gaze as his fingers moved between her thighs. His cock twitched again when he pressed one finger inside her. He pumped in slowly in and out, then dragged the same finger back to her clit.

"Oh, God," she whispered.

"Don't hold back, Edie. If you want to get loud, get loud. If you want to bite me, bite me. Don't hold back."

She spread her thighs wider, rocking against his hand. "Will you put your finger inside me again?"

He nodded, his jaw twitching as he slid his finger back down to her entrance.

"Yes," she moaned, her voice soft as the pleasure wrapped around her.

He brushed his thumb over her clit, and her hips jumped. "More?"

"Yes, yes," she said, her words stilted.

His finger pumped into her slowly, dragging his thumb over her clit with each gentle thrust.

Edie's hands went to his shoulders, using him for leverage. She rocked with his movements, thrusting against his hand with more and more urgency. Her body took over, remembering the feeling, enjoying the pleasure coursing through her.

Her breasts bounced in his face, smacking him a few times. His hand on her hip moved to grasp one breast, rubbing over her nipple as he continued to fuck her with his fingers, adding a second one and speeding up the strokes.

"You're so beautiful, Edie," he whispered. "So fucking gorgeous."

She listened to his words and felt his pleasure at what he was giving to her. Everything came together, and the waves started.

"Pryce," she groaned, teetering right on the edge.

"Let go, Edie. Come for me, my beautiful Edie."

His loving words were the last piece she needed before she shattered into a million pieces, never to be the same again.

She moaned and panted and begged him for more. She flooded his hand and her panties, her orgasm rolling over her in an endless stream of pleasure that she couldn't get out of, and didn't want to.

"Yes, Edie. God, yes," he encouraged, not letting up after one orgasm.

A second one followed the first, the aftershocks of the two nearly sending her into a third. She eased her hips to a stop, his hand still inside her, his other hand still holding her breast.

She collapsed onto him, throwing her arms around his neck as the relief and joy of what she felt overwhelmed her. Pryce moved his hand from her breast around her back and simply held her, letting her feel all the things she was feeling.

After a minute, she sat up and looked at him. "Thank you."

"That was beautiful."

"Yes, but if you're willing, I'm not ready to be done."

"Anything you want, Edie. Absolutely anything."

"I want you, Pryce. All of you."

"Yes, ma'am."

13

PRYCE WOULD BE LYING IF HE SAID HE WASN'T MORE THAN excited to fulfill Edie's every wish. Watching her come apart was the single greatest moment of his life. Better than seeing her laugh or seeing her smile or seeing her breasts on full display for him.

He was pretty sure she was ruining him for all women. And he was a ready and willing participant.

He meant it when he said he'd do anything she wanted him to do. Stand on his head, close his eyes, anything. As long as she felt good, it was worth it.

But he was beyond thrilled he was able to watch the magnificence that was Edie finding her pleasure. That was a sight.

So was seeing the look in her eyes when he removed his hand from her. She moaned and shivered, her entire body revolting at his leaving it.

"You must think so little of me," she whispered, turning her face from him.

"Why would I think little of you?"

She bit her lip and shrugged. "I'm being very greedy. Not

acting like a woman who—"

"Stop. Whatever it is you're supposed to be acting like that you think you are not... You only need to be yourself with me. I want Edie, not some version of yourself you think you should be."

She nodded but kept her gaze away.

Pryce gripped her chin gently and eased her face so he could look her in the eyes. "I don't know who you think you're supposed to be, but that was beautiful. And sexy. And amazing. If you're done, I will happily take you home. If you're not, I'll happily take you to my bed. But whatever you want, I am not wishing you were anyone other than exactly who you are, Edie."

"Thank you."

Her eyes sparkled with the pleasure from moments ago, like she was allowing herself back to that time. Back to where she was allowed to find joy.

"It's been a long time since... I'm not sure."

"We go slow," Pryce said. "As slow as you need. And if you say stop, at any moment, we stop."

"I don't want you to think—"

"I would never."

She seemed to absorb his growled words, internalizing them like she knew he meant it.

He did. He knew where she was going with her statement, and he hated that she had to worry about that. Too many women were blamed for things that happened to them and ended up afraid to be real. Afraid changing their minds meant it was okay to be assaulted. Afraid to be alone with a man for fear of the same.

Pryce knew it was huge that Edie was there with him. Hell, it was huge she agreed to a date at all. For the date to continue in private was an even bigger deal. One Pryce had zero intention of fucking up.

"Thank you."

Pryce leaned forward slowly, giving Edie time to react. She met him halfway, throwing herself into the kiss that had Pryce's cock painfully aching to continue the evening.

One of Edie's hands snuck between them, her palm against his body. Pryce tried to hold still while she explored his skin, but it was nearly impossible. He twitched with each press of her palm, each drag of her nails. His hips lifted more than once, thrusting his pulsing cock against her without conscious thought.

"Can I touch you?" she whispered against his lips.

Pryce nodded. If he tried to speak, he would have said far more than either of them was ready for.

Edie's hand flattened on his belly. She leaned back, giving herself space. Pryce sucked in his belly, giving her room to slide her hand into his jeans.

They watched her hand ease beneath the edge of his jeans together. They groaned together when she wrapped her hand around his erection. Then she stroked him once, and Pryce's eyes rolled back in his head.

He yanked the button on his jeans free and tore the zipper down, needing to give her more space. He watched the tent in his boxer briefs change from the edge of his cock to her fist over and over as she stroked him from root to tip.

"Edie," he warned, knowing he was going to make a mess if she didn't stop soon.

She slowed her strokes and looked up at him.

"You feel really fucking good. So good, I'm going to come if you keep going."

"Is that... do you want to?"

"You're leading here, Edie. You don't owe me this, and I

don't expect it. But if you want me... if you want me inside you, regretfully, I need you to stop."

She giggled, her smile brightening at the pained look he knew was on his face. "I have a hard time regretting that I want to feel you inside me."

Pryce groaned, surging into her fist at the mention of sinking into her.

"You're going to be to blame if you keep going."

Pryce chuckled, struggling to grip his sanity and control again. She was too important for him to lose his mind and risk scaring her. "Sorry."

"It was good. I... It makes me feel powerful to know I can make you feel good."

Pryce knew what she wasn't saying. He surged forward, capturing her lips before she could retreat from him like she always did after one of her confessions.

Edie squeaked in surprise, then moaned and leaned in to the kiss. Her hand didn't move from where it was wrapped around him, everything forgotten but the kiss that had them both panting and fighting to get closer.

"Bedroom," Pryce whispered against her lips, pulling her in for another kiss before he released her and helped her stand.

Edie was shaky on her feet, something that made Pryce pretty damn proud until he tried to stand and was just as wobbly. They laughed together, then reached for each other, stumbling and kissing on the way to his room.

Pryce's bedroom was nothing special, but it was more comfortable than the couch. When they reached the door, he stopped, pulling back to look at her. "Lights on or off?"

"On," she said without hesitation. The look in her eyes was not one of fear, but one of excitement. She wasn't afraid of the dark, she wanted to watch them.

Pryce ached at the thought. And agreed completely.

They both worked to kick off their unbuttoned jeans, leaving them in the doorway before they were back in each other's arms. Pryce touched as much of her as he could, his hands caressing from her waist to her shoulders down to her breasts and across her belly.

Edie was an active participant, her hands exploring just as freely as Pryce's. She cupped his butt, squeezing his cheeks and bringing him against her.

"Pryce," she whispered.

Pryce eased her toward the bed, stopping before they climbed in. He pulled back from her, dropping his boxer briefs to the floor and digging a condom out of his nightstand. Then he laid on the bed.

"You want me on top?" she breathed.

Pryce sat up immediately. "You don't have to be. I just thought you wouldn't feel trapped. I told you, you're in charge here, Edie. I didn't mean to presume."

"No, I…" She exhaled slowly. "Thank you. I don't know how good it'll be, but—"

"It's with you. It'll be fucking amazing."

Edie slid her panties down her legs, giving Pryce his first view of her completely naked. If he wasn't already on the edge, he would be with that picture. She was perfect. Slick and plump and ready for him. He wanted to lick her, but she was already moving to straddle him.

"Let me get the condom on," he said, stopping her before she sank on him. Pryce tore the package and rolled the condom down with shaky hands. He wanted them on her, not on himself.

As soon as the condom was in place, he reached for her, holding her hips while she positioned herself over him. Pryce wrapped one hand around his cock and held still as she lowered onto him, both of them groaning at the feel of her wet heat welcoming him in.

"Holy fuck," Pryce breathed. His eyes were glued to where he disappeared into her, her brown skin and dark hair framing his cock like the sexiest picture ever.

"Yeah," she whispered.

Pryce dragged her gaze to her face. He knew it was the first time she'd been with anyone since she was taken. His chest was overly full at the reminder of not only what she'd been through but her strength to reclaim her body and her life after.

The look on her face said she was there with him completely. Her lips were slightly parted, her eyes closed. Her nipples were hard, her body soft. She was perfect. Like a fantasy.

Then she moved. "Oh, fuck, yes," Pryce moaned.

She lifted and squeezed, tugging on his cock, then released her muscles and sank down onto him. She set a slow pace that had his eyes crossing and his throat tightening and his balls begging to let go.

"Fuck, Edie. Oh, fuck." Real words evaded him. All he could do was watch and feel and hope she was enjoying herself as much as he was.

A glance at her face said she was. Her mouth was pinched in an expression that would have looked like pain in any other situation. The way her body sagged with each downstroke told him she was enjoying the feel of him fully seated inside her.

He needed to get in on the action.

The next time she sank down on him, Pryce thrust up into her, pressing against her inner channel. She gasped, hands falling to his chest. Her fingers curled on his next thrust, nails digging into his chest.

"Pryce," she whispered.

"What do you need?"

"More," she gasped. "Oh, God, yes."

Pryce grabbed her hips, sensing her energy was failing and her body was claiming what was left for her orgasm. Her inner walls rippled around him, sending flutters of need through him. He clenched his jaw and focused on the beautiful woman riding him like she was meant to be right where she was. In his fucking bed.

Pryce guided her into a faster pace, forcing her down on his strokes up into her and pulling himself away. Sweat beaded on his forehead. His muscles burned from holding back and driving forward at the same moment.

Edie's hands didn't move from his chest, the only thing keeping her from collapsing onto him. She moaned with each thrust, her muscles twitching as she chased her orgasm.

"Pryce," she whimpered.

"Can I flip us, Edie?"

"Yes, please. Oh, God, please."

She'd barely finished the words when Pryce rolled them. He positioned himself inside her again, loving the feel of her body welcoming him in. She blinked her eyes open and smiled at him, and he was gone.

He lifted to his knees, cupping her butt to tilt her hips up. He surged into her, watching himself slide in and out of her beautiful body. With his hands free, he pressed her thighs wider, giving himself full view of her.

"Can I touch you, Edie?"

"Yes," she begged, like she'd been waiting for him to offer.

Pryce slid his thumb over her clit, and she jumped. She

moaned, her body tightening around him. He rubbed over it again, feeling the answering flood of moisture inside her.

"That's it, Edie. Come for me."

"Oh, God," she moaned. "Yes. Pryce. Yes."

She came with a beautiful, glassy look in her eyes, and a thrust of her hips that had Pryce bottoming out inside her.

He wanted to check with her, to make sure she was okay, but he was gone. He couldn't control his hips as they pistoned into her, following her over the edge three thrusts later and calling out her name. After waiting her out, his orgasm poured from him like a flood and took the last of his energy.

Pryce collapsed onto her, but he immediately rolled them so she wasn't pinned beneath him. She held him, ending up on top of him as their bodies cooled. He kissed the top of her head.

"You're really good at that," she said, her jaw moving against his chest.

Pryce chuckled. "I was not the only active participant."

"Yeah, well, I was mostly along for the ride."

"It was the best ride I've ever had," Pryce said.

"Me, too."

Pryce couldn't remember the last time he felt so content. The last time he wasn't wondering when the other shoe was going to drop. Instead, he was just happy. He finally found a woman who made him feel like everything was going to be okay. A woman who fit him in every possible way.

A woman who made him believe there was no other shoe to drop. Because they were good together. That was a damn good feeling.

"You slept with him?" Stacey gasped. She schooled her expression and drew a deep breath. "I'm sorry. I didn't mean to sound like I was judging you. I'm trying to be supportive and encouraging here, and the last time we talked, you seemed unsure of him."

Edie laughed. She asked Stacey for another session. Charlotte kept her promise and went to see Stacey, and Edie realized having someone to talk to was a good thing. She trusted Stacey's thoughts and opinions, and she trusted Stacey to be honest with her about the way she was feeling.

"You can be shocked," Edie said. "I didn't go into the date planning to sleep with him, but I kept thinking about all the times he and I talked. He's the reason I've been able to even consider a normal life again."

"What do you mean?"

Edie shrugged. This was the hard part. The reason she wanted to talk to Stacey. "I know the fear is never going to go away. I hate that, but I'm trying to accept that all I can do is face it. Part of that fear was that I'd never be normal again. That I was destined to be alone because I'd never trust another man. I'd never have an interest in sex or a relationship or anything. That I'd stay here forever and never try for more."

"Some people take longer than others to find what normal looks like. There's nothing wrong with needing more time."

Edie shook her head. "That's not what I'm saying. I never considered I could get there. I assumed I'd just be this same shell forever. Chasing bad guys and hiding everything about myself. Wearing a mask when I'm out there, no matter who I was. But Pryce... I felt like he saw through that."

"He knows you're the vigilante?"

"No," Edie said quickly. "No. I mean in general. The first

time we met, he talked to me like I was anyone. Every time since then, even once he knew who I was, he never treated me like I was fragile. He was careful with me, don't get me wrong, but he doesn't act like I'm going to break. It's refreshing. It made me want to feel that way myself."

"That's good." Stacey looked confused, like she was trying to figure out where the bad news was coming from.

"Why him?" Edie asked.

Stacey chuckled. "I think that's a woman question."

"What do you mean?"

"We all ask that. About the person we fall in love with. I can't tell you how many times I asked myself that about Wray. Especially after we almost lost everything. I couldn't bring myself to walk away from him, but I didn't feel like I could trust him either."

"What changed?"

"I put our family at risk. I'm not saying that was a good thing, but it gave me perspective. He's gotten help for his gambling, and he stays away from all of it, but he was still a victim. People preyed on him. Just like they preyed on you and Raina and Karli. At the end of the day, he's the person I want to spend my life with. The man I want beside me for every major moment in life. I don't know why, and I'll never know why, but he's it for me."

"Pryce and I barely know each other."

"True, but you have a connection."

"Is that why he's the only man I've been able to touch?"

Stacey's face went all soft. "You trust him, Edie. There's nothing wrong with that. After everything you've been through, being able to have sex again and not freak out is amazing."

"So, I should have freaked out. I knew there was something wrong with me."

"No, I didn't say that." Stacey chuckled. "I'm saying if you had freaked out, I wouldn't have been surprised. But you didn't, which tells me Pryce is a good man and he's good for you."

"He really is," Edie whispered.

"So, what's the problem?"

Edie chewed on her lower lip and debated her next words.

"Just say it, Edie."

"What if the only reason I feel like I can handle normal is because of him? If he's some kind of grounding force for me, but then things end. If he finds out I'm the vigilante and he hates me. Or meets someone else and doesn't want me anymore. Or—"

"Edie," Stacey said calmly, breaking into Edie's fear. "Are you more afraid of losing him or losing yourself?"

"Both," Edie whispered. "What if I don't know who I am without him?"

"Then you come ask me, or Frannie, or Lorelei, Karli, Jessica, Raina, and Mackenzie. We'll remind you of who you are. We'll tell you about the strong, beautiful, intelligent woman we know. The woman who wasn't afraid to stand up to the man who kidnapped her. The woman who's working with the FBI to bring down the organization that held her for months. The woman who has not been swallowed by the darkness, even though you were in it for far longer than you ever should have been. Edie, you are amazing. We are all in awe of you and honored to be your friend. And if you think Pryce is the only reason you're thinking about normal, he's a lucky man to be gifted with your attention and your love."

"Love? I don't love him."

Stacey smiled. "Maybe you're not willing to admit it yet, but it's there. And he'd be lucky to have you fall for him."

"I don't..." Edie broke off, thinking about the things people have said about love. There was no way she was there.

But maybe she was headed there.

"I think we should all get together soon. Next week?"

Edie nodded absently. Maybe a night with her friends was exactly what she needed.

14

———

THE COP EASED AWAY FROM THE STATION, NOT IN A HURRY. HE didn't want to draw unnecessary attention to himself. He followed the patrol car from a few spaces behind, knowing what he was doing was a risk, but he had no choice.

If Officer Murphy was helping the vigilante, like so many people suspected, he needed to know. He needed proof. Proof that would give him cause to have Officer Murphy in jail like he should be, and the vigilante in the ground. Like she deserved to be.

The call earlier said another present was left for the police. That was what she called them, the people she picked up. And the more presents she left, the more heat was on the cop. Trevor was getting pissed as his network was shrinking. People were afraid of getting hauled off to jail for work they'd done for years. The Company's promise of protection was no longer enough for get those lazy assholes to do their fucking jobs.

Which was why Trevor was putting the pressure on the cop. Trevor was still sure Edie Warren was the vigilante, but there was no way. Not when she lived with the captain. He was barking orders daily to find the vigilante and put her away, and the captain was not that good of an actor. He was pissed.

But he wasn't nearly as dangerous as Trevor.

Murphy pulled into the parking lot of Bob's Diner, a shitty rundown garbage place in the middle of the city. The place made dumps seem fancy.

The cop parallel parked on the street, close enough that he could see the inside of the place but far enough away that he wouldn't be noticeable unless someone was looking for him.

And no one should be looking for him.

After Murphy brought in the latest collar, courtesy of the vigilante, he handed over the perp and headed out again. And went to a diner?

The cop watched as Murphy climbed from his vehicle and looked around the lot. A smile lifted the edges of his mouth, like he saw something that made him happy. The cop tried to figure out what it was, but all he saw was a bunch of vehicles that looked like they belonged at that shitty diner.

He did his time working the shit jobs. He paid his price. He was done living like a pauper. He listened to the rumors around the station and he knew how to stay undetected. And he knew how to get to the people who would make his side-work worthwhile for both of them.

The cop was the one who approached Trevor. Offered to make things easier on him, if Trevor was willing to make it worth his while. Trevor was eager to trade.

He was never overly interested in the women or the drugs, even though the cop knew both were abundant in Trevor's world. Cash was easier to hide, and it meant a lack of proof. The cop knew that. If Trevor gave him a woman, he had proof of trafficking. Cash was cleaner. Cash meant the cop could buy his own property, one no one knew about. One he planned to go to when the time was right.

With the one woman he did want. The blonde Trevor promised him.

But first, he needed to find the vigilante and bring an end to the problems she was creating for Trevor and the Company.

Murphy waved to the woman behind the counter, clearly familiar with her, as the cop watched him. Murphy spoke to the woman for a few seconds, then turned toward the back of the diner, smiling as he made his way to a booth as far from the door as one could get.

Where Edie Warren was sitting.

"Well, isn't that interesting," the cop murmured to himself. The suspected vigilante herself was cozying up to the officer who always reported to her crime scenes.

Murphy sat on the same side of the booth as Edie, kissing her quickly before smiling and helping himself to a bite of her pie.

"That's cozy."

The cop took a few pictures of the two of them, zooming in to get the look on Murphy's face. The look that said they weren't just friendly and sharing pie. They were fucking.

He hated being wrong, but he was definitely wrong about Edie Warren not being the vigilante. There was no way he was going to argue against Trevor after seeing Murphy and Edie together, all snuggled up in a booth in a shitty diner, clearly celebrating their latest victory.

Guess it was time to change tactics. If Trevor's people hadn't been able to take her down yet, maybe they were focusing on the wrong one in the partnership. Maybe they needed to take Murphy down instead.

And the cop knew exactly how to begin.

Pryce was still smiling when he made it back to the station. He couldn't get enough of Edie. They still hadn't had a second official date, but she kept showing up at the diner, so he knew she was still interested. That and she kissed him back every time he leaned in.

And Pryce leaned in for a kiss a lot.

He was still thinking about the kiss she gave him in the parking lot before he left when he stepped through the door. The smile on his face faded when he nearly ran into James Hampton. Not in handcuffs.

"What the hell?" Pryce muttered.

"I told you nothing would stick," Hampton said with a smirk.

His slick-suited attorney barely glanced at Pryce before shuffling his client out the door. Free.

"Why is he leaving?" Pryce asked to no one in particular.

"Lawyer got him off," Maxwell grumbled. "Said it was entrapment. Made a case that the vigilante is working with us."

"What?" Pryce gasped.

Maxwell shrugged. He jerked his thumb toward his partner. "That's what Dempsey said. Hampton's lawyer is some big shot with a lot of pull with judges. Called in a favor when he heard the police officer who picked him up let the woman who attacked him go."

"How in the hell is that relevant?" Pryce asked, his cheeks burning.

"Because you don't know how to do your fucking job," Foster snarled from right behind Pryce. "If you'd actually done something right, he wouldn't be leaving. Hell, if you'd done something right, you would have brought in the criminal we had evidence for."

"What are you talking about? Hampton's on the damn board! We have a witness. And a shit-ton of evidence or we wouldn't have a case against him and a picture of him on the fucking board."

Maxwell and Dempsey eased away, leaving Pryce to face Foster alone. Chickenshits.

"Are you a detective now?" Foster asked, his snarl turning to a straight-up sneer. "Because I missed the part where you were allowed to speak to me that way."

"It seems like you aren't much of a detective if you can't make charges stick on a man the entire fucking department knows is guilty. Why is he walking? What the hell happened?"

"The witness is dead, so the lawyer got a judge to throw out the charges. Said when you brought him in, you had no cause. You didn't even read him his rights, because you weren't charging him with anything. You saw him and decided to arrest him, even though he was the victim that night. I told you your girlfriend should have been the one you arrested, but instead, you bring in the guy you think will look better. The guy who's on the board. For what? You think the brass is going to give you some award or something?" Foster laughed. "Not now."

"He was the bigger threat to the community," Pryce growled. "He was the more dangerous one of the two. And if you were even a halfway decent detective, you would have had a case against him that wouldn't have the city's biggest known drug dealer back out on the fucking streets right now!"

"Murphy!" another voice barked from across the room.

Pryce winced, knowing the voice belonged to his captain. He didn't know Captain Patrick was still in the building, but it didn't matter.

Foster smirked at Pryce before Pryce turned to face his captain.

"My office. Now."

Snickers followed Pryce across the bullpen. The captain never yelled at them in front of others, something Pryce always respected about the man, but that didn't mean he wasn't going to yell.

Pryce knew he deserved it, too. Foster was an asshole, but that didn't mean Pryce should be, too. He didn't say anything he didn't mean, but there was an order, a ranking that meant the way Pryce spoke to Foster was not okay.

"Shut the door," Captain Patrick said when Pryce stepped inside.

Pryce closed the door, catching grins from his coworkers watching avidly for Pryce to be ripped a new one. Fuck.

"I expected better from you," Captain Patrick said.

"Sir?"

"You're already getting too much attention for your presumed connection to the vigilante, and now you start a fight in the middle of the shift with Foster?"

"I didn't start that, sir." Pryce leaned forward.

"Stop." Patrick closed his eyes and drew a deep breath. "I should be home by now, Murphy. Instead, I'm here working on this case. And instead of helping, you're in a pissing contest with a detective. In the middle of everyone. Do you really think that's going to win anyone over?"

"With all due respect, sir, I don't care about winning them over."

"No? It doesn't bother you that more of them out there think Foster's right than wrong? Or that a few of them have talked about following you to see who you're spending time with? Or that they could go after Edie if they see you together and assume she has something to do with this?"

"She's not involved."

"They don't know that. I thought you were going to take care of her."

Pryce's palms were suddenly damp. "Did something happen to Edie? I just saw her, sir."

Patrick's brows jumped up. "You were on a date during shift?"

"No, sir. I went to Bob's Diner. Some of the patrons and one of the servers are CIs. I go there regularly to keep in touch with them."

"Edie was there?"

"The first time we met was there. She was looking at pie, and I startled her and spilled her coffee. I bought her a new coffee and a slice of pie as an apology. We've been meeting there ever since."

"And you still do?"

Pryce nodded. "Yes, sir. But again, is something wrong with her? Did something happen?"

Captain Patrick shook his head. "No. Not that I'm aware of. But it's only a matter of time. Do you know why Foster is good at his job?"

Pryce shook his head. He never thought of Foster as good, but he also never gave the guy a chance.

"Foster has a good record. He gets convictions on most of his investigations. He's not phoning it in. He's doing the work. And part of that is exactly what he did to you tonight. He goads them into a reaction. He waits for the right moment and digs in to that one spot where it hurts. He lets them sink themselves. Either during his initial questioning or after he's gathered enough evidence for charges. He knows what he's doing."

Pryce couldn't argue. Foster's record was good. Even if the guy was an asshole with a grudge who Pryce resented.

Or was Pryce the one with the grudge?

"You don't have to like him. You don't have to trust him. But I trust him. He's good at what he does. He gets the job done. I think if the two of you worked together, you'd actually be able to solve the vigilante case, and others. But it would mean both of you putting aside your egos, and I'm not sure either of you has the fucking balls to do that."

Pryce swallowed roughly because the captain was right. Pryce never shared information with Foster, not if he could help it. He made Foster dig up everything on his own. Pryce was not a team player when it came to Foster.

And he needed to change that.

"I apologize, sir."

Captain Patrick leveled Pryce with a glare that made him squirm. After a minute, he shook his head and said, "Good. Now go do your job and catch some bad guys."

Pryce stood, making his way to the door when something Foster said made its way to the front of his mind. "Sir, Foster said the witness is dead. I thought we had the witness in custody."

Captain Patrick sighed heavily and shook his head. "Big H was taken out. The official report says it was a turf battle and he was caught in the middle, but we know that's not the case. It was a hit, and he was the target."

"And we can't put that on Hampton?"

Patrick snorted. "Do you think I'd have let him out of here if I could?"

"Sorry, sir."

Captain Patrick shook his head and rubbed his hands

over his face. He looked more tired and defeated than Pryce could remember ever seeing his boss.

"This isn't an easy job, Officer. None of us have it easy. But if we stop trying to stop the bad guys, they win."

"Sometimes they win anyway," Pryce said.

Captain Patrick looked up at him and nodded slowly. "Sometimes they do. For a little while. But we can't let them win forever. We have to keep trying and wait for them to mess up. They always do."

"Always?"

Captain Patrick glared at Pryce. "Always, Officer. Always."

Pryce nodded, hoping his captain was right, and let himself out of the office. Foster was standing along the far wall, watching Pryce with a smirk.

Pryce wanted nothing more than to ignore the asshole and walk out the door, but Patrick was right. If they worked together, they had a better chance at success.

Pryce walked across the room to where Foster was standing. Foster straightened as Pryce grew closer, scowling at him until Pryce stopped right in front of Foster and extended his hand.

"You were right. I brought in the wrong person. I wanted the bigger threat off the street, and I believed Hampton was the bigger threat. But I didn't catch him doing anything, so I made your job more difficult."

Foster tentatively reached forward to shake Pryce's hand. "True."

"Captain Patrick wants us to find a way to work together. I know you don't trust me, but I'd like the chance to prove to you I can be valuable."

Foster nodded once. "You don't get a lot of chances with me."

"Nor with me," Pryce growled back.

"Noted," Foster said.

They released each other, a glare of truce exchanged between them, followed by a mutual retreat.

EDIE SAT at the table with a drink in her hand and a smile on her face. Spending time with her friends was exactly what she needed. The beautiful women she was surrounded by were more like family to her than strangers who became friends. They were her reason for doing what she did.

"Okay, okay," Raina said, commanding the attention of the room. "Adam has been after me to set a date. I'm thinking about this summer. Do you guys think I'm crazy?"

"No!" everyone said together.

"You deserve to be happy," Karli said, stepping forward to hug Raina. "After all you've been through, you should celebrate. You found a man who makes you feel good. Who's one of the best out there, and you love each other. Why in the hell would you wait?"

Raina wrinkled her nose. "I feel like we're not done yet. We haven't stopped everything."

"Bad things are always going to happen," Mackenzie said. "I hear it every day. Bad things happened before Damon and bad things are going to keep happening."

"But—"

"I think that's all the more reason to get married," Edie said quietly.

The others looked at her. Seven women waiting for her to impart her wisdom. She nearly laughed.

"We don't know how much time we have. We all want to believe our time will come when we're old and gray and have lived a full life and we are surrounded by loved ones. The harsh reality, that we all know too well, is that we don't all get that story. Some of us are brutalized by someone who was supposed to love us, like Holly."

Stacey clasped her hands together and nodded. "Some of us are in the wrong place at the wrong time, like Tonya."

Karli, who it still sometimes hurt for Edie to look at, nodded thoughtfully. The similarities between Karli and Tonya took Edie off-guard more than they should, but it was also a comfort to look in the face of a woman who was so familiar.

"People die every day. Horrible things happen every day. It sucks, but it's reality. So, when something good happens, we need to grab hold of it and fight like hell to keep it there." Edie wanted them all to live in their happiness, not the despair they'd been through.

The others nodded, each looking lost in her own thoughts.

"Well, if there's any of us who knows what it's like to grab hold of happiness these days, it's definitely you," Raina said with a wide grin.

"What?" Mackenzie said, spinning on Edie. "Are you seeing someone?"

Edie sucked in a breath and shook her head at Raina's smirk. She looked around the room at the other women. "I am. He's a cop."

The room erupted in a combination of cheers and disbelief. Followed immediately by demands for more information.

"We met at Bob's Diner. He snuck up behind me and scared me. I spilled my coffee, and he bought me a new one, and a slice of pie."

"Peach?" Mackenzie asked, knowing it was Edie's favorite.

Edie nodded.

Mackenzie, not one for dramatics, swooned. "That was all it took, wasn't it?"

"Well, it's a bit more complicated than that." Edie glanced at Frannie, unsure how to explain the connection she had to Pryce without revealing to the police captain's wife that she was the person the police were spending their time chasing.

Then Frannie leaned in and said, "He's the cop who keeps showing up when Edie's leaving her presents, so complicated isn't even the half of it."

Edie was pretty sure she stopped breathing.

15

———————

"You know?" Edie gasped. Her gaze was locked on Frannie, wondering if the woman was waiting for confirmation so she could turn Edie in or if she was on Edie's side.

Frannie snorted. "Of course I know. Who do you think was the first one to wear that mask you keep in your handbag?"

"You?" Edie's breathed word was definitely one of shock. It was also one of respect and admiration.

"I assumed you knew, but I guess not. I spent my twenties as an exotic dancer. On my way home one night, I witnessed a murder, which I've told you. Marcus was one of the officers who investigated the murder. That was how we met. But I went after the man who killed the woman."

"You what?" Edie asked.

"It's a long story, but I was lucky. He was going to kill me, and he would have if it weren't for Marcus. I kept that mask as a reminder of a time when I felt unstoppable. I gave it to Stacey when she went after Holly's killer."

"And I gave it to Jessica when she went after Tonya's killer," Stacey said.

Jessica nodded.

"And Jessica gave it to me when Cade and I were after Damon," Karli said.

"Karli gave it to me," Mackenzie said. "Then I gave it to Raina for strength."

"And obviously, I gave it to you," Raina said. "We're all connected. We're all doing what we feel is right. And none of us judge you for trying to help. Or for not trusting the police to handle things."

"Does Marcus know who I am?" Edie asked, staring at Frannie.

Frannie leveled Edie with a look perfected by years of telling people what they needed to hear, whether it was what they asked or not. "Do you honestly want to know the answer to that question?"

Edie sucked in a breath and leaned back in her seat. If Marcus knew and wasn't stopping her, it meant he was on her side. But if he didn't know, it could mean anything.

"What I will tell you is Marcus has said if he knew who the vigilante was, he would thank her for helping the department."

"That's what Pryce told me. I wasn't sure I believed it," Edie said.

Frannie smiled. "He meant it. He knows things happened that never should have happened. Everything with that Officer Bernard and the others he investigated. Marcus was so angry and hurt. And shameful. He never thought something like that was going on right under his nose. That you could have been missing and his department could have done something, but it was all hidden. He'll never forgive himself for it."

"It wasn't his fault," Edie said. She knew Marcus was a

good man. And she knew if he'd had any idea of what was going on, he would have put a stop to it.

"He's in charge. He sees that as being the one to blame."

"I wish he wouldn't."

Frannie chuckled. "That's Marcus. That's one of the many things I love about him. He wants things to be good. He wants to believe people are good. Finding out Bernard wasn't really rocked him. In a major way. And ever since you started talking to Officer Murphy, he's been doing every check possible on the man to make sure he knows Pryce is a good man."

"Is he?" Edie whispered, afraid of the answer as much as she craved it.

Frannie nodded, smiling as she did. "Marcus has found nothing bad about Pryce Murphy. He's a good man."

Edie sighed heavily. "Thank God."

"You already knew that," Raina said. "You told me you thought he was a good man."

"I also thought Damon was going to save me from Trevor," Edie said wryly.

"You weren't in your right mind then," Mackenzie said. "That's not fair to yourself."

Edie sighed heavily. "I know. I just don't know how to trust again."

"He showed you who he is," Raina said. "More than once. I think he's proven you can trust him."

"I hope so. But what about him trusting me?" Edie asked in a small voice.

"What do you mean?" Karli asked.

Edie met her gaze. "He's after the vigilante. He thinks she's wrong to bring people in. Says it's assault and kidnapping. Says she deserves to be arrested."

"I guess we can assume he doesn't know it's you," Jessica said.

Edie shook her head.

"I think he'll understand one day," Frannie said. "It's easy to think we understand a person or their motivations, but when we get a peek inside, it's a different story."

"He knows about my past," Edie said.

"I'm not surprised, but does he know the people you're going after are ones who are part of that organization? That you're working to take down the people who held you? What you're doing isn't random."

"How do you know that?"

Frannie smirked. "I pay attention. As well as you do."

Edie's cheeks burned with embarrassment. All the times Edie snuck a look at Marcus's files, she wasn't being as sneaky as she thought.

But the files kept getting left out, which meant...

"What you're doing takes a lot of bravery," Mackenzie said. "I sit behind a desk and answer phones. I'm not doing anything."

"We wouldn't be here if it weren't for you," Raina assured Mackenzie. "Damon was going to kill all of us, and God knows what else he would have done to me. You are a hero to me, Mackenzie. And you're a hero to every person who speaks to you on the phone when their life is falling apart. Don't doubt that what you do matters, because it does. A lot."

Mackenzie smiled. "Thank you, Raina."

"All of you impress the hell out of me," Lorelei said. "I meet a lot of brave people in my line of work, people who've gone through the same training I have. They're great people, and we've committed our lives to helping others. But we don't see a lot of civilians with the same level of commitment to helping others. You ladies are the first people I'd call if I needed backup."

Karli laughed and hugged her cousin. "Hopefully you never need it."

"Oh, I definitely hope I never need it, but if I do, I know where to find support," Lorelei said.

"We all know where to find support. And for the record, I think you should grab on to that happiness you were telling Raina to grab on to. You deserve it just as much as she does," Jessica said to Edie.

"Thank you," Edie whispered.

"You all deserve that happiness," Frannie said. "That's why I started Shelter in the Storm. I wanted to create a place where women had the chance to believe that. Where women could come when they had nowhere else to go and rebuild their lives in a place where they were safe. It took me a lot longer than I'd hoped, but I'm proud of what I've created, and I am so damn proud of every single one of you. You ladies are the best of them. The ones who are fighting for a happily ever after for everyone, and doing what you can to get it for them."

"You are our inspiration," Stacey said.

Edie nodded with the others, feeling the love and affection around the room. She felt the same way Frannie did. She was doing what she was doing because of the women in the room, and all the women who couldn't be in the room. All the women who were still living their personal hell. The ones who would never be able to have their happily ever after. The ones who were gone and forgotten.

The unclaimed, as Mackenzie called them. The people who disappeared and were never missed.

Edie was almost one of them. If it weren't for Tonya, she would have been. Tonya fought for Edie, and died for her.

And every night Edie put on her mask and found a person who was trying to destroy their city, Edie was fighting for Tonya.

She would never stop. The risk to her didn't matter. What mattered was bringing home the ones who had no one fighting for them. Edie would fight. Until she ended their suffering.

PRYCE TOYED with the bracelet Edie wore, needing to keep a connection to her. He couldn't seem to stop touching her soft skin or leaning in for a kiss.

They were finally on their second date, but it felt more like a much higher number. They still met at the diner almost every night, and he stole kisses from her every time they were there. One night they kissed so much when they were leaving that Edie threw her head back in lust and rode his thigh until she came right there in the parking lot.

Sexiest fucking thing ever. Except then Pryce had to go back to work with her scent all over him and an erection that would not go away.

Totally worth it.

"What are you thinking about?" Edie asked, bringing him back to the real live version sitting across from him. Her head was tilted to the side, studying him like she'd asked him something and he was so zoned out he missed it.

"The parking lot," he said, letting his voice tell her exactly what he meant. He lifted her hand, kissing the inside of her wrist.

She inhaled sharply, her eyes dilating. She clenched her fist, like she was barely holding on to something.

"I seem to be having trouble holding on to my sanity around you."

She laughed huskily. "Same. I was telling my friends about you over the weekend."

"You told your friends about me?" Pryce sat up straighter. He understood what it meant when a woman talked to her girlfriends, even more when it was a woman like Edie who spoke about her friends with a high level of admiration and affection. "What did you tell them?"

"That I really like spending time with you."

"That's good," Pryce said, trying not to push her for more information.

"And that I think I can trust you."

Pryce sighed, his insides going soft. The woman never ceased to amaze him. She was constantly making him feel like he was a better man than he ever thought he was. "You can trust me, Edie. But I know that's not easy. Thank you."

She shook her head. "You've shown me who you are. That's what they reminded me of. You aren't just here to get me naked. You want to know me."

Pryce nodded. "I do." More than she realized. Pryce felt a little crazy when he thought about what Edie was doing when he wasn't with her. He knew it was too soon to be in love with her, but he was pretty damn sure he was. He wanted to be around her every minute. He missed her when she wasn't next to him. He couldn't keep his hands to himself when he was near her.

And the real kicker? He was letting himself imagine a future for the first time ever. A future that meant finding a new place to live, with a secure building where she would feel safe and would have her own space to make it her own.

When she was ready. If she was ready. And willing to move in with him. One day.

Yeah, Pryce was definitely a goner for Edie Warren.

"I'm really not sure how I got so lucky."

Pryce chuckled. "It's hard to resist a woman who likes peach pie."

Edie laughed. "Oh, so, if there'd been another woman in there who wanted peach pie, I'd have been out of luck?"

Pryce shrugged. "I guess we'll never know."

Edie laughed with him, shaking her head. "I guess I'm lucky I was in the mood for pie that night."

"No, Edie, I'm lucky. I am definitely the lucky one."

She sucked in another breath, her chest lifting with the move.

Pryce's gaze dropped to her perfect brown swells, the delicate lace of her top teasing him with hints of more flesh. He nearly swallowed his tongue when she walked outside in that shirt, the way it clung to her breasts like it defied gravity and wrapped around her neck to fall in a drape behind her, Pryce ached to work his way beneath the top and rediscover her warm skin once more.

"Pryce," she whispered.

He lifted his gaze to hers, noting the lust-drenched look in her eyes.

"Let's get out of here."

He nodded, thankful he'd already paid the bill. He reached for her, wrapping his arm around her waist and letting his fingertips clutch her hip and hold her tight against his body. They walked side-by-side, their bodies bumping and rubbing with each step they took toward the door, the car, privacy.

Pryce forced himself to slow down once they made it outside. If it was any other woman, he would have taken her suggestion as an invitation to take her back to his place, or her place, and spend the rest of the evening in bed. But with

Edie, he not only wasn't willing to make assumptions and risk hurting her, he wanted to hear her say what she wanted.

"Where to?" Pryce asked. The evening air had a slight chill to it, not so much that it cleared his head, but enough to remind him they were in public and he needed to treat her with the respect she deserved.

"Your place," she whispered, not a hint of hesitation in her voice.

Pryce held her until he got to his SUV, opening her door and making sure she was safe inside before he went around and climbed in next to her.

His fingers gripped the steering wheel tight, his mind wondering when he was going to choose somewhere for a date that was closer to his place. Closer meant he didn't have to wait as long to get his hands on her. Closer meant they would have already been at his place and her body would have already been in his hands.

Edie didn't say a word on the drive, just shifted in her seat like she was as uncomfortable as Pryce was. He parked and met her next to the vehicle, his hand on her back as he led the way to the building and up the stairs to his apartment.

He fumbled the keys more than once, something that made Edie laugh. "I'm sorry," Pryce said, feeling like an idiot for being so clumsy.

"It's okay. I dropped my mascara three times when I was getting ready."

Pryce chuckled, his nerves settling a touch at the idea of her being just as nervous as he was. He finally fit the key into the lock and let them into his apartment. He flicked on a light, the whole place coming into view.

Edie stepped inside, giving Pryce space to close and lock

the door behind them, then she was pressing him against the door and herself to his chest.

Pryce grunted his approval as she lifted onto her toes to kiss him. His hands went to her hips, drawing her body tight to his and letting her feel how ready he was for her.

Gone were the tentative teasing and the unsure moves. Replacing both was an assurance in her body and who she was that made Pryce want her even more.

She shoved her fingers through his hair, catching a few strands and tugging. He winced, but she didn't seem to notice. She was a woman on a mission. And it appeared he was the mission.

"I'm sorry," she whispered against his lips. "I feel like I can't control myself right now."

"No apologies necessary. I feel that way every time I'm with you."

Edie laughed softly, lowering to flat feet and taking her lips away from Pryce. He ached to have them back.

"I want to enjoy life. I was telling my friends that you made me feel like there was something to enjoy, and they encouraged me to go for it. But I feel like I'm not that person anymore."

"What person?" Pryce rubbed her sides, not willing to lose contact with her, even though he wanted to know every thought in her mind and didn't mind the interruption in the slightest.

"I'm not who I used to be. That Edie would go home with a guy without a second thought. She was always up for something different. I didn't live the most exciting life ever, but I wasn't afraid to try things."

"And now?"

She shrugged. "I feel like I'm afraid of everything."

"Are you afraid of me?"

She shook her head. "I think that's why I went a little crazy just now. Being with you makes me remember who I used to be. It makes me think she might still exist."

"Do you want to be her again?"

Edie bobbed her head for a second before she shook it. "No, I don't think I do. I know there are things I miss about who I used to be, but more than that, I know I can't really go back."

"Letting go of that isn't always easy."

She laughed mirthlessly. "No, it isn't."

"You know you can be whatever version of you that you want to be with me. I lo— like them all."

Her eyes went wide and her mouth opened into an O. She bit her lip and nodded. "Me, too."

Pryce sucked in a breath, wondering if she was saying what it sounded like she was saying. Then he decided he didn't care. If Edie loved him, she'd tell him when she was ready. And if she wasn't there yet, she wasn't running out the door, so he had a chance.

But until then, he was going to show her exactly what those words meant to him. For as long as she'd let him.

16

———

EDIE DIDN'T KNOW WHAT TO SAY WHEN PRYCE ALMOST SLIPPED that he loved her. She was starting to wonder if she felt the same, but she was nowhere near ready to utter the words yet, so she hedged.

When he smiled at her and moved closer, pulling her in with one hand on her hip and the other teasing the fabric of her shirt that was barely holding on, Edie went willingly into his arms. She always went willingly into his arms. She felt safe there. Like she was meant to be there.

His fingertips grazed her bare skin beneath the edge of her shirt. Then his entire hand was on her, and she was lost to him. She let herself sink into his kiss and his touch and knew he would catch her. No matter how hard or far she fell.

His lips were soft but encouraging. He always let her lead, but he wasn't holding back how he felt. He licked at her lips, getting her to open for him. He groaned when her tongue slicked alongside his. He tightened his grip on her waist and pulled her body against his growing erection.

Edie didn't think about the men she'd been with over

the last year. For not the first time, she was grateful she couldn't remember everything that happened to her. She was grateful for so many things, but that was the big one. She could enjoy sex without the memories clouding her pleasure. She could touch Pryce and feel his hands on her body and not be thrown right back into the past.

Pryce eased his hands up her sides, drawing her top up her body until he had to stop kissing her to remove it.

She pulled back and tugged the tie that held it all together, watching his face as the fabric fell away and left her in the lace bra she treated herself to the previous weekend. In hopes it would put that exact look on his face.

Pryce's eyes bugged out, his jaw slack.

Edie grinned, loving that she could excite him the way something simple like a lace bra did.

"I'm glad I didn't know you were hiding this all night. I'm not sure I would have been able to restrain myself. It was hard enough without knowing what was under that top."

"I thought of you when I got it."

"This is for me?" he whispered, his voice reverent and awed. He looked up at her, a melty, soft expression in his eyes.

Edie nodded. "I wanted to see that look on your face."

"What look?" His voice dropped to a low timbre that sent a shiver up her spine. "What look, Edie?"

"That one," she whispered, barely able to get the words out. "Like you want to eat me up."

"Oh, I definitely do. Will you let me taste you, Edie? Will you come for me like that?"

"I... I didn't mean like that. You don't have to."

He shook his head and reached for her hand. "Oh, Edie. It's not because I feel like I have to. I want to. I want to feel you lose control on my tongue. I want to feel your body grip my fingers. I want to have your scent on me for days and your taste something I never get enough of. There's no *have to* here. Just want to."

"Okay," she whispered.

"Yeah?"

She nodded, and before her head stopped bobbing, he had her in his arms and his tongue between her lips. He groaned like he was already on the edge of his own orgasm and walked them toward his room.

Her bra was gone by the time they made it into Pryce's room, and her breasts were supported by his greedy hands, molding and teasing her nipples until she thought her knees would give out. Edie wasn't about to be outdone and brought her hand beneath his shirt to feel the warmth of his skin. She pressed her palm to his abs, loving the way they rippled at her touch.

Pryce bent at the waist, pulling his skin from her touch, and brought one breast to his lips. He kissed her skin, licking it before catching her gaze. With his eyes locked on hers, he drew her nipple into his mouth.

Edie groaned at the sight, an answering moisture pooling between her thighs. She cupped his head, holding him in place as he toyed with her nipple and readied her even more for him.

"Pryce," she whispered.

He released her nipple and kissed his way to the other one, licking around her nipple before sucking it hard and rolling it against the roof of his mouth.

"Oh, God," she murmured, letting her eyes close while Pryce took care of her.

"On the bed, Edie," he whispered, his lips moving against her breast.

She let him back her up until her calves hit the mattress.

He held her as she sat, then urged her to lie back. He continued to kiss and lick her breasts while he worked the button and zipper of her jeans. With them free, he withdrew from her breasts to slide her jeans and panties down her thighs, leaving her bare to his gaze.

"Every time I see you, I can't believe you're real," he said, his gaze skipping around her body like he couldn't figure out where he wanted to look. "You're so beautiful, Edie."

"Thank you." She was working on accepting compliments from men and trusting they weren't delivered with ulterior motives. Pryce already had her naked, and he'd proven he was a good man. His only motives were ones Edie was all on board with.

"How do you want me, Edie?"

She looked up at him in confusion. How many ways were there for him to go down on her? "On your knees?" she suggested.

He chuckled. "I'm happy to hear you're on board with the plan, but I meant do you want my clothes on or off?"

"Off," she blurted. "Always off."

He laughed again, not taking his time to strip the clothes from his body. When he caught her watching, because why would she not be, he winked at her and took a few extra seconds. Seconds where his jeans slid down slowly, giving her a peek at him springing free before Pryce reached for a condom.

Nope. A strip of condoms.

"No pressure," he said. "Just too much in a hurry to separate them at the moment. I have work to do."

He dropped to his knees next to the bed. Edie's legs were bent over the edge, her thighs pressed together in anxiety.

Pryce skimmed his hands up her calves and over her knees. He teased her inner thighs, then retreated again, caressing her skin in a way that had her forgetting to be nervous.

When he leaned forward, he kissed her rounded belly, dipping his tongue into her belly button, then nipped at the folds of her belly. He licked the crease of her thigh, pressing her thighs apart gently to give himself space.

"You're stunning, Edie," he breathed. "So damn beautiful." He kissed her thighs again and lifted one leg, setting it on his shoulder. "Are you ready for me?"

She nibbled her lip and nodded.

"I want to do this, Edie. It's killing me to not already know what you taste like, but I want to make sure you're okay with it."

"I am," she choked out.

He brought his hands between her thighs and spread her entrance wide with his thumbs. "So perfect," he groaned before he lowered her mouth to her. His tongue speared inside her, and Edie's hips lifted in response.

Pryce groaned, and Edie moaned. He licked her folds and her entrance, sucking her skin like he couldn't get enough of her.

Edie was not complaining. She was pretty sure she was going to be addicted to his mouth on her pussy, just like she was addicted to his mouth on hers. The man had a talented tongue.

"Pryce," she moaned, reaching for him.

He lifted a hand to her, holding on to her hand with one of his. He moved his lips, kissing his way through her folds until he reached her clit. One finger pressed into her in a slow thrust as he licked over her clit.

Edie thrust against him. Deeper, more. He added a second finger, giving her what she didn't realize she asked for out loud.

Pryce did not seem to be in a hurry to bring Edie to her climax, but she was already building up to that point. She had been all night, since she saw him waiting outside for her. Stretched out on his bed and surrounded by his scent had her even closer to orgasm, not counting the feel of his hand and mouth on her.

His tongue explored the intimate folds between her legs, taking detours to other folds instead of focusing on her clit and giving her the orgasm she was almost desperate for.

"Pryce," Edie begged, needing relief.

He pressed a third finger into her and finally returned his tongue to her clit, using the flat of his tongue to cover the entire nub. She shifted her hips, using his tongue to give her the friction she needed.

Pryce speared the tip of his tongue against her, the sudden change enough to send Edie over the edge. She called out his name, letting herself fall as he kept up the strokes inside her.

"Damn, Edie. That was amazing," Pryce growled. "More, Edie. Let me have more."

The man was relentless with one orgasm out of the way. He focused on her clit again, licking it with the tip of his tongue until her body tightened around his fingers. Then he sucked hard on her clit and made her scream, her orgasm flooding her body and sucking his fingers in deep.

"I need to feel you, Edie," Pryce groaned. He surged to his feet and grabbed the strip of condoms, cursing himself for not separating them when he ripped two open in his haste to get them apart. He grabbed one and rolled it on, stroking himself in the process.

"Inside me," she begged, her body coiled tight and ready to go off again.

Pryce slammed into her in one swift move, triggering an

aftershock that had her muscles clenching and her thighs wrapping tight around his hips.

"You feel so fucking good. Nothing has ever felt like this."

"Same," she whispered, her mind going back to his retracted word.

Did she love him? It was so much more than just sex with him, but was it love?

And if it was, how did she keep her secret from him?

"Are you with me, Edie?" Pryce asked, his hips still. He was buried inside her, but not moving as she contemplated their relationship instead of paying attention to the man who was in the middle of making her feel like she could do anything.

"I'm with you."

Pryce held her gaze and nodded. Then he eased back, sliding deep again. His pace was slow, designed to build Edie back up to where she was before. His jaw was clenched tight, his body ready to let go, but he was waiting for her.

No one had ever treated her the way Pryce did. Edie wanted to love him. She wanted him to be the one who adored her for the rest of her life. But it wasn't fair to him to say she loved him if she wasn't sure.

And until she shared her secret with him, she knew she was holding a part of herself back.

"Don't hold back," Pryce grunted, as if he was reading her thoughts.

No. He was talking about her orgasm. It was building again, climbing, clawing, desperate to get out.

Edie didn't want to fight it. She wanted to let go. She wanted to feel it and feel Pryce and feel good. She wanted it all.

Her muscles rippled around him, clenching and

releasing in rapid pace before he slammed in hard, his orgasm taking him where he needed to go.

"Edie, come with me. Are you there?"

"Yes, Pryce, yes," she moaned, the train barreling down on her, taking over as she let go and came hard.

"Fuck," he growled, her body's reaction triggering his. He slammed into her, sending more aftershocks through her as he tipped over the edge and followed her into an orgasm that might have woken the neighbors.

Pryce fell forward, catching himself on his elbows before his weight rested on Edie. She wrapped her arms and legs around him, pulling his weight onto her.

Another test. Another challenge. Another moment she could enjoy again, that Pryce allowed on her time.

Another reason to love him.

Another reason the truth between them hurt. Not just her, but him.

She had to tell him. Before someone else found out and told him. But first she had to figure out how.

"You're gonna tell him?" Mackenzie half-screeched from the bedroom.

Edie stopped by to get Mackenzie's advice a few days after her second date with Pryce and found her getting ready for work. Mackenzie insisted Edie come in, and Edie blurted the whole thing out at once.

"It feels wrong. How did you tell Holden about me and what you were doing?"

Mackenzie stuck her head out of the bedroom. "Um, you showed up at the station. It kind of blew all hope of keeping things quiet."

"Yeah, but you said you were looking into things before then. That you were reviewing old calls."

"I was," Mackenzie shouted, back in her room. "But I didn't tell Holden about any of that until after you showed up. He's a paramedic, and when you dropped into our laps, I knew I couldn't treat you. I needed his help."

"I'm confused. I thought you told him."

"I did," Mackenzie said, coming out of her room again. She pushed her glasses up her nose and fluffed her long hair. She wore jeans and a green tee and had a sheen of lipgloss, which was as much makeup as Mackenzie liked. "I was looking into things, but when you showed up, I hadn't told him anything. I had to call Marcus and let him know you were there so he could make arrangements to get you somewhere safe, and Holden was there. That was when I told him."

"Wow. Okay. I thought you decided it was time to trust him."

Mackenzie shook her head, finally understanding why Edie sought her out. "You wanted to know when I was ready."

Edie nodded. "I like Pryce. A lot. He's amazing, and he makes me feel safe. I can see myself falling for him. I might be."

"But?" Mackenzie prompted.

"But I'm keeping this huge thing from him. I'm not telling him about this secret, and it's a secret I don't think he's going to be okay with. If someone else tells him, it'll ruin us. But if I tell him..."

"It still might ruin you," Mackenzie finished for her.

Edie sucked in a breath and nodded. "Yeah."

"Shit, Edie. I wish there was an easy solution."

"Me, too." Edie was quiet for a minute, trying to figure

out how to balance the part of her that believed in what she was doing with the part of her that loved Pryce and wanted him—

Loved Pryce. She actually thought those words. She did love him.

"What? You look like you just had a realization," Mackenzie said.

Edie looked at her friend and smiled. "I think I love him. I know the people I'm bringing in are bad. I know I'm helping, even if Pryce can't see that. I know it's getting me closer and closer to Trevor and the rest of the organization. But Pryce—"

"Doesn't agree," Mackenzie said.

"Yeah. He thinks I'm breaking the law."

"What if you were able to find a way to get him to understand what you were doing? If you could explain it to him in a way that makes him see how you're helping? Like Frannie said, you're not just going after random people. It's the people involved in the group that held you hostage for months. That would have made you disappear. That did the same to others."

"I don't know if it would matter to him. If he would see all of that."

"Is that part of what scares you?" Mackenzie asked, more perceptive than Edie expected her to be.

"Yeah, maybe. He doesn't think there's a gray area in right and wrong. You can't be both. There is no wrong for the right reasons."

"Shit." Mackenzie was silent for a minute. "So, what are you going to do?"

Edie shook her head. "I don't know. That's the problem. If I love him, I owe him the truth, but if I tell him the truth, he's not going to love me."

"You never know, Edie," Mackenzie said.

Edie smiled. "I do, actually. I know him. And I know he's never going to be okay with it."

"Then you have to pick."

Edie sucked in a breath and nodded. She knew that was the answer, but she didn't like it. She couldn't imagine giving up either. But it was the only way.

Pryce or the vigilante.

17

———

Pryce closed the folder he'd been reviewing and pushed it aside. He was missing something. He knew he was. It bugged him. He wasn't a detective, so he didn't have an obligation to solve this, but he wanted to. He wanted to stop the vigilante. She was putting people at risk and going to end up dead herself.

Another woman had channeled her inner-vigilante and wound up in the hospital for it. A purse snatcher tried to run off with her handbag, and the woman fought back. Good for her, but the man was a foot taller than her and had fifty pounds on her, according to witnesses. He easily over-powered her and shoved her to the ground. The ground was unfortunately next to the road, and she ended up in the path of traffic.

The driver stopped, the witnesses called nine-one-one, but the purse snatcher disappeared into the crowd, and the woman was in a coma.

Pryce didn't know the answer to any of it. Fighting back rarely worked with a criminal, but people needed to feel safe. And they didn't. Which meant Pryce was failing. The entire department was failing.

And the vigilante was still out there.

Pryce needed a change of perspective. All the calls went through the emergency station not far from the police station. Maybe someone there would have more information.

He parked in the visitor lot, nodding to the paramedics washing their ambulance and waiting for a call to come in. Pryce headed toward the door where the call center was located, hoping he would get lucky.

"Can I help you, Officer?" a woman asked, meeting him almost as soon as he walked in.

"Yeah, I'm Officer Pryce Murphy. I was wondering if I could speak to someone about the vigilante."

The woman blanched, blinked a few times, then shook her head. "I'm not sure what we can do for you, but you're welcome to whatever information we can provide."

"You seem surprised."

She shook her head. "I apologize. It's just... around here we see her as helping. People are being brought in. The calls we've received about overdoses has decreased, not a ton but some, and we are seeing a shift. You appear to be here to find out who she is to stop her."

"I am," he said. "What she's doing isn't legal."

"But it's helping people."

"Do you have proof of that?"

"Amanda, do you— Oh, sorry. I didn't see you," another woman said. She had long brown hair and wide glasses. She glanced at Pryce's badge, and her eyes widened before she shoved her glasses higher on the bridge of her nose.

"Mackenzie, perfect. The officer wanted to speak to someone about the vigilante. Since you've answered more of her calls than anyone else, maybe you can answer his questions," Amanda said.

Mackenzie looked shocked. Or like she was going to be sick. Either way, talking to Pryce seemed to be the last thing she wanted to do. "Um, sure."

"Thank you. I'm going to pull some data for the officer. I'll come to your station in a few minutes."

Mackenzie nodded woodenly and turned toward the collection of desks in the middle of the room. Pryce followed her, looking around at the others as they stared at him and Mackenzie.

Mackenzie sat down at a desk and gestured behind her toward a table surrounded by chairs. Pryce grabbed one and pulled it up to Mackenzie's station.

"Um, so, what do you want to know?" Mackenzie asked in a stammer.

"Anything you can tell me. Anything about the calls or her voice or actually, can I listen to the calls?"

Mackenzie logged in to her computer and clicked a few buttons. She picked up a headset and handed it to Pryce.

Pryce put on the headset. Mackenzie clicked a button and sound filled the headset.

"Nine-one-one. What is your emergency?"

Pryce recognized Mackenzie's voice.

"Hi. Um, I need the police."

"Are you okay?"

"Yeah, um, yes. I'm safe. But there's a man here. He's a bad man. A man who hurts people. He sells drugs to people and people die because of him."

"Okay. Can you tell me where you are?"

"Springfield and Calloway."

"Can you tell me who you are?"

"No. But send help quick. Please don't let him get away."

"Help is already on the way. Someone should be there in less than three minutes."

"Thank you," the caller breathed, relief evident in her voice.

"You're welcome. Be careful."

"I will be."

The call ended, and the muffled sound of silence greeted Pryce. He looked at Mackenzie. She was watching him with something that looked like unease.

"That was you?" Pryce asked, removing his headset.

"Yes, sir."

"You don't have to call me sir."

"Okay."

"You've spoken to her again?"

Mackenzie nodded.

"Can I listen to those calls?"

"Of course."

Pryce put the headset back on, and Mackenzie started another recording. One after another, Pryce listened, trying to place the stranger's voice. It changed just enough to tell him she was trying to disguise it, but not enough to make him believe there was more than one vigilante out there.

As Pryce listened to the calls as they came in, he struggled. The things she said about the people she targeted were right on, like she had inside information about the criminals. It wasn't random. But Pryce didn't know her pattern or who she was targeting.

All he knew was she thought she was helping. Even though he didn't agree, he could feel her desperation in each call. Her desire to stop the people she was after from hurting others. It wasn't selfish. Not to her.

Pryce's mind went back to Edie and the way she spoke of her cousin. How she defended the vigilante and said she appreciated that people were trying to make the city a better place.

If he was honest with himself, part of why Pryce was looking into the vigilante was because of Edie. Because he was afraid Edie would be like one of the other women who fought back. That she might go after the organization that killed her cousin. The organization the police had yet to find and dismantle.

Some believed it died with Damon Street, but Pryce wasn't one of them. Where there was one evil, there was always another. Men like Damon Street didn't operate alone. He had a network, a group, and in his absence, someone else was in charge.

And if Edie realized that, she might do something rash and try to find them.

Which was why Pryce needed to stop the vigilante.

"Has she ever revealed anything that's not on these calls?" Pryce asked.

"What? No. All of our calls are recorded. How could she tell me anything?"

"Everything is recorded?" Pryce asked.

"Everything," Amanda said, joining them once more. "For our protection and that of the callers. The calls we take are used in court cases all the time. A phone doesn't ring in here without a recording picking it up."

"What about personal phones?" Pryce asked.

Amanda shook her head. "We would never do that to an employee. They are allowed their privacy."

"Do you know who the vigilante is?" Pryce asked Mackenzie directly.

The color drained from the woman's face. She shook her head.

"Officer, you can't come in here and harass my employees. Mackenzie is an amazing resource for this department. She's been instrumental in bringing down so many criminals, including Damon Street."

"Damon Street?" Pryce's gaze swung back to Mackenzie. "How was that?"

"Mackenzie was the one who stopped him at that safe house. The one who fought back and held him off until the police arrived when those two FBI Agents and the other two women were attacked."

"You saved Edie?" Pryce breathed.

Mackenzie nodded. "Edie is a good friend of mine. We both care about her very much."

Pryce felt like he'd been punched. He was interrogating Edie's friend. He wasn't a detective, and not only had he overstepped and questioned someone, but he questioned a woman who was friends with the woman Pryce was in love with.

"I didn't know."

Mackenzie nodded. "I figured. Edie talks about you a lot. When I saw your badge..."

Pryce nodded. "I'm sorry for making you uncomfortable. I appreciate you taking the time to speak to me."

"Any time, Officer," Amanda said. "Do you want to see these reports?"

Pryce nodded and let Amanda lead him away from Mackenzie's desk. Pryce glanced back to see Mackenzie sit down and put on the same headset she'd handed to Pryce. She swung the microphone into place. Ready to help.

"I know the vigilante isn't always doing exactly what's right, but for us, she's a hero, Officer. We work day and night to help people, and she's stopping crimes before they happen. That's not a bad thing in my book."

Pryce nodded at Amanda and took the paperwork she

gave him. He carried it to his vehicle and flipped open the pages. He read as he signaled dispatch he was available for calls.

Almost immediately, a call came in. A present. From the vigilante.

Pryce set the folder on the passenger seat and flipped on his lights and siren. It was time to go.

EDIE COULDN'T EXPLAIN why she went back to Bottom's Up, but as soon as she stepped inside, she knew she had to be there. If she was going to give up being the vigilante, she had to make sure the man who drugged her and stole her away from her old life wasn't able to do it to anyone else.

She hoped she didn't have to give up what she was doing, but she had to tell Pryce the truth. She knew that. It was too painful to live the double life she'd created for herself. Even if she never intended it to be a double life, that's what it was. By day, she was a regular person trying to piece her life back together after tragedy. By night, she was taking control and getting revenge on the people who decided they had the power and were going to use it to control others by stealing their lives.

Edie still believed in what she was doing, but she knew Pryce had gotten close too many times. He would find out, and when he did, she didn't know what he would do. She needed to tell him. She owed him that much. She'd figure out the rest after that.

Edie walked to the bar, pasting a smile on her face that she hoped would fool the bartender. He was familiar, possibly the same one who'd been there the night she was taken. She shook off the thought that he was in on the whole thing.

Edie made sure she looked nothing like her normal self with a sassy blonde wig, fake lashes, and stage makeup that amped up her features. She wore a pair of tight jeans that were cut way too low and showed off the fake tattoo she carefully applied just above her waistband. Her top was as tight as her jeans and cut low enough to show off half her breasts, lifted and on display thanks to the push-up bra Edie bought for Pryce.

The bartender did a double take and grinned lecherously at her. He made his way over and asked her breasts what they wanted to drink.

"Slippery nipple," Edie said, dropping her voice to a husky tone.

His grin widened. He mixed the drink with quick precision, setting it in front of her with a soft thud. "You need anything else, you tell me. I'm here all night."

"Yeah? What time to you get off?"

"Whenever you want me to," the bartender returned with a wink.

Edie grinned at him and lifted the drink, her gaze locked on his as she wrapped her lips around the straw.

He watched her, shifting himself before he was called away to help another customer.

Edie watched him, laying it on thick. She wanted him to call his friend and get her on the list.

She didn't have to wait long.

"Hi," a voice said, taking the seat next to Edie. "Mind if I take this seat?"

"Help yourself," Edie cooed. It was Jason, the man who'd taken her from the very same bar. The man she believed took another woman weeks earlier, even though Adam never found proof.

Edie fought against the panic threatening to take over. She looked him up and down, waiting for a hint of recognition to spark in his gaze. None did.

He smiled. "Drinking alone?"

Edie shrugged. "Not any longer, I hope."

Jason grinned and signaled to the bartender.

The bartender approached with a scowl. "Yeah?" he growled.

"Beer. Whatever's on tap. And another drink for my friend here."

Edie giggled, letting her gaze fly between the two men. Hook, line, and sinker. It was almost too easy now that she was in on the game.

Bartender mixed her another drink and set hers and Jason's beer on the counter.

Another customer called out, dragging the bartender away.

Edie turned her attention to Jason. "So, why are you drinking alone?"

Jason shrugged. "I'm not. I'm here with you."

Edie smiled widely, licking her straw into her mouth. She was sure this one had drugs in it, so she sealed her tongue over the top of the straw to avoid drinking anything.

"You hungry?" Jason asked.

"Are you offering to buy me dinner?" Edie teased him.

"Anything you want, beautiful."

The nickname turned Edie's stomach, the sharp reminder of what she was doing there. It wasn't fun and games. It was death and torture.

And she was ready for it to end.

"Sounds perfect. But first, I need to go to the ladies' room. That first drink went right through me."

Jason nodded, offering her a hand as she slid off the stool.

Edie put her hand on his chest in thanks, then swung her hips as she walked away. She kept up appearances until she was behind the closed door of the stall.

She sank hard to the toilet seat, the jolt bringing tears to her eyes. Or maybe it was the reality of what she was doing that brought her tears. All Edie knew was this was her one and only chance to put an end to Jason and his easy path to women. She had to get this right.

Edie went back to the bar, grabbing an empty beer bottle from a vacated table as she passed. She rubbed the edge of the bottle against her pants to get rid of whatever germs were on it and decided it was better than the drugs inside her drink.

Edie laughed with Jason and pretended to be interested in everything he had to say. Little by little, she acted more and more tipsy. She leaned against him and let herself fall off her stool onto his side, so he had to catch her. All while the contents of her drugged drink were in the beer bottle instead of her stomach.

"Whoa. Maybe we should get you out of here."

"No," Edie protested drunkenly. "I should get another drink."

"I'm not so sure that's a good idea. It seems you've had enough," Jason argued. "Hey, man, can we get the check?"

The bartender was quick to bring a bill and pocketed the cash Jason handed over, including an extra hundred, Edie noticed. For his assistance, no doubt.

"She okay?" the bartender asked loudly.

"Yeah. Those drinks you make are pretty potent. Just too

many for her," Jason cooed sympathetically. "I'll make sure she gets home."

Edie played her part, tripping over her feet and leaning on Jason for help, letting him half-walk-half-carry her outside.

Jason led her toward a large black truck parked along the dark edge of the parking lot. Edie allowed it until they got a bit away from the door.

Then she spun on him, knocking his hand free.

"Whoa, what's going on?" Jason chuckled. "You going to be sick?"

"You'd love that, wouldn't you? The hero, taking care of the woman. The good guy."

"What... what are you talking about?"

"We've met before," Edie said in a menacing tone. "A year ago. In this very bar. Except I never made it home that night. I was locked in a house and drugged and raped repeatedly until I got out."

Jason's face went white, fear sinking into his eyes. He looked around and found he had no backup.

"I... I don't know what you're talking about."

"Well, maybe the police can refresh your memory," Edie growled. She lunged at him, surprising him enough to catch him off guard. She got one hit in on his cheek, sending him flailing into the car parked behind him.

"What the fuck, you bitch?" Jason growled and came at her. "Who the fuck do you think you are?"

"I'm the woman who's going to take you down." Edie pulled a zip-tie from her pocket and raised her foot, kicking Jason square in the balls before he had a chance to realize what she was doing.

He went down like a stone, grabbing his dick and howling in pain. Edie grabbed one of his hands and looped the zip-tie over it. She was about to drag him to his truck when the whoop of a siren stopped her in her tracks.

"Stop. You're under arrest."

Edie looked up into the eyes of the man she loved.

"Edie?" Pryce whispered.

18

____

Pryce blinked twice, but Edie was still there. She wasn't an apparition or a dream. More like a nightmare. The woman he loved, with a zip-tie and a bruised and beaten man on the ground.

"She attacked me. I was trying to be a nice guy and help her get home, and she came at me," the man on the ground said with a groan. He was a foot taller than Edie and had at least thirty pounds of muscle on her.

Pryce had his doubts about what actually happened, but he was a cop. He was trained to read a situation and see what was in front of him. "What happened?"

"He tried to drug me," Edie said.

"She's lying. I didn't do a damn thing to her. Bought her drinks. You can ask the bartender!"

"He's done it before. To others. And to me." Edie looked up at Pryce, the meaning of her words and the plea in her gaze hitting him square in the chest.

"He's the one?" Pryce breathed, barely able to contain his fury. The man on the ground was the one who drugged and kidnapped her and sent her into a life of sex slavery.

"She's lying. I've never seen her before in my life," the guy growled, sounding much stronger than he did a minute ago. He scrambled to his feet, the poor beaten man act forgotten. "She's a crazy fucking bitch who wants to pin this shit on me. I didn't do a damn thing."

"I think we should go down to the station and have a talk about that. See if there's any chance she's telling the truth," Pryce said, pulling out his cuffs and approaching the man.

The guy made a move like he was going to run. Resisting arrest. "I didn't do anything wrong. You can't take me in for buying a woman a drink."

"I can if she has drugs in her system."

"I didn't drink the drinks. I pretended I did so he'd try to take me again."

"What the fuck?" the guy barked. "You played me?"

That was enough of a confession for Pryce. He moved on the guy before he had a chance to run. Pryce grabbed him and spun him against his truck, slapping the hand-cuffs on him. "We're going to ride to the station and have a chat."

"Fuck you, asshole. I'll be out in no time. I didn't do shit. You can't prove a fucking thing."

"I guess we'll find out."

"What about her? She attacked me. She kicked me in the fucking nuts. I want to press charges! That's assault."

"Self-defense," Edie growled. "You tried to drug me."

"Can't prove it."

The guy fought against his cuffs, trying to get to Edie.

She stepped back, fear warring with anger in her gaze.

A war built inside Pryce, too. He'd spent months chasing the woman who was right in front of him the entire time. Months of criminals he brought in. Months of searching for her.

"Mackenzie," Pryce breathed, something clicking in his mind.

Edie's head whipped toward him, her gaze widening. "You know Mackenzie?"

"I met her earlier. I went to find out more about the nine-one-one calls that come in. She played them all for me. And she said she knew you, before I left. She knows, doesn't she? She knows you were the one calling her. That's why she always told you to be careful."

"Mack had nothing to do with any of this. She is not involved."

"Jesus, Edie. How many people are in on this? How many know what you've been doing?"

"It was all me. No one else knows anything. Leave them all out of it."

Pryce shook his head. "I'm not sure I can do that. Was I just a game for you? A part of the adventure? Fuck the cop who's chasing you? Was it fun to know you were getting me to fall in love with you when you were toying with me?"

"It wasn't like that," Edie said with a gasp. She stepped toward Pryce, but he backed up, holding up his hands so she couldn't touch him. "I never set out to know you. And I never..."

"Wanted me to get so attached," he finished for her. "I see that now. It was easy for you to get information from me. Find out things about open cases. God, I was such an idiot. I thought we had something, Edie. I thought you were in this with me. Do you know what this is going to do to me? Do you have any idea? I'm going to lose my job. Lose everything. Because I trusted the wrong person. Again."

"Pryce," she whimpered, reaching for him again.

Pryce backed up, shaking off her touch. "I can't do it, Edie. I can't. I need to take him in. Get this sorted. I can't have you in the same vehicle as him. I will be back for you. Or someone will be. Now that I know who you are, it's going to be a lot easier to bring you in."

"Pryce, please. Let me explain."

Pryce shook his head. "If you wanted to explain, you would have by now. I'm not the one you need to explain anything to. I don't care anymore, Edie. You're on your own. Don't ask me for any favors. You knew what you were doing. Don't blame me for it."

Pryce walked away, escorting the guy Edie attacked into the backseat of the SUV. Pryce got in the front and lifted his radio.

Before he could call anything in, he thought twice. He set his radio back on the dash and pulled out his phone. With his gaze on Edie, he called the one man he knew would make sure everything was handled appropriately.

"Foster," he barked into the phone.

"The vigilante is at Bottom's Up. I have her latest gift in custody."

"Why don't you have her in custody, Murphy? What the hell is wrong with you?"

"I'll explain everything, but I need you to get her, Foster. She's in the parking lot."

"Are you going to stay there until I get there? Make sure she doesn't leave?"

"She won't leave." Pryce hung up as Foster argued. He didn't want to hear it. Foster would get the credit for bringing Edie in, and the case would be closed.

Pryce knew she had to pay for what she'd done. She had to answer for her crimes. But he wasn't strong enough to be the one who put cuffs on her and walked her through the station.

He was only strong enough to drive away.

EDIE WATCHED Pryce pull out of the lot, lights on but the siren silent. She stared until the flashing lights on the nearby buildings disappeared with whatever turn he made.

She collapsed onto the gravel of the parking lot. Sobs wracked her body, her shoulders shaking as regret poured from her.

A horn lifted her head with hope that was dashed as soon as she saw the car. Not Pryce.

"You need to come with me," the man said. He flashed a badge at her. The cop Pryce called.

Edie nodded and stood. He eyed her closely, watching her every move until she got to his side. "Do you need to put cuffs on me?"

The edge of his mouth quirked up. He shook his head. "Are you going to be a problem?"

"No," Edie breathed. She was done. Pryce was done with her, and she was done fighting the inevitable. She was doing the right thing, bringing in people who were hurting others, but she crossed a line to do it. A line that was easy to cross. One she didn't ever think she'd cross.

She never meant to hurt anyone. Especially Pryce.

The cop put his hand on her arm and held her loosely while he opened the back door to his car. He guided her head into the vehicle, making sure she didn't hit the door-frame before she was seated in the back.

He closed the door and climbed into the seat in front of Edie. She stared at her hands instead of at the man Pryce sent to retrieve her. He pulled out of the lot slowly, like he had all the time in the world to get her to the station.

It was for the best, though. If he took his time, maybe she wouldn't see Pryce.

The cop didn't say anything to her as he drove, just wound through the city streets. After a few minutes, Edie started to wonder how long it would be. She didn't love the scent of his cologne and was more than ready to be away from him.

She looked up and didn't recognize the street they were on. She tried to catch a street sign, but he was going fast.

Busy streets became quieter. Traffic drifted away, left behind in the city. Where Edie thought she was going.

"Where are we going?" she asked.

He looked up at her in the mirror, then turned his attention back to the road.

"I asked you a question."

"And you think you deserve an answer?"

"Who are you?"

"That doesn't matter. I'm doing as I was told."

"By whom?" Edie whispered, even though she already knew the answer.

"By Trevor," the cop confirmed.

Bile rose up in Edie's throat. Tears stung her eyes. Sweat pooled in her palms. She could not sit there and disappear again. She couldn't give up. She couldn't let it happen again.

She tried the handle on the door, but nothing happened when she pulled the latch. Locked. Child locks where it didn't matter what she did, the door wouldn't open.

She leaned back and kicked the glass. The vibration traveled up her legs and into her spine, jolting her with immense pain.

"What the fuck do you think you're doing?" the cop barked at her.

"I'm not going back to him."

The cop laughed. A chuckle that grew louder when she kicked the window again, then louder still when she turned and kicked the expanded metal guard between them.

Edie was trapped. In the backseat of the vehicle of a madman. A man who was delivering her to the person she feared most in the world. Not Jason and his drugged drinks, but Trevor and his insatiable need for more and more from her. Trevor and his demands and his drugs and his dick.

Edie remembered Trevor. Not every moment they spent together, but she knew he kept her as one of his favorites. He would loan her out to others, like Damon, but Trevor had a thing for Edie. She was one of his personal collection.

He liked to test out when was best to give her the drugs. Too early and he complained she wasn't into it. Too late and he complained she cried too much.

Trevor was as much of a monster as Damon was, but Trevor was Edie's monster. He toyed with her for months. He would have killed her if she didn't get away when she did.

He would kill her. Once the cop behind the wheel handed her over to him.

Edie couldn't stop the tears that streaked down her cheeks. She couldn't stop the pain that sliced through her body. She couldn't stop the ache deep inside her that the last time she saw Pryce was during a moment of anger.

Pryce hated her, but she loved him. She never told him. She never told him the truth about who she was or how she felt about him. She didn't know if he felt the same before he learned who she was, but it no longer mattered because she'd never know.

She'd never see him again. She would die at Trevor's hand. All she could pray for was that he made it quick.

Knowing Trevor, that wasn't going to happen.

THE CAR ROLLED TO A STOP, and the cop got out. He wanted to make sure he got his reward. He wasn't going to let anyone else take credit for bringing the whore Trevor was looking for right to his doorstep.

"I need to see the boss," the cop barked at the man by the door.

"He's busy."

"He'll want to make time for this. Trust me."

The guy rolled his eyes but nodded to his partner to go find Trevor.

The cop knew Trevor wasn't the boss. Trevor was just the person between the boss and the rest of them. The boss stayed isolated. Hidden. He didn't care. He was going to get what he wanted as soon as Trevor saw what he had.

"What the fuck are you doing here?" Trevor barked when he walked outside. "Are you out of your fucking mind?"

"I brought you a gift."

"What the fuck...?" Trevor peered through the window and saw the woman in the backseat. A lascivious grin spread over his face, making him look truly heinous. "Well, well, well. Someone did his fucking job."

"A call came in saying she had another present, but when I got there, she was talking to another cop."

"Where's the other cop?" Trevor barked. He pulled a gun from behind his back and pointed it at the cop's head.

"Gone. Do you think I'm that stupid?"

Trevor raised a brow. "You brought a wanted woman here in your personal car. I wouldn't call that smart."

The cop rolled his eyes. "No one knows I'm here. She nabbed Jamison, though. Had him on the ground when I got there. The other cop took him into custody."

"What for?"

The cop shrugged. "I don't know. They talked a lot. The other cop? It's the one I've been following. Pryce Murphy. He didn't seem to know who she was until tonight."

"Isn't that interesting? Officer Murphy was sleeping with the enemy the whole time. And he had no idea."

The cop snorted. "Definitely seemed that way. He just left her in the parking lot. Like he trusted her."

"He left her? Did he call it in?"

The cop shook his head. "I was listening to the radio. He didn't tell anyone she was there. No one knows. Except me."

"Good." Trevor glanced at the truck and grinned. "I should say hello to my guest."

The cop put his hand on Trevor's chest before he walked by. The man at the door took a step forward, but Trevor stopped him with one raised hand.

Trevor turned to the cop with a raised brow.

"What about my payment?" the cop asked.

"Payment?"

"You agreed I could have the blonde in your restaurant," he growled. "If I don't get her, you don't get her."

Trevor smirked, his gaze locked on the cop's face. "Are you going to sit here until Maya arrives? Keep me from saying anything to her?"

The cop crossed his arms and leaned back. "If I have to."

Trevor chuckled. He rubbed his chin and focused all of his attention on the cop. "Okay. I can respect that. You don't trust me. You think I'm going to pull a fast one on you, huh? I can't really say as though I blame you."

The cop sneered. He knew not to trust Trevor or the rest of them. Criminals were all the same. Give them an inch and they'll take a mile and all that shit. The only reason he did this was because they made it worth his while. Once he had Maya, he could disappear. None of them would ever know where to find him or where he went. He could hide on the property he bought and make a life for the two of them.

Whether she wanted it or not.

"Call Maya. She's needed here. Now." Trevor shouted to the guy at the door.

The guy nodded and went inside to make the call.

Trevor glared at the cop. "She's on her way."

"We can wait until she gets here."

"What's your plan? You just going to lock her up in your basement?"

The cop shook his head. "Of course not. I'm not a monster. Is that what you do? What you're going to do with her?"

Trevor chuckled and looked through the window at Edie again. "Nah. I have bigger plans for her than that."

"Like?"

Trevor glared at him. "Why do you want to know? Are you wearing a wire?"

"Why would I do that?"

"Let me see your phone?"

"What?"

"Your phone."

The cop retrieved his phone from his pocket and handed it over. It was off, so it couldn't be traced, but Trevor didn't care. He slammed it against the hood of the car, then smashed it on the ground, grinding it into dust under his boot.

"What the fuck? I need that. I'm going to have to pay for it to be replaced."

"Guess you should have asked for money instead of a woman."

"Fuck you, Trevor."

Trevor snorted.

"When is she going to be here?"

Trevor looked at the door as Maya emerged with the man who'd been guarding the door. She looked different. Her hair was stringy and limp. Her eyes were sunken and vacant. She didn't have the same curves the cop admired just a few weeks ago.

"What the hell did you do to her?"

Trevor shrugged. "Nothing. She took those drugs all on her own, Officer."

The guy at the door shoved Maya toward the cop while Trevor went to the backseat. Edie screamed, trying to get away from Trevor as he advanced on her. The screaming only stopped when the click of a trigger could be heard.

"Get out of the fucking car or you die in it," Trevor snarled.

The cop watched as Edie followed Trevor from the car, tears flowing freely down her cheeks. A part of him felt bad for her, but Maya whimpered in his arms and he forgot all about Edie.

"Nice doing business with you, Officer," Trevor said as he followed Edie to the door, the gun pointed at her head the entire time.

The cop guided Maya to the front seat and helped her in, hating what Trevor did to her. "You're safe now," he whispered. "I'm not going to let anything else happen to you."

He buckled her into the car and pulled away, disappearing into the night.

19

———

PRYCE SAT AT HIS DESK WITH HIS HEAD IN HIS HANDS. He already booked the Jamison guy Edie was trying to bring into custody. The guy had a rap sheet a mile long and a list of things he was suspected of. He protested the entire damn time, but Pryce knew Edie would testify against him.

Jamison was going away for a long time. Because of Edie. Because she...

Pryce stopped. Something was off. He'd had the feeling since he pulled into the Bottom's Up parking lot and saw her there, but he thought it was just because he didn't expect to see Edie there. It was more.

Edie wasn't the one who called nine-one-one.

She couldn't have been. She hadn't secured Jamison yet. She wasn't wearing her mask.

Which meant someone else was there. Watching her. And knew what to tell the operator so a cop would rush right over.

Who the hell could have been there? And why didn't Pryce notice someone else?

"Murphy!"

Pryce shook his head at Foster's bellowed word. All he wanted was to ignore the man who brought Edie into the station, but Foster was always quick to remind Pryce who was the higher ranking officer.

Pryce stood and faced a furious Foster as he stalked across the bullpen to where Pryce was. "Was that your idea of a joke?"

"What?" Pryce asked.

"Sending me on a wild goose chase? Telling me she'd be there. Did you get a good laugh at my expense?"

"What are you talking about? She was there."

"No one was there, Officer," Foster growled. "I pulled into the lot, sirens and lights blaring, gravel flying, and nothing. Not a soul was in the parking lot. Until they heard the sirens and came outside to find out what was going on. Did you think it would be funny to call me directly and send me there? To a bar? On duty?"

Foster got up in Pryce's face, forcing Pryce to back up. His legs hit the edge of his desk and the crazy look in Foster's eyes had Pryce leaning farther back to get away from the other man.

"Foster! Murphy! My office. Now," Captain Patrick shouted.

Pryce waited for Foster to give him some space. Silence echoed in his ears, the normally bustling office deadly quiet for the altercation.

Foster shoved Pryce's desk and stomped toward Captain Patrick's office.

Pryce took a second to take a breath. He didn't understand why Foster was so angry at him. Or why Edie wasn't there. There was no way she would run. Not when he knew who she was and where she lived.

Pryce had to do what he should have done when he walked in the door. He had to tell his boss what he learned.

Pryce trailed a bit behind Foster, ignoring the stares and snickers from his coworkers. Again.

"Close the door," Captain Patrick ordered when Pryce stepped inside.

Pryce did as he was told and stood in front of the door, unsure where he should be. Both men outranked him, and neither of them sat. Foster paced the short length of the office, and Captain Patrick stood behind his desk, glowering at both of them.

"What the fuck is going on?"

Pryce glanced at Foster and found the other man looking defeated and broken.

Pryce stepped forward. "I got a call on the radio earlier. It said there was another present. I raced to where it was, a bar called Bottom's Up. When I got there, the vigilante was fighting with a man, trying to zip-tie him to his truck."

Captain Patrick sucked in a breath but said nothing.

Pryce lifted his gaze to his captain's. "Sir, it was Edie."

Captain Patrick nodded once. "Then what happened?"

"Did you hear me, sir? Edie is the vigilante."

"Is that why the two of you are shouting at each other in the middle of my station?"

"No, sir, but—"

"Officer."

Pryce snapped his mouth shut at the tone.

"What happened after you found her there?"

Pryce swallowed thickly. "She said the man was the one who drugged her. That he'd slipped something in her drink. Tonight... and before. She was sure of it."

"Was she intoxicated?"

Pryce shook his head. "I don't think so. I... She didn't sound like she was."

"Is Jamison Child the one she said drugged her?"

Pryce nodded. "Yes, sir."

Patrick nodded and looked up from the computer he was studying. "So, she said he was the one who drugged her, and then what happened?"

"I arrested him. I brought him in."

"You left her there?"

Pryce nodded.

"Fucking liar," Foster growled.

"I'm not lying," Pryce argued.

Foster spun on him and took two big steps, getting in Pryce's face. "Then where the fuck is she? This Edie. Did she run off?"

"Drake, stand down. We'll get to that. Pryce, what happened when you left?"

Pryce swallowed and glanced at Foster.

Foster backed off, sinking into the chair on the visitor's side of the desk.

"I was going to call it in on the radio, but I didn't want to have every cop in the city going to get her. I knew... I knew if I called Detective Foster, he would do what needed to be done."

"And when you got there, she wasn't there?" Captain Patrick asked Foster.

Foster shook his head. "No one was there. There was no one in the parking lot."

Captain Patrick smoothed a hand over his face, dragging his jaw down until he gaped at both of them. "I need to make a call. Both of you give me a second."

Pryce made a move for the door, but Captain Patrick stopped him.

"Stay here. No one outside this room can know what's going on."

Pryce wasn't sure what that meant, but he did as he was told and resumed his position against the wall. Foster didn't move from the chair.

"Is Edie back?" the captain asked the person he called.

Pryce assumed it was his wife.

And he assumed it was bad news when the captain's face fell.

"Find the van. Now. I need to know where it is."

He was quiet as the person on the other end of the phone presumably tracked the vehicle.

"That's what I thought. I'm sending a unit to you right now. No one in or out until you hear from me. Be careful, Frannie. I love you."

A second later, Captain Patrick hung up the phone. He hung his head for a long moment before meeting the eyes of the two men in the room. "We all need to understand a few things. And I need the two of you to agree right now that you will listen to me and we will work together."

"I can't work with him," Foster growled.

"He doesn't know your history, Drake," Patrick said.

Foster's shoulders slumped.

"Drake?"

Foster nodded.

Captain Patrick focused on Pryce. "Detective Foster is an alcoholic. He's been in rehab and is excellent at his job. He has never relapsed, but he stays away from bars. I found out because his sponsor is an old friend of mine. We all ended up at the same coffee shop one day."

Pryce was shocked, but he understood why Foster was angry at Pryce for sending him to a bar. "I didn't know. I wasn't trying to... anything. I trusted you to bring her in."

"Which brings us to the next part of this," Captain Patrick said. "Edie has been dating Pryce. She also lives at the shelter with my wife and me."

It was Foster's turn to be shocked. His gaze flickered from Pryce to the captain and back. "You wanted me to arrest your girlfriend?"

"She's breaking the law," Pryce said weakly.

"Did you know what she was doing?" Foster asked Patrick.

The captain nodded. "I've been leaving information lying around. Stuff that would help her."

"Fuck," Pryce breathed.

"What?"

Pryce shook his head, his gut churning as he realized exactly what that meant.

"We're airing the laundry. If we're going to move forward and find Edie, we can't have anything in the dark now, Murphy. What is it?" Patrick asked.

"I... I accused her of using me to get information. I said she was only sleeping with me to find out about the guys she was taking down."

"Edie never used you, Pryce. She cares about you. I think what she was doing weighed on her. Made her feel like she shouldn't be doing it because of the way you felt."

"And I threw it in her face."

"What matters right now is that we need to find her."

"What do you mean?"

"She didn't come home. The van is still at the bar. And if Edie isn't, it means—"

"Someone took her," Foster finished for Patrick.

Pryce's stomach took a dive. He lunged for the trashcan, barely getting his face above it before he was spilling his guts.

He yelled at her. He made her feel like shit. He sent someone to arrest her. And she was gone. Someone else was there. Someone else got her.

"Someone else was there," Pryce managed to choke out after the vomit. He wiped his mouth on the back of his hand and sank to the floor. "Someone else called it in. There's no way Edie called nine-one-one. I was there before she'd tied the guy up. Someone was watching her."

"And that someone could have been the person who took her," Foster said. "We need that call."

"I've got a contact," Patrick said, lifting the phone and dialing without hesitation. "Mackenzie, I need a favor. Edie's missing."

Mackenzie? The same Mackenzie?

"I need the call that came in tonight. The one that said they had a present." Captain Patrick was quiet for a minute. "We're going to find her. Thanks, Mackenzie."

Captain Patrick hung up the phone and sat down behind his desk. He clicked a few buttons, then a voice filled the air around them.

"Nine-one-one, what is your emergency?"

"There's a present waiting for the first cop who can get to Bottom's Up."

"Can you tell me who you are?"

"Doesn't matter. Just hurry."

The call ended. It was not Edie who made the call. It was a man's voice. One Pryce thought he recognized.

Captain Patrick moved past Pryce to the door. He yanked it open and stood there for a minute. "Where the hell are Maxwell and Dempsey?"

Pryce lifted his head. Maxwell. That was who the voice belonged to.

When no one answered Captain Patrick, he returned to

the office and closed the door. "We need to find those two. Now."

"They're not on tonight," Foster said. "Asked for the night off."

"Both of them?"

Foster nodded.

"Find them. One of them, or both of them, knows where Edie is."

Pryce leaned over the trashcan and heaved again.

OFFICER MAXWELL NODDED to the guard and stepped into the house. When the boss called, he showed up. Especially when the entire fucking operation took a dump.

The sound of flesh hitting flesh met Maxwell's ears. He knew it wasn't the good kind of flesh pounding. This was a punishment. Intended to do damage.

"You thought you could get away from me?" Trevor barked. His laughter filled the room before Maxwell walked in. "You thought you were going to be free."

Maxwell took his post inside the door and watched as Trevor beat the woman on her knees in front of him. Her brown skin didn't show the bruises yet, but her bloody lip and swollen eye were enough indication that the boss hadn't taken it easy on her.

Good. The woman had been a pain in the fucking ass for months. Maxwell wouldn't pass up a chance to throw a few punches himself.

"Is it done?" Trevor asked.

Maxwell knew the question was directed at him, even though Trevor hadn't bothered to look at him. Maxwell stepped forward. "Yes, sir. The entire cabin is rigged to go seven minutes after they get inside."

"What the fuck for?"

"When he left here, he was carrying the woman. I wanted to make sure they were both inside when the blast went off. If he goes inside to turn on lights or something, then goes back to the car for her, it could go too early or when he's the only one inside."

Trevor rubbed his jaw and nodded slowly. "Okay. I can go with that. As long as it goes boom and they both die."

"They will, sir." Maxwell understood the role he played. Dempsey was a fucking pussy, but Maxwell was smart. Where Dempsey only saw cash and that blonde when he talked to Trevor, Maxwell knew there was a lot more than that. His skills as a cop could be valuable to Trevor and the Company. Not to mention the drugs, women, and stacks of cash that were always being thrown around.

Dempsey took his peanuts and bought a place he thought no one would find. Dumb fucker looked at the place on his phone all the damn time. It took Maxwell five fucking seconds to find the place and figure out the fake name Dempsey used to buy it.

Stupid fuck.

Maxwell wasn't going down like that. He saw what Bernard did. He aligned himself with the wrong person. Between him and Dempsey, Maxwell knew what lines to cross.

None. That was the answer. Don't cross any fucking lines or Trevor would put a bullet in your head. He was a crazy motherfucker who didn't think twice about killing someone.

Edie Warren whimpered, and Trevor's attention returned to her.

"I was going to take such good care of you, Edie. You

were my favorite. But you had to listen to that sick fuck, Damon, and take off." Trevor reached for the desk and came up with a needle. "Want something to take the edge off? A little reward for coming back to me?"

Edie cried and shook her head. Her hands were bound in front of her, her ankles the same. She wore the clothes she had on at the bar earlier. Black pants and a dark top. Tight and ready to draw the attention of the stupid fuck, Jamison, who didn't recognize her.

Maxwell had to admit, the bitch was smart. Once Trevor told him to watch for her, he found her in the crowds. All the crowds. She always came back to watch her prizes getting taken away. Dressed in bright and colorful clothes, so she wasn't in all black, but always there.

Hiding in plain sight.

Trevor plunged the needle into Edie's arm and depressed the syringe, shooting the drugs into her veins.

Edie screamed. She fought her restraints. She tried to get to Trevor.

Trevor gripped her jaw and yanked her chin to force her gaze to his. He sneered at her. "You're so anxious for me. Did you miss me as much as I missed you? Aw, Edie. It won't be long now. Once those drugs work their way into your system, so will I."

Trevor tossed her down, the restraints keeping her from bracing herself before she slammed onto the hard floor. Trevor walked out the door laughing like the sick fuck he was.

"Maxwell, with me."

Maxwell glanced at Edie, curled on her side and sobbing, then followed Trevor. Trevor sat in a recliner in the next room. Maxwell stood.

"I need you to take care of her."

"Sir?"

"Kill her. Dump her body. Make sure she never makes noise again. Make sure she can never tell another soul about any of us or any of this."

"You're not going back in there?"

Trevor snorted. "Fuck no. She was never that good of a fuck, but she didn't complain. Bitch has teeth, but you're welcome to have a go at her before you get rid of her. Too bad you couldn't leave her at the cabin and get all three of them with one bang."

Maxwell nodded, thinking about what he wanted to do.

"Light this place up when you leave. She can stay if you want. I don't care if it looks like an accident or not. As long as she's dead when the day is over."

Trevor stood, accepting his trench coat from one of his men. He looked like a fucking porn star in the velvet trench coat with fake fur trim. It was fucking spring, but the asshole didn't care.

Maxwell watched as they walked out the front door. Trevor took his entire crew with him. Car doors slammed and tires crunched on the gravel driveway as they all left.

Maxwell grinned. He had the place to himself. With Edie. The vigilante who thought she was bigger and badder than the rest of them.

Maxwell rubbed his hands together and grinned.

He was going to have some fun.

20

———

EDIE LISTENED TO THE DOORS CLOSE AND VEHICLES DRIVE away. She held her breath. There was no way they left her alone. Not unless they also rigged the building to blow up.

But even that she didn't trust. Trevor wouldn't take anymore chances with her.

Edie fought against the restraints, knowing she had to get out of there before they came back or the place exploded or whatever was going to happen next. Her wrists were raw from the zip-ties Trevor pulled too tight, and her brain was already getting fuzzy from the drugs.

She didn't have long before her body would give up and her mind would go blank. When that happened, she wouldn't be able to fight anyone.

Edie slammed her wrists against her bent knees, hoping the force would snap the zip-ties like all those videos she watched online. All it did was make her cry out in pain as the hard plastic cup deeper into her skin.

She wanted to cry. Just sit there and give up. Cry for everything she'd lost and pray someone eventually found her, but Edie wouldn't do it. For Tonya, for Holly, for all the other women, she was going to fight.

She slammed her wrists onto her knees again, still not getting anywhere. She shifted her position, looking around the room for another option, then heard the sound.

A whistle. Low. A haunting tune that seeped into Edie's mind and brought back a forgotten memory.

She shivered. One of the other women told her about a man who liked to whistle before he came in. Said he was mean and violent and hated everything. He would beat her before he raped her, choking her until she nearly passed out.

Sweat beaded Edie's forehead. Was this the same man? Did it matter? If someone was left, he wasn't there because he was a nice guy and wanted to help her.

The doorknob turned slowly, Edie's heart pounding with each second it took before the door creaked open. The squeak was long and loud, the only sound in the entire house.

Then he was there. The man who'd come in just before Trevor left. He looked familiar, but Edie wasn't sure who he was.

"You've been a royal pain in the ass, Edie Warren," he said, his voice low and soothing, like he was talking to a dog he intended to train instead of another human. "But I'm so happy to finally meet you."

"I must have missed your name," she said. Her voice sounded foreign to her ears, raw and strained.

"My name isn't important," he said. "I knew Bernard, though."

Edie gasped. "You're a cop?"

The man nodded, moving closer to Edie. He left the door wide open, letting her see the vacant space beyond the room they were in. Not a sound existed outside the ones the two of them made.

His hair was dark and cut short. He looked like he had six inches or so on her, and a few dozen pounds of muscle. He was not someone she could overpower. Not without catching him off-guard, and with her hands and feet bound, the chances of that were slim.

He pulled out a knife and came toward her, letting her see the blade. "We should get these binds off you. Make it a little more exciting for us. Don't you think?"

Edie's gut screamed at her not to trust him. Aside from the obvious signs that he was a dirty cop, he was coming at her with a knife, but she couldn't defend herself against him.

He slid the blade between her hands and pulled upward to cut through the zip-tie at her wrists. She gasped at the painful relief it brought. He repeated the process with the tie at her ankles, then stepped back. He flipped the blade into the handle and put it back in his pocket. He reached for Edie, offering her his hand.

Edie tentatively let him help her up, putting her hand in his. He pulled her to her feet, then socked her in the stomach with his other fist.

Edie's breath rushed out in one startled gasp.

"Fucking whore. You've caused your last problems for the Company."

Edie stumbled, trying not to lose her footing as she also fought to keep her stomach from giving up.

The cop came at her again, punching her in the side, then catching her jaw. He only stopped when Edie fell to the floor again.

"Oh, come on. It's not as much fun when you don't fight

back. I know you can. I've seen the reports on the men you've taken down."

"Fuck you," Edie growled.

"We'll get to that. But first, I want to make sure you know the damage you caused. If it weren't for you, we would have been able to continue our operation without any issues. Instead, you had to get involved and start bringing people in. I couldn't keep my involvement out of things when every other shift someone I knew was walking into the station."

"Maybe you shouldn't be a dirty cop," Edie hissed, clutching her side.

"You want me to be squeaky clean like your boyfriend? You think Pryce Murphy is so good? Why did he let you go tonight?"

Edie gasped. "How...?"

"How did I know? Ah, Edie, you really haven't figured anything out, have you? I've been following you. For weeks. Trevor told me you were the vigilante. He needed proof, so I was on your ass. Really enjoyed you and Murphy getting to know each other. Some great shots of you two. It'll be a nice addition to the report I file. The report that'll include him finding you in the parking lot, him letting you go, and your dead body."

Thinking he was going to kill her and him admitting it were two very different things for Edie. His words weren't laced with hope or belief. He was speaking the truth. He was going to kill her. He had no doubt he would kill her, and get away with it, and put the entire thing on Pryce.

Her only option was to keep him talking until she could figure something out.

If she could fight the drugs that long.

"You called nine-one-one tonight, didn't you?"

The cop clapped, his grin one of praise. "Good job, Edie.

When you walked out with Jamison, I knew you weren't high. Stupid fuck wasn't paying any attention. He almost ruined the entire fucking thing. But he's already dead, so that doesn't matter now."

"Dead?" Edie breathed.

The cop shrugged. "You don't get many second chances in this organization. Too dangerous. He knows too much. He can't be out there. So, he's dead."

"He's in custody. I saw Pryce drive him away." A dark thought occurred to her, and she gasped, "Pryce?"

The cop chuckled. "Don't worry, your precious boyfriend is fine. Although maybe I should call him your ex. He was not very happy to learn you'd been lying to him. Fucking him two ways." He shook his head and tsked. "Not very nice of you, Edie."

"I was going to tell him," Edie whispered. She hated that she was admitting that to a man who would never tell Pryce. A man who would be witness to her last breath. But she needed to tell someone. She needed to put it out there.

She regretted not telling Pryce. She didn't think it would have made a difference, but if she'd told him on her own terms, she might have been able to make him understand.

It took a minute, but the cop laughed. "Do you really think it would have been okay if you told him? Although knowing you didn't is going to make everything so much better. First, his sister is fucking his best friend behind his back and the two of them try to get Murphy involved in their shit, and now you. Wow. I guess he never told you that story."

Edie closed her eyes. She knew the story. And she knew it was why Pryce was so upset with her. He valued honesty above just about anything else. And she lied. Many times.

"Oh, you did know that story. Wow. And you still lied to

him. I guess it's a good thing you're going to be dead so you don't have to face him."

Her wounded stomach revolted at his words, flipping and demanding attention.

Edie coughed, choking up whatever wanted to come up. She spit, vomited, whatever, erupting with a dark red substance.

"Fuck," the cop growled, narrowly escaping her spray.

"Blood," Edie whispered.

"Jesus. You're disgusting. Trevor was right about you. Said you weren't a very good fuck. I can see why. Can't even take one punch. What the hell am I supposed to do with you now?"

He glared at Edie like she was supposed to answer. "Let me go," she suggested, figuring she had nothing to lose.

He snorted. "Not happening. I'm not looking to get a bullet in my head." He shook his head and looked around. "I guess it's time for me to go. Trevor will give me someone more resilient."

He came at Edie faster than she expected. Another punch to her face, one more to her gut, and she went down like her bones were made of spaghetti.

She gasped for breath, finding none there. Panic clawed at her throat. She tried again, her jaw giving way so she could suck in a breath.

It burned the entire way in, and again on the way out. Everything hurt. She was broken and bruised, but she was still alive. For now.

The cop moved around the room, doing something out of Edie's line of sight. She coughed and wheezed, fighting for every breath. Something was wrong with her. Seriously wrong. Each breath was harder than the one before. Blackness threatened the edges of her vision. What used to be a blissful escape when the drugs wrapped around her nerves and dragged her under now came with fear. More than before. Because Edie knew this time, she wouldn't wake up when the drugs wore off.

She wouldn't wake up ever again.

The acrid scent of fire hit her nose on the next breath she struggled for. Edie lifted her gaze enough to see the first flames around the edges of the room.

Her eyes widened as the curtains flickered over the flames, teasing and toying with the fire before two became one. It would have been beautiful if it weren't so terrifying.

She was going to be burned alive.

Edie tried to crawl toward the door, but a boot on her back stopped her.

The cop leaned down close to her ear and hissed, "Now, be a good girl and don't fucking move. I'll be outside, making sure you don't escape. If you do, I'll know you're strong enough for whatever I want to do to you, blood or not."

He kicked her in the ribs, and Edie rolled. She didn't know if the crack was a rib breaking or the fire mating with more of the house, but it didn't matter. The blow did what he intended, and she stopped trying to escape.

Her breath wheezed in her chest. Her lungs screamed for the oxygen that fed the fire around her. Flames danced and played with the house, caressing the walls like a lover.

Edie tried to search for the cop, but the smoke grew thick in the sealed house. No windows offered relief, all keeping the flames and smoke inside the house.

Edie refused to lie there and do nothing. The cop could be lying. Even if he wasn't, she'd rather be raped than die.

She almost laughed at the thought. How many times had she wished to die so she wouldn't be raped again? Now, she struggled to pull herself across the floor, trading in the opposite way.

Time lost all meaning as Edie pushed herself. Every few inches, her body shut down. The fire roared above her, finding pleasure with the ceiling of the small house and becoming one with the drywall and beams that held the ceiling above her head.

Edie was vaguely aware it was only a matter of time before the ceiling gave way. Before the entire building collapsed on top of her. Before she was buried under the rubble and never found again.

Would she make it to the door? It still looked so far away.

And if she did make it, would the outside bring any relief? Or was it just a different kind of death waiting for her?

PRYCE VIBRATED in the front seat next to Captain Patrick. They raced through the city streets, following instinct and what Pryce hoped was good police work.

Once they realized Maxwell was the one who made the call that sent Pryce to Bottom's Up and caught Edie in the middle of bringing in the man who took her, the pieces started to fall into place. Foster admitted Maxwell and Dempsey both asked a lot of questions about the vigilante case. They were more curious than any other cops, but Foster wrote it off as being diligent.

None of them realized the partners were playing both sides, neither telling the other what they were doing. They were smart.

But not smart enough.

Pryce paced the office while Marcus made calls. He got

records on both Dempsey and Maxwell's phones and found the locations they both went to most frequently. When they were narrowing down a likely location for Edie, a call came in about a fire close to one of the locations.

They all took off.

Pryce resisted the urge to tell Marcus to go faster, knowing his boss was just as worried about Edie. Pryce gave up thinking about Marcus as Captain Patrick after the shit-storm of the last few hours. Marcus knew what Edie was doing, helped her do it, and never told a soul.

Pryce had questions, but none of them were as important as getting to Edie in time.

Three hours and seventeen minutes. That was how long she was missing. A lot could have happened in that time. Things Pryce didn't want to even consider. Things his mind wouldn't let him stop thinking about.

The glow in the sky told Pryce they were close to the burning building. A house, according to the information they got. One without neighbors for a mile or so, but someone drove by. Said there were a bunch of vehicles there earlier and they couldn't tell if there were any left.

Pryce prayed for both. He didn't know which he hoped for more. To find Edie at the house that was on fire, or for her to not be there.

One would mean she wasn't missing. The other would mean she still was. One would mean she could be dead. The other didn't guarantee anything.

Marcus cut the lights half a mile from the house. Sirens were off miles earlier when they left the city and stopped passing other vehicles. Pryce was about to ask what the hell Marcus was thinking, but Marcus pointed.

A figure was moving around the house. Someone was there.

"Edie," Pryce gasped.

Marcus shook his head, whether in disagreement or uncertainty, Pryce didn't know. All he knew was they didn't want to let whoever it was know they were there until they had to.

Marcus pulled over on the side of the road, cutting the engine and climbing out. Pryce followed him, getting low and hoping they could sneak up on whoever was skulking around the engulfed house before the person jumped in their vehicle and took off.

Marcus signaled for them to stick to the shadows, indicating Foster should take the lead. The other officers with them followed, fanning out and keeping their guns trained on the building, waiting for their spectator to show their face.

Pryce was behind Marcus, shuffled to the back of the line. Pryce tried not to take offense. He wanted to charge in there and find Edie, so it was probably for the best he was at the end of the line.

They moved toward the house, keeping in sight of each other. They got twenty feet from the front door when someone shouted, "Freeze! Put down the gun!"

It was Foster. His gun was trained on the person who'd been making their way around the house.

Pryce watched, the whole scene playing out in slow motion. The other man heard the order, but instead of obeying, he pointed at the officers and fired a shot.

Foster went down, and shots were returned to the man near the house. He jerked as one bullet, then a second hit him, then he sank to the ground.

"Get him," Marcus barked.

Two officers raced toward the man near the house,

kicking his gun away and grabbing him by the shoulders to drag him away from the burning house.

"Foster," Marcus shouted, dropping to his knees next to the detective.

Foster wheezed and grabbed Marcus's arm. "Caught it in the vest. I'll be fine. Was it him?"

Pryce turned with Marcus and looked at the man the other cops were dragging over.

"Maxwell," Marcus sneered. "Where's your partner?"

"Dempsey? Don't worry, Captain, you won't have to worry about him anymore."

"What did you do?"

"Same thing I did to Murphy's girlfriend. Although it's a bit slower for her. Same result, though."

Pryce stared at the house, completely engulfed in flames. Edie was in there.

And she was going to die.

Someone grabbed Pryce as he turned toward the house. He fought them off, unable to think. He might have thrown a punch. He didn't care. He had to get to Edie.

21

Pryce raced into the burning house, choking as soon as he opened the front door. The entire place was full of thick, black smoke. He couldn't see or breathe or think. None of it mattered. Edie was there somewhere.

Pryce dropped to his knees, knowing the advice probably didn't matter when the entire fucking place was on fire and the smoke was too thick to see his hand in front of his face, but he wasn't giving up.

He crawled forward, the fire deafening. Pops and smacks split the roar, like standing behind a plane as it was about to take off.

Pryce had no idea where Edie might be. He didn't know what the house looked like. She could be on the ground floor, upstairs or downstairs, or even hidden in some room they would only find when the fire was out and recovery was the name of the game.

Pryce didn't care. He wasn't leaving the flames of the house until he had Edie.

A chair burned in front of him, the fabric melting to the wooden frame and dripping to the floor. Pryce tried to see if other chairs were there. A dining room maybe? He kept going.

The floor creaked under his weight and the damage already inflicted by the fire. It could give way at any moment. Or he could find Edie at any moment.

"Fire department!" came from behind him, followed quickly by a whooping siren.

"Here!" Pryce shouted, waving his hands uselessly in the pitch black room. "I'm here."

The siren grew louder, coming toward Pryce, until a figure in full fire gear was right in front of Pryce. "I need to get you out of here!" the man shouted.

"Edie's in here somewhere. I'm not leaving without her."

"We'll find her," the guy said.

Pryce shook his head. "I'm not leaving."

The guy swore. "I knew you were going to say that." He pulled his mask off and pressed it to Pryce's face. "They're going to have my ass for this."

Pryce nodded, understanding he was breaking protocol to let Pryce stay inside and look for Edie. He sucked in a few quick breaths, then nodded for the firefighter to take the mask back.

"With me," the firefighter said. "We're going to go straight back. Stay low."

Pryce nodded, following the firefighter into the darkness. They barely made it five feet before he stopped and turned his siren on.

"Got her!" he shouted.

Pryce's chest tightened with relief.

"Not breathing. Coming out fast."

The relief Pryce felt was swamped by fear.

The firefighter scooped up Edie and turned back to the

door. He moved slowly, not offering Pryce oxygen again, and walked Edie to the door.

He carried Edie down the front stairs and handed her off to another firefighter. The other firefighter raced away with Edie, leaving Pryce to stare after her and fight to breathe.

"You need to get checked," the firefighter said to Pryce.

"I will once I know she's okay."

The firefighter put his hands on Pryce's shoulders. "She's not okay. I know that's not what you want to hear, but she's not okay, Pryce. They're going to take her to the hospital and try to save her, but she's not okay."

Pryce sank to the ground, all the emotions of the day gripping him and sending him into a tailspin. Pryce heaved, his stomach demanding it empty immediately. Again. The firefighter scooped Pryce up and moved him away from the house before letting him sink to his knees again.

"Water!" shouted someone from farther away.

"Clear!" came the reply from the firefighter who helped Pryce.

"She has to be okay."

"I get it. I've been there. The paramedics are going to do everything they can. She'll be at St. Nicholas Memorial. Want us to give you a lift?"

Pryce shook his head.

"Thanks, Wray," Marcus said, joining their little circle. "This would have gone much differently if you guys hadn't shown up when you did."

"Glad we were able to get them both. We wouldn't have been allowed home."

Marcus chuckled. "Same. Stacey with the boys?"

"Yeah. Jessica and the others were going to go over there, too."

"Anyone check on Mackenzie?"

"She's still at work. Holden's with her," another voice said.

"Good. They're all going to need each other."

"So are we," Wray said. "You should get that checked."

Pryce finally lifted his head, looking at the three men above him, chatting as though their worlds weren't hanging on the brink.

Marcus glanced down at Pryce and rubbed his jaw. It had already started to bruise, the color darker in the light from the fire. "Not my first hit."

"Shit," Pryce groaned.

Wray looked down at Pryce and chuckled. "You? I thought for sure it was the one in the back of the car, not the one who ran into the burning building."

"He had someone important inside," Marcus answered for Pryce.

"You know we get that."

Marcus and the other firefighter nodded.

A whistle split the air, catching the attention of the firefighters. They both jerked their heads at whoever whistled, then reached out to Marcus.

"Dinner soon?" Wray asked.

"Sounds good."

"Make sure he gets checked out. He sucked in a lot of smoke inside."

Marcus nodded. "Thanks, Braden. Will do. You two be careful."

Wray and Braden shook hands with Marcus, nodded at Pryce, then jogged off to help their crew.

"I apologize, sir," Pryce said.

Marcus shrugged and reached his hand down to Pryce. "I should have known you'd do exactly what you did as soon as he said that. You were faster than me."

"I shouldn't have hit you."

"Do you remember it?"

Pryce thought for a second, then shook his head. "No, sir."

"I love Edie like a daughter, or a favorite niece. I don't know. She's important to me. Twenty years ago, I would have been right there next to you running into that fire."

"Really?"

"There's a lot about me you don't know, Officer Murphy."

Pryce nodded, understanding it wasn't the time for all of that. "I'd like to go to the hospital, sir. I know I'm in the middle of my shift, but—"

"Did you really think I was going to put you back out there?"

"I... You asked me to keep her safe, and she wasn't breathing when Wray pulled her out of that building. I'm the one who left her in that parking lot. I'm the one who led Maxwell and Dempsey right to her. I'm the reason she's fighting for her life right now."

"And you're going to be the reason she fights. Listen, love doesn't have to make sense. I certainly don't understand it. All I know is without my wife, I'd be a different man. A man I'm not so sure I'd like. Meeting her wasn't... It was a fucking disaster. But she's the best thing that's ever happened to me. I have a feeling you think the same about Edie."

Pryce nodded.

"I know you need answers, and I know you're not all on board with what she's been doing, but you need to know a few things about it. About Edie."

"What things?"

Marcus glanced around. The fire was mostly out, the firefighters shooting water into one window but darkness around the rest of the house. Maxwell was already gone, taken to the station for processing. Foster and the other cops who'd gone out there were all gone.

"Let's go for a ride."

Pryce nodded and followed Marcus to the car.

Marcus pulled away from the side of the road and drove in silence for a few minutes.

Pryce ached to fill the silence, but he knew this wasn't his story.

"Edie is one of the kindest people I've ever met. She's funny and friendly. She's become a confidant of some of the others who've stayed at the shelter. Many of them have said they wouldn't ever feel like they had a chance at a real life without Edie."

Pryce nodded and swallowed roughly. His throat burned, and he wondered if he should have taken that ride with Wray to the hospital.

"What no one else knows is that Edie doesn't sleep. She has nightmares almost every night. She used to wake up screaming, but now she doesn't. Some nights she gets a snack and other nights she stays in her room, but her nightmares are regular."

"How do you know this?"

"I don't always sleep well. There have been times I've thought I heard something upstairs and have gone to check. The house has alarms on all the windows and doors, but we want the people who stay to not feel like prisoners. There are no cameras in rooms or hallways upstairs, but there are cameras outside everywhere. When I hear a noise upstairs, I check it out to make sure someone didn't get around our system and get into the house somehow."

"You hear Edie?"

Marcus nodded. "A lot of the time. She's not the only

one. But she gives everything of herself. Including what she's been doing as a vigilante."

"How do you figure?"

"Edie got out. She has her own life. She doesn't have to get involved. She doesn't have to be trying to bring down these criminals. But she wants to end the organization. She wants to give all the others she saw, women she was held with or who were taken and went somewhere else, woman who were killed, all of them, she wants them to have justice. To have a life, if they can. She wants to take down the people who did this to her and killed her cousin."

"Okay. But she's still breaking the law."

"Maybe. But she's only going after people who are bringing drugs into our city. She's not going after just any criminal. It's the people who have ties to this organization."

"Are you trying to tell me it's better that she's being selective? That if she was going after anyone and everyone that would be wrong?"

Marcus shook his head. "No. I'm telling you this is personal for Edie. This is about doing what we failed to do when she went missing. This is her chance to feel like she has some control over her life and for her to overcome her fears. And being with you? I think that might have been her biggest fear of all. And you threw it in her face."

Pryce felt like a scolded child. His cheeks burned, his hands slicked with sweat. He wanted to run and hide and not face what he'd done.

But Marcus was right. Pryce made things worse.

"I've worked hard to get to where I am. I've sacrificed. I almost didn't get here. What happened to her never should have happened. But how do I balance what she's doing with what I believe?"

"Maybe you don't. Maybe you can't. Maybe you report

me up the chain and get me fired. Maybe you never talk to Edie again."

Pryce's chest squeezed at all those maybes. Was that what he really wanted?

"In my experience, a person who's willing to run into a burning building to save another person, with the exception of a firefighter, is doing it for one reason only."

Pryce waited.

"Love," Marcus said. "I can't tell you how you feel, Officer Murphy. All I can tell you is if you love her, you might want to take a look at who she is and what's she's been through."

Pryce opened his mouth to tell the captain he'd read the report, but Marcus cut him off.

"I'm not talking about reading the report. Half the department has read the report. But none of them have talked to Edie about it. None of them have asked if she's okay. None of them have tried to help the woman who fought back and survived something none of us will ever understand. If you love her, you need to understand what she's been through. And try to accept how she's fought back to remember who she is. And maybe then you can be proud of the woman she is, because I sure as fuck am proud of her."

Marcus shifted the vehicle into park, and Pryce realized they were at the hospital.

"She's likely in surgery, but you need to get checked out. You've been rubbing your neck. Your voice is rough. I need to go find Dempsey."

Pryce nodded.

Someone tapped on the window, and Marcus got out. Pryce followed him.

"Police officer. Ran into a burning building without a

mask. Smoke inhalation and possible burns, although he hasn't said anything about that. His girlfriend is Edie Warren. Edie lives at Shelter in the Storm with my wife and me. She'll be back shortly to see Edie. If you need verification of who she is, call Director Alexander."

The nurse who met the vehicle nodded and encouraged Pryce into the wheelchair next to the car. Pryce took a seat and stared at Marcus until he was turned and rushed into the emergency room.

OFFICER DEMPSEY PARKED his vehicle in front of the little bungalow. He left the car running while he got out, using the headlights to shine on the front door.

"I'll be right back," he whispered to Maya. She slept in the front seat.

Dempsey hurried to the door, quickly unlocking it and stepping inside. It looked exactly as he left it three days earlier. Right down to the dusting of baby powder by the front door to make sure no one was there.

Dempsey flipped on lights and turned the temperature up, knowing Maya was cold. She was shivering on the drive. She'd feel better once he got her warmed up and sobered up and she realized she was safe.

He went back outside, reaching in and lifting the woman into his arms. She was lighter than he'd expected. Fury coiled through him. Trevor had no right to do this to her. Trevor knew Dempsey wanted Maya. Knew she was the one and only thing Dempsey wanted. And instead of letting her be, leaving her alone and allowing her beauty to shine through, he poisoned her with the filth he pushed onto the streets and ruined lives with.

Maya deserved better.

"I'll make sure you never have to worry about anything ever again," Dempsey whispered as he carried her into the house. He settled her on the couch and smoothed the hair back from her face. "I'll be right back."

He went back to the car. He grabbed the bags he had in the trunk, some clothes and food that would get them through a few days before they could leave it all behind and truly disappear. This was just temporary.

He turned off the vehicle and pocketed the keys. A quick inhale of the fresh, clean, open air, and he hurried back inside to the woman he was going to take care of for the rest of their lives.

Dempsey put the bags down inside the door and closed and locked it. Not that it mattered. No one knew where they were.

He settled on the couch next to Maya and finally allowed himself to relax. Everything was going to be okay now.

Then he heard the click. Before he could process what it was, the blast ripped through the small house, igniting the entire structure in less than a second and blowing every inch of it to bits.

Including Dempsey and Maya.

EDIE DRIFTED in and out of consciousness. The sounds and smells around her were unfamiliar. She fought to stay awake every time she thought she was going to wake up, but sleep and darkness dragged her down again.

She felt like she was floating. Like she was barely attached to the ground. It was a peaceful feeling, like floating in a pool with her eyes closed. Or facing an opponent at the start of a tennis match. Nothing could be wrong there.

"How long until she wakes up?" a voice asked, filtering in through the fuzziness around Edie.

She didn't hear the answer.

"What if she doesn't wake up by then?"

Another fuzzy answer.

Edie groaned, trying to get in on the conversation.

"Edie!" someone shouted.

A bright light flashed in her eyes, like the headlights of oncoming traffic.

Edie tried to scream, but she couldn't. Something was stuck in her throat.

"Don't touch that," a stern voice said.

Edie's hands were pulled down from her face before they made it to whatever was choking her. Panic flooded her and a beeping noise grew louder and more insistent.

"Ms. Warren. There is a tube down your throat to help you breathe. You inhaled a lot of smoke. Your throat is severely damaged, and it still needs to rest. Do you understand me?"

Edie searched for the face of the person who was shouting at her. When she landed on it, it was unfamiliar but commanded calm and authority. Edie held the woman's gaze and nodded.

"Okay, good. The tube is still helping you. I know it's not comfortable or easy, but we wanted to wake you up and talk to you for a minute. We're going to put you under again soon."

The same panic Edie felt before clawed at her. She fought, frantically searching for someone to understand her. Her gaze landed on Frannie.

Edie grabbed for Frannie's arm and squeezed it tight. Edie shook her head.

"You don't want to be put under?" Frannie asked, understanding Edie's plea.

Edie shook her head.

Frannie looked up at the doctor. "Is there another option?"

Edie followed Frannie's look and pled with her eyes for the doctor to have pity on her.

"There's a lot of swelling. The tube has to stay in."

Edie nodded, squeezing Frannie and nodding more.

"She's okay with that. What about keeping her awake?"

Edie looked at the doctor again.

"It's possible, but you can't fight the tube or rest. And you're going to be in a lot of pain, Ms. Warren. Your lung collapsed, and you had internal bleeding and a lot of damage to your organs, plus three broken ribs. I think it would be better for you to allow your body to rest for a few more days."

Edie finally felt the pain her brain was hiding from her. Her entire stomach felt like it had been ripped open. Her head hurt, her ribs, everything.

She didn't want more drugs. She hated the idea of relying on them. But she knew the doctor was right. She would be in pain if she didn't let them put her under again.

A tear slid down her cheek as Edie nodded.

"Edie? Are you saying you're okay with the doctor putting you into a coma again?"

Edie nodded once more.

"Okay." Frannie nodded at the doctor. "There are a lot of people here to see you, Edie. Mackenzie and Raina, and the others. Pryce. Some of your old coworkers."

Edie shook her head. She didn't want to see anyone.

Especially not Pryce. Not after the things he said to her last time she saw him. She couldn't face him when she couldn't defend herself.

Frannie kept talking, but the doctor was quick. Sleep pulled at Edie again, then blissful silence wrapped around her and pulled her under.

Peace.

Pryce paced the hallway outside Edie's room. He hadn't been allowed in to see her. He tried. He did everything, including flashing his badge, but the nurses knew who he was and knew he wasn't allowed in without permission from Edie.

Which she wasn't able to grant since she was in a fucking coma.

Frannie walked out of Edie's room looking exhausted. She smiled at Pryce.

"Did she wake up?" Pryce asked.

Frannie nodded. "She did. She was able to answer some questions, which is a good sign for her brain."

"And?"

Frannie's smile faded, and she shook her head. "She shook her head when I mentioned visitors."

"Even me?"

"I didn't have time to specifically ask about you, Pryce, but..."

"But?"

"She started shaking her head when I said your name."

Pryce laughed mirthlessly. "So, I'm the one she really doesn't want to see."

Frannie tried to offer him a smile or something, but Pryce couldn't stick around for more pity.

It had been four days since he almost lost her. Four days he hadn't been allowed to see her. Pryce went to Bob's Diner for pie and found himself staring at the plate and pushing it away when Jenny asked if he wanted anything else.

His apartment smelled like Edie. His thoughts were consumed by Edie. Pryce replayed all their conversations and put them together with his knowledge that she was the vigilante.

And he got it. He listened to the things she'd been telling him all along, and Pryce understood why she did what she did.

She was no different than any other cop out there. Good cops. She wanted to make a difference. She wanted to help others and give back. But she didn't believe in the system Pryce worked within.

After everything that happened to her, he wasn't sure he did either.

22

———————

Edie looked out the front window and sighed. She was finally getting out. Her second time in rehab was a lot easier than her first, even though both times were emotionally painful.

Raina and Mackenzie tried to talk her out of going once she was released from the hospital, but Edie felt the pull of the drugs Trevor injected into her. She didn't want them, but after the medically induced coma and the pain she was in from the beating and the smoke inhalation, she needed a safe place where she knew she wouldn't give in to temptation.

Now she was done. She felt stronger, better, more like the person she believed she could be.

More like the person she wanted to be.

A month had passed since that night, and the nightmares had stopped. Edie was proud of what she'd done, but she was hesitant to go back out into the streets and keep fighting.

She was exhausted. And she wanted a life.

Her heart squeezed at the thought, but she'd given up

hope that Pryce would forgive her. He didn't visit her at the hospital or in rehab. No one told her he asked about her. He said everything he needed to say the night he stumbled into the truth about who she was. It was time to move on from Pryce Murphy.

The van pulled up in front of the rehab center, and Edie smiled. She turned to Rosie, the nurse waiting with her, and said, "That's my ride."

Rosie nodded. "Good. You'll feel better when you're home."

Edie gave her a noncommittal noise, knowing home was still up in the air, but she appreciated Frannie and Marcus holding a room for her.

Frannie came to the door and smiled when she saw Edie. "You look good."

"Thanks," Edie said with a laugh. Frannie always greeted her that way. A compliment that boosted Edie's spirit and made her feel like she made the right choice going there.

"Are you ready?"

Edie nodded. She turned back to Rosie and hugged the other woman quickly, then grabbed the handle of her suitcase and looped her arm with Frannie's. "Thank you for getting me."

"Of course. There's nowhere else we'd rather be. The other girls want to see you. Stacey invited everyone over tonight. If you're up to it."

Edie nodded. "I'd like that. It would be good to feel normal and see everyone."

"Good. We'll get you settled, then head over there for dinner. Does that work for you?"

Edie nodded again. Her heart squeezed again. She didn't like hiding things from the people who'd been so good to her, but Edie knew they would understand her need to leave town. If Trevor wasn't enough of a reason, Pryce was.

Trevor was still out there. Edie knew the chances were high that Trevor would try to grab her again, and if she kept risking her life, he would succeed. Knowing him, he also wouldn't leave the job to someone else next time.

Getting away felt like the right choice. And a night with all her friends in one place was a good time to tell them all.

The drive back to the shelter was quick. Frannie didn't push her to talk. Marcus helped carry Edie's suitcase up to her room when they got back, then they left her to get settled.

Edie put her things away in the dresser and closet, wondering why she bothered but not pulling it all back out again. She'd give herself a few days before she left. A few days to feel back to normal again.

A knock on her door had Edie looking up from her task with a smile when she saw Charlotte.

"Hey," the young woman said. "You're back."

Edie nodded at the obvious. "How are you?"

Charlotte shrugged and nodded to the bed.

Edie waved her hand for Charlotte to come in.

Charlotte sat on the edge of the bed. "I wanted to thank you."

"For?"

"For? Um, everything. I mean, for one thing, you were out there every night kicking ass and putting away the assholes who were hurting people."

"You know about that?" Edie gasped. No one came to arrest or question her in rehab, so Edie assumed Marcus did something to keep her name out of the news and all police reports.

"I kind of wondered, but when it all stopped when you went away, I put it together."

"What I did was reckless and dangerous."

"It was badass and strong. You're an inspiration."

"Charlotte."

"Don't worry. I'm not here to tell you I'm following in your footsteps. I just wanted to say thank you for showing me we can be both badass and vulnerable. I'm still seeing Stacey."

Edie was surprised but happy to hear it. "How's it going?"

"She thinks I'm doing well."

"And what do you think?"

"I think I'm always going to be afraid, but I have a friend in Oregon who said I could go live with her for a while. See if it's a place I might want to stay."

"That's great news," Edie said, feeling proud and already missing the woman in front of her.

"Stacey said that, too. I think I'm ready."

"Then you are."

"You think so?"

Edie nodded. "Absolutely. You know how you feel. You should go out there and live your life."

"Is that what you're going to do?" Charlotte's gaze was far too precise.

Edie nodded. "Yeah."

Charlotte held her gaze for a long moment, then nodded. She stood and walked back to the door. "I guess we're both ready."

"I guess so."

Charlotte stared at Edie again, then took a few hurried steps and threw her arms around Edie's neck. "Thank you for being here for me."

Edie hugged her back. "Thank you for being here for me."

Charlotte chuckled and nodded, then pulled back, wiping her eyes. "Say bye before you leave if you go first."

"Of course. You do the same."

Charlotte nodded, then walked out of the room, her door closing a few seconds later.

Edie looked around. She was ready.

AT FIVE, Edie met Frannie in the foyer. Frannie smiled. She'd been giving Edie space all day, more than Edie expected. Like Frannie knew the end was coming.

Edie was quiet on the drive to Stacey's. It would take time for her to feel normal again. For everything that happened to sink in. She never asked why she wasn't arrested, but she was curious. Even though he hadn't turned her in, Pryce could change his mind at any time. Frannie admitted Marcus knew all along and would protect her secret, but Marcus was no longer the only cop who knew Edie had been handing over criminals.

Two of whom were killed.

The details of the night everything blew up came in slowly over the last month, but Edie knew the parts that mattered. Officer Maxwell followed her and called in her location. Officer Dempsey followed Pryce and picked Edie up after Pryce took Jamison, not Jason, away. Maxwell killed Jamison while Dempsey took Edie to Trevor, then Maxwell set charges on a cabin Dempsey owned, killing him and the woman he was with. Maxwell then came to the house where Edie was with Trevor and almost burned the place down with her inside. Would have if Pryce, Marcus, and the other officers hadn't shown up when they did. Stacey's husband, Wray, carried Edie out of the fire after Pryce ran in to get her.

It was that last point that kept sticking in Edie's brain. Why did Pryce go into the fire to get her?

She told herself it didn't matter. But it kind of did. Too bad she'd probably never know.

"Are you ready to go in?" Frannie asked.

Edie looked up and realized they were parked in front of Stacey's house. The engine no longer ticked, telling Edie they'd been sitting there a while. "Sorry."

"No sorry necessary. I know this isn't easy."

Edie laughed mirthlessly and nodded. "It'll be okay."

They walked together to the door, which swung open before they made it there. Stacey stepped out and wrapped her arms around Edie. The hug felt good. It had been a long time since Edie had any real physical contact, and it brought tears to her eyes.

"I'm so happy you're here," Stacey whispered.

"Thanks for getting everyone together."

Stacey nodded and pulled back, wiping the tears from Edie's cheeks and leading her inside.

Edie was immediately met by the rest of her friends. They all wrapped her up in tight hugs that healed a part of Edie she didn't realize could be healed. A piece she thought was shattered and beyond repair.

"Can I get you a drink? Water, juice, we have wine, but I don't know how you feel about that," Stacey said.

"Just water is good. Thank you."

Stacey nodded and went toward the kitchen. Frannie followed her.

Raina and Mackenzie flanked Edie on the couch, each of them holding one of her hands. Edie squeezed their hands back and let herself breathe. It was good to be with her friends again.

"How are you?" Karli asked.

Edie looked up at the woman who could have been Tonya's twin and forced a smile. "Stronger than I was."

"Are all of your injuries healed?" Jessica asked.

Edie nodded. "Thankfully, on the way. I still have moments with my ribs, but as long as I'm careful, I'll be okay. It doesn't hurt to breathe anymore, so I'm taking that as a good thing."

"That's definitely a positive," Jessica said with a smile.

"We're still looking for Trevor," Lorelei said. "We're not giving up."

"I know," Edie said. She was grateful for everything the FBI was doing, but Edie still doubted the chances they would find Trevor.

Stacey and Frannie came back into the living room with trays of drinks and food for everyone.

"We thought this would be easier. Relax and eat and talk. If that's okay with you," Stacey said to Edie.

Edie smiled. "I'm good with whatever. I don't want you guys to treat me like I'm going to break."

"We know," Raina said. "But we also know what you went through wasn't okay. We want you to know we're here for you."

Edie took a breath and nodded, knowing that was her opening. "Speaking of that, I want to tell you all something."

The other seven women in the room stopped what they were doing and looked at Edie. Having their attention was a little overwhelming, but she was strong.

"I've decided to leave Niagara Falls," Edie said.

The room was silent for a long moment. No one spoke or moved or breathed.

Finally, Raina squeezed her hand, and Edie looked at her friend. "We will support whatever you want to do."

"Thank you."

"We're going to miss you," Stacey said.

"Are you sure that's what you want to do?" Mackenzie asked.

Edie breathed a laugh. "No, but I need to figure out what my life is going to look like going forward. Trevor is still out there. And I can't stay at Shelter in the Storm forever."

"Sure you can," Frannie said. "Marcus, Stacey, and I wanted to offer you a job. A live-in position that includes doing exactly what you've been doing."

"Draining your resources?" Edie joked.

Frannie shook her head. "Helping. Talking to the others about moving on. Figuring out what they want to do when they get out."

"I... Thank you. Can I think about that?"

Frannie nodded. "Of course. But we want you to know we see you as an asset to Shelter in the Storm. A big one. You offer something we've never had."

"A criminal presence?"

"You know that's not how we see you," Frannie admonished, leaving Edie feeling bad for her remark.

"I know. I'm sorry. I'm grateful for that. I know Marcus had to do something to keep me out of jail, and I'm grateful for it. I hope it didn't damage his career."

Frannie shook her head. "Marcus didn't do anything. You're not in jail because you were never charged with anything."

"How is that possible? Pryce knows."

The other women in the room exchanged glances that made Edie's throat itchy. Something was going on.

"Pryce resigned from the police department," Frannie said.

"What? Why would he do that? Because of me?" Edie gasped.

"No. Because of me," Pryce said from behind Edie.

Edie gasped and faced him. It had been a month since she'd seen him, and he looked like she felt. Like he was held together with duct tape and a prayer.

"What are you doing here?"

"I wanted to talk to you."

Edie laughed. "You've had a month. I heard what you said the last time we spoke. I got the message."

Pryce winced and took a step forward. "I was wrong. About so many things. But there was one thing I should have said to you that I was too afraid to say that night."

"Oh, yeah? What was that?" Edie asked, fighting her emotions. She could do this. She could hear what he said. Then she would leave.

"I love you, Edie Warren."

Edie gasped. That was the last thing she expected him to say.

And maybe the only thing he could have said that would erase his other words.

"I don't believe you," she whispered.

His heart cracked at her words. He waited. He gave her time. He did the things he thought he needed to do to become the man who was worthy of her. He was a work in progress, and always would be, but he hoped telling her how he felt would at least give him a chance to win her back.

But she thought he was lying.

"It's the truth. I love you. I have for a long time, but I didn't think you would accept it when I wanted to tell you. That night... I said a lot of things I regret. Everything I said, I regret. I never gave you a chance to explain."

"You've had a month to ask me. I was a captive audience," Edie joked.

Pryce chuckled, her wit giving him the tiniest bit of hope. "I wanted you to be able to heal. I didn't want to risk setting you back or upsetting you. I knew you didn't want to see me."

"I ached every day that you never showed up."

"In the hospital... It doesn't matter," Pryce said, thinking of the day he went to her and she didn't want to see him.

"What are you talking about? You weren't at the hospital."

"Yes, he was," Frannie said, catching Edie's attention. "The day the doctor woke you up. I told you he was there. You shook your head."

Edie stared at her lap as if trying to bring back the memory. She shook her head. "I don't remember that at all." She turned back to Pryce. "Why did you come?"

Pryce took another step toward her. "I wanted to be there for you. I wanted to be the one sitting at your side and telling you to fight. I wanted to be the first person you saw when you woke up."

A single tear rolled down her cheek. She drew a breath and closed her eyes. "I wanted that, too."

"I should have pushed, Edie. I'm so damn sorry I didn't. I thought I was giving you the space you needed. After everything I said... I can never apologize enough for that. Marcus explained a few things to me, and I... I spent the last month making changes. You were doing the same thing the police should have been doing. You were helping the community and saving people. I wasn't willing to see that, but I do now."

"I can't keep doing it," Edie whispered.

"I'm not going to stand in your way. But I am going to ask you to let me help you."

Edie shook her head. "I can't. I... Trevor wants me dead. And he'll make it happen."

"I won't let it happen," Pryce growled. He'd do anything to keep her safe.

"Why did you quit your job? You love being a cop."

"I love you more. And Marcus refused to accept my resignation until I spoke to you."

"Why would he do that?"

Pryce looked at Frannie. Frannie nodded.

"I've been offered a job at Shelter in the Storm. Security. Live in."

"What?" Edie gasped on a laugh. "You're going to be living there?"

"Marcus also offered to get me into the detective exam. Detective Foster is supporting that option."

"You can be a detective?" Edie asked, a smile lighting up her face.

Pryce nodded. "Marcus has ordered a full investigation of the entire department. After Maxwell and Dempsey were both found to be working with Trevor, separately, Marcus insisted on everyone being reviewed and vetted. Again."

"What do you want to do?" Edie asked.

Pryce exhaled and shook his head. "I want to be with you. I get to help people no matter which job I decide on. But if you're leaving the area..."

"I didn't know how to live here and risk seeing you."

"Oh, Edie," Pryce said, moving around the couch to her.

She met him halfway and fell into his embrace. "I missed you."

"I missed you, too," he whispered against her lips. "I love you."

Pryce didn't wait for her answer. He kissed her hard, one arm around her waist and the other cupping the back of her head.

Edie threw her arms around his neck and held on. Tears leaked down her cheeks, mixing with their kiss, but Pryce didn't care.

He had her back. That was what mattered.

"I love you," she whispered as they pulled apart. "I'm sorry it took me so long to admit it."

"I was willing to wait for those words forever," Pryce said.

"You should be a detective," Edie said. "It's what you've always wanted. And it'll mean you can keep investigating. You can find the women who disappear."

Pryce closed his eyes and nodded. His heart squeezed. That was what he wanted, too, but he would have given it up for Edie. "Are you sure?"

She nodded. "You have to figure this out. You have to save the rest of them."

"I'll do my best."

"Then I know it'll happen," Edie said with a smile. "I'm really happy you're here."

"I'm sorry I waited so long."

"It's okay. You were worth the wait."

Pryce chuckled.

The crunch of a chip brought Pryce's head up.

Lorelei was across the room, her mouth full and a sheepish smile on her face. "Sorry," she mumbled.

The others laughed, then followed Lorelei to the trays of

food.

Edie kissed Pryce once more, then pulled him toward the food. Pryce sat with the women and ate, enjoying the friendly camaraderie they shared. Wray and Braden came in a little while later, grabbing food for themselves and Wray's boys and refreshing the trays.

Pryce spoke to Wray and Braden. Both men had become friends over the last month, since Pryce realized Wray was the one who saved Edie. Braden was in the house with them, too, although Pryce only remembered him from outside. Pryce owed both men everything for saving both him and Edie that night.

"Everything good?" Wray asked.

Pryce smiled at Edie. She laughed at something Karli said. "All good. Thanks to you two."

"Just doing our jobs," Braden said. "We've been there. This whole thing is so fucked up."

"It really is," Pryce agreed. "It goes deep, too. Into places we never would have suspected. Whoever's behind all this is smart."

"And rich," Wray said.

"What did you say?" Lorelei asked.

Wray shrugged. "I was just saying whoever is running this organization must have a ton of money. It can't be cheap to have cops on your payroll, not to mention properties you can blow up and all the other people working for them. I know they're selling drugs, but they're also using a lot on the people they take."

The entire room was silent as everyone processed what Wray said.

"Follow the money," Pryce whispered.

"Exactly," Lorelei said. "How did we miss this?"

"What are you guys talking about?" Stacey asked.

Pryce and Lorelei exchanged a glance.

"Money always leaves a trail. We knew Damon was putting it through his company, but he's gone. Which means the money has to be going somewhere else," Lorelei said.

"And if we can find where, we can find Trevor, and everyone else who's working for him," Pryce said, meeting Edie's gaze.

"And finally stop him," Edie whispered. "For good."

FLEE IS COMING MARCH 8...

Dawn had been caring for Robert Davis for the better part of a year. Atoning for her sins and making things right in her life so she could move on. But moving on wasn't supposed to include inheriting a fortune and getting a target on her back. The only one who can help her is Gage Stevens, the lawyer who handed her the keys to the kingdom.

If the man who wants the money doesn't get to her first.

PREORDER FLEE TODAY!

Everyone deserves justice. Even when they're no one.

Witnessing a murder was not on Frannie's bucket list. Marcus had to find out what the curvy dancer knew. They made a deal. She would help him, and he would find the murderers. No one would know she was involved. She hoped.

Frannie and Marcus's story is available only to subscribers.
Sign up at https://dl.bookfunnel.com/y9ms2k2dq8 to get FORSAKEN now.

*T*URN *the page to read chapter one of FLEE.*

FLEE

CHAPTER 1

Dawn Patterson blinked away tears as she read the latest text from her ex-husband.

> Savannah doesn't want to go to dinner Friday night.

Dawn's first instinct was to threaten Owen with a call from her lawyer, reminding him of the custody agreement they had and that she was entitled to one dinner a month alone with their daughter, but Dawn was trying to be better. It wasn't easy, but she was trying.

> Okay.

Dawn shoved the phone back into her pocket and drew a deep breath. She always saved her favorite patient for last, and today, she needed the confidence and joy from the man more than most days.

Dawn waved her hand beneath the automatic hand sanitizer dispenser and rubbed her hands together as she walked into the room.

Robert Davis laid in his bed, his head propped up with too many pillows as he struggled to breathe. His pale skin was wrinkled and weathered, but his eyes were still bright and full of life. It was like his body was trying to drag his mind out of the world and into the afterlife.

"Jeez, what did they do to you?" Dawn asked, hurrying to Mr. Davis. She pulled one of the pillows from behind his head and lowered the head of his hospital bed.

"You just take my breath away," Mr. Davis joked.

Dawn chuckled with him and shook her head. "You're good for my confidence."

"If I were only five decades younger..."

Dawn laughed at the old joke. It had become his favorite line with her over the last year. A year where Dawn had fought with everything she had to begin to rebuild her life.

A life where her daughter still wanted nothing to do with her and her ex-husband was the eternal good guy.

"How are you feeling now that you can breathe again?" Dawn unwound her stethoscope from around her neck and checked his heart and lungs. Still okay, but slower. Every day they were getting slower.

"Like I'm fifty years old again."

Dawn grinned. She knew he didn't feel fifty again, but he never complained. She sat on the edge of his bed. "How do you really feel?"

He sighed, the sound pulling his eternal grin down just a touch. "I'm tired, honey."

"I know." Dawn patted the man's hand. She loved the work she did. What started as a penance enacted on herself became work she had a passion for. A part of her felt guilty for enjoying the job when she went into the work to atone for her many, many sins, but she knew what she was doing was helping people.

"How come you're still here? I thought you got off at five."

Dawn shrugged. "No reason to rush home."

"That'll change one day. Owen and Savannah will realize what they're missing by keeping you at arm's length."

The kind words brought tears back to Dawn's eyes. Not because she wished Mr. Davis was right, but because he had such faith in her, even though he knew everything she'd done. "I don't think that's going to happen. Savannah just canceled dinner for Friday night."

"I thought that was court ordered," Mr. Davis barked. He tried to push himself upright, indignant that her life wasn't going as planned.

Dawn pushed his shoulders so he'd lie down again. "It is, but I can't force her to have a relationship with me."

Mr. Davis shook his head. "You can't give up on her. I gave up on my sons. Both of them became people I didn't recognize. I put all of myself into work and didn't pay enough attention to them. I wish I'd made different choices. It's my biggest regret. I don't want you to have the same one when you're on your deathbed."

"You're not on your deathbed just yet," Dawn told him, not wanting to think about the man not being there.

"Dawn," he said, gripping her hand with far more strength than she expected from the frail man. "I know you think I'm a crazy old man, but please listen to me. Do whatever it takes to fix your relationship with Savannah. If you're not interested in getting back together with Owen, don't think twice about that, but Savannah matters."

Dawn nodded, knowing the man was speaking from experience and not just offering bland advice.

"When my wife died, I let myself get lost in work. I let myself ignore my sons. If I could go back, I would, but I lost them both a long time ago. By the time I tried, it was too late to reach them."

"I will. I promise."

Mr. Davis nodded, relaxing once more, his grip failing as he sank against the bed. His face relaxed, sleep coming for him. "I apologize. I hate to see you repeating my mistakes."

"Thank you. I know. I'm not sure Savannah will ever forgive me, but you're right. I need to try. I need to make sure she knows I've changed."

Mr. Davis nodded. "Good. I apologize for fading on you, but I know I'm not going to be awake much longer."

"You never have to apologize to me for anything. Rest. We'll talk tomorrow."

Mr. Davis nodded, his eyes falling closed as he fell asleep just that quickly.

Dawn finished her work for the day and headed home. Her apartment was empty and lonely and depressing, but it was one more piece of her penance. One more thing to remind her she owed her life to others. To the nine-one-one operator who kept Savannah calm that night, and to the firefighters and paramedics who saved Dawn's life.

Rock bottom hurt. But it worked. Dawn turned her life around after that night, but she couldn't erase all the pain she caused. All she could hope for was forgiveness one day.

Clearly, not today.

Gage Stevens reached for the phone as he keyed in his password to unlock his computer. He'd barely made it into his office and had just spoken to his assistant, Betsy.

"Yeah?" Gage asked into the phone.

"You have a call, Mr. Stevens." It didn't matter how many

times Gage told her to call him by his first name, the older woman refused. Said she'd never called a boss by his first name and didn't intend to start now, even though she claimed to be old enough to be his mother.

"Can you take a message?"

"It's Mr. Davis."

Gage sighed. The man was nearing the end of his life. Gage knew it, and Mr. Davis knew it. Gage never refused the man's calls. Not when any of them could be the last one.

"Line two," Betsy said, knowing Gage was going to take the call.

"Good morning," Gage said into the phone.

"I woke up, so I guess I'll agree with you for now," Mr. Davis said. Robert was a friendly man, and a wealthy man. Over the years, Gage had grown to respect him.

But Mr. Davis had secrets. Secrets Gage had never been able to get out of him.

"What can I do for you today?" Gage asked, knowing Mr. Davis didn't tolerate small talk or beating around the bush.

"I need to make an amendment."

"Excuse me?"

"I want to change my beneficiary."

"You can't possibly be serious," Gage said. As much as Gage hated it, Mr. Davis's only son was his heir and would inherit a seven-figure company. They'd spoken many times about it, and Mr. Davis was reluctant to hand that kind of money over to his son, but without any other family, he had few choices.

"We both know the end is coming for me, Gage. And Trevor is getting more and more erratic. I can't. I have no proof, but we both know what he's doing isn't good. I can't sit back and know my company is going to be used for criminal activity. My name will be tarnished, and my employees will be out on the streets. If they survive."

"He's going to be furious," Gage whispered. Trevor Davis was a crazy son-of-a-bitch. The man was unhinged and deadly. Gage had no proof either, but he had every reason to believe Trevor was involved in some of the events happening in Niagara Falls recently.

And attorney-client privilege kept him from sharing his worries with the police department.

"Yeah, he is. But you know with my money, he's going to burn the city. It won't be safe for anyone."

Gage sighed. Robert was right. Gage knew he was right. But it was going to be hell when Trevor found out. "Okay. Who do you want to leave everything to?"

"Dawn Patterson."

"Who is that?"

"She's a nurse here. She's had a lot of shit happen in her life, and she's a good person. She deserves this more than Trevor. She will honor my company."

"Trevor is going to go after her."

"That's why you're not going to let him know about her."

Gage sucked in a breath. "I'll draw up the paperwork and come by in an hour." There was no time to waste when the client was so close to the end. "I need witnesses."

"I'll have the doctor here," Mr. Davis said. He understood. Someone had to be there to confirm Mr. Davis was of sound mind when he was making a decision like the one he proposed. Otherwise, it would all be for nothing.

"See you then." Gage hung up the phone and dropped his head into his hands. Dealing with clients at the end of their lives was always tough, but this was pushing it.

Gage pushed aside his thoughts and started on the new paperwork. He made all the changes that needed to be made and printed out everything Mr. Davis needed to sign.

An hour after their call, Gage walked into Mr. Davis's room. Both a doctor and a nurse were in the room, talking to Mr. Davis.

"Mr. Stevens?" the doctor asked.

Gage nodded and shook her hand.

"Dr. Walden. Mandy and I were doing the cognitive exam, and I can certify that Mr. Davis is of sound mind and capable of making this change of his own free will."

"Thank you, Dr. Walden. And Mandy."

The nurse nodded.

"Will you both be willing to sign as witnesses to Mr. Davis?" Gage asked them.

"Of course," they said at the same time.

Gage went through the changes he made, including the name of the woman Mr. Davis had chosen as his new beneficiary. At her name, the doctor and nurse both gasped.

Gage spared them a glance, but Mr. Davis didn't flinch.

"Sign here, sir," Gage told Mr. Davis. They'd been through this before. Every few years, Mr. Davis updated his will with his current assets, ensuring nothing was left out. He signed his name with the familiar care he always used, his hand moving slowly so there was no mistaking his signature.

Gage took the paperwork from him when he was finished and set it on the table in front of Dr. Walden and Mandy. "If you would both sign beneath his as witnesses to his signature."

Dr. Walden signed first, then slid the paperwork in front of Mandy. When both were done, Gage confirmed their signatures and names, then stamped it as the notary of record.

"I will file this with the court today and keep the originals in my office, as always."

Mr. Davis nodded, understanding what Gage wasn't saying. If it was only in his office, and Trevor got to it, he could destroy the will and claim he was the sole heir.

"Do you need anything else from us?" Dr. Walden asked.

Gage shook his head. "Thank you both for your time."

They nodded and excused themselves from the room, their whispered voices disappearing when they were outside.

"I take it they know Ms. Patterson?"

Mr. Davis nodded.

"Is there something I should know about her?"

Mr. Davis shook his head. "All you need to know is she's the best person to do this. It won't be easy for her, but Dawn deserves a break."

Gage sighed. Mr. Davis had a big heart. He was always giving back, donating his entire salary to local charities for the last decade he worked. Without any major expenses and with plenty of savings, he insisted on helping others. He was generous with his bonus structure and rewarded loyalty and exceptional work.

Gage took his answer to mean Dawn Patterson had some trouble, and Mr. Davis decided she was his latest charity project.

Maybe he'd change his mind. Maybe she'd never know about the lottery ticket he would be handing her.

But like any lottery ticket, it came with strings. Ones that could either set a person free or kill them.

Gage hoped the woman knew how to free herself.

Trevor Davis walked down the hallway toward his father's room. He hated the place, but it was the only way he could see his father anymore. And the only way the grumpy bastard would give Trevor money.

Trevor stepped into the room, spotting a fat nurse sitting on the edge of the bed.

"It'll get better," his father said, patting the woman's hand like she was important. Like she mattered. Instead of like she was the damn help.

"Dad," Trevor growled, letting them know he was there.

The fat nurse jumped, spinning to face him with a guilty look on her face. She smoothed the purple scrubs over her chunky stomach and pressed her hands into wide hips.

Trevor let his gaze trail over her. He liked the big ones. Once they got hooked on drugs, they lost weight, forgetting to care about food and choosing drugs only. She'd be a good fuck. Fat bitches had tight pussies because no one else liked to fuck them.

"Trevor," his father said, the encouraging tone he'd used with the fat chick replaced by one of disdain. "What are you doing here?"

"I'll just let you two talk," the nurse said. She made her way around Trevor, giving him space like she couldn't bear the thought of touching him.

Trevor stepped in her path and ran a hand down her cheek.

She swallowed roughly. "Excuse me."

"Let her be," his father barked.

Trevor smiled, letting his gaze run down her chunky body again. Yeah, he'd enjoy a go at her. It had definitely been a while since a man put his hands on her. Trevor would take pound her into submission.

She stepped around Trevor and hurried out of the room, closing the door behind her.

Trevor sneered. He delighted in making others uncomfortable. Made him hard. If his dad wasn't glaring at him, Trevor would have stroked one out right then and there, but the miserable bastard was glaring at him. "What?"

"You're the one who showed up at my home. What do you want?"

"Money. I'm almost out. I need ten grand."

"I gave you ten grand last week."

"And I spent it. Now, I need more."

"What are you doing with all this money, Trevor?"

"What the fuck do you care? You haven't worried about me since I was nine and mom died. Fuck, you probably didn't worry about me then. She did."

"I always worried about you."

"Could have fucking fooled me," Trevor spat. He hated his father. All he'd ever done was disappear. Trevor and his older brother, Clyde, had to learn to take care of themselves. And they did. By taking what they wanted.

Their father never gave a shit. Not until Trevor no longer needed a father.

"One day you're not going to be able to get my money," his father said, almost sounding sad at the admission.

"Because you'll be dead? Yeah, I'm counting the days, old man."

His father grimaced. He swung his legs over the side of the bed and eased himself to a stand. He walked across the small room to the dresser where he kept his cash. He unlocked the safe and retrieved rolls of bills. He counted it quickly, then locked the box again and turned to Trevor.

"I'm sorry I was such a horrible father."

"Whatever. When I inherit all your money, I'll appreciate the fact that you only cared about your company and never about me." Trevor turned to leave.

"You're not going to inherit my money," his father whispered.

Trevor stopped halfway to the door. He had to have heard him wrong. "What did you say?"

His father straightened when Trevor turned back to him. He held himself upright, but the exhaustion on his face betrayed the false bravado of his posture. "I said you're not going to inherit my money. I changed my will."

"The fuck you did."

"It's already done, Trevor. I can't have you destroying my company. You'll—"

Trevor was on his father so quickly he didn't even remember moving. He wrapped a hand around the man's throat and guided him to the bed. "You never cared about me. That company was all that ever mattered to you."

His father shook his head, the movement just enough to break Trevor's hold. His father sank to the bed, knocking a pillow onto the floor. "That's not true. I loved you and your brother. I would have done anything for you two."

"Except give me your company. You are treating me no better than a dog in the street, rejecting me and refusing to give me what I've earned."

"How did you earn it? You've never worked there a day in your life!"

"I earned it by being born. I earned it by surviving. I earned it by sharing your blood. And I will have what I earned."

Trevor picked up the pillow from the floor. He held it between his hands and pressed it over his father's face.

The old man's feet kicked. He fought against the pillow.

He tried to scream, but the pillow drowned out the sound. He grabbed at Trevor's hands, but Trevor held still.

Until his father stopped fighting.

Trevor removed the pillow from his father's face. Terrified eyes stared up at him. Vacant. Hollow. Dead.

It was the most loving look his father had ever given him. The one Trevor would remember for the rest of his life.

He fluffed the pillow and put it behind his father's head. He positioned him so it looked like he was sleeping. Then Trevor left the room with his money and a promise to himself that he would get what he deserved. Every last penny.

PREORDER FLEE TODAY!

ABOUT THE AUTHOR

USA TODAY Bestselling Author Mary E Thompson spent most of her childhood wishing she had a few less curves. She hid in the pages of books because her favorite characters never cared what size her clothes were. Now, neither does Mary, and she writes stories that celebrate women like her. Real women who have curves, chase dreams, and find love, because we should all be happy, no matter our dress size.

Mary spends her non-writing time with her husband and two kids, watching too much TV, cheering for her hometown football team (Go Bills!), and hiding chocolate from her family.

Visit https://MaryEThompson.com/ to sign up for Mary's newsletter, **Romancing the Curves.** Subscribers get free ebooks and other fun stuff, like exclusive, members only content and giveaways, plus are the first to know about new releases and sales!

www.ingramcontent.com/pod-product-compliance
Lightning Source LLC
Chambersburg PA
CBHW060806190726
48285CB00002B/561